Never Touch a Dead Body

J. W. HODGE

CAMEL
PRESS

Kenmore, WA

CAMEL
PRESS

A Camel Press book published by Epicenter Press

Epicenter Press
6524 NE 181st St.
Suite 2
Kenmore, WA 98028

For more information go to:
www.Camelpress.com
www.Coffeetownpress.com
www.Epicenterpress.com

This is a work of fiction. Names, characters, places, brands, media, and incidents are either the product of the author's imagination or are used fictitiously.

Cover design by Scott Book
Design by Melissa Vail Coffman

Never Touch a Dead Body
Copyright © 2024 by J. W. Hodge

Library of Congress Control Number: 2023945663

ISBN: 978-1-68492-135-5 (Trade Paper)
ISBN: 978-1-68492-136-2 (eBook)

This book is dedicated to my husband Jerry Hodge.
He's had my back from the get go.

Acknowledgments

I'd like to express my gratitude to Carol Cartaino for helping Sadie find a home with Camel Press and to Jennifer McCord Executive Editor and Associate Publisher of Epicenter Press who is responsible for making me dig deep as an author and adding any coherence the book possesses. A special shout out to my critique partners Georgia Wright and Barbara Larson for their encouragement and insight. A special thanks to Dr. Lonna Gerstner DVM for her expert knowledge about animals. And finally a big thanks to my husband, family, and friends for their unending support.

ONE

MOTHERS LOVE TO GIVE ADVICE. Words of wisdom: Take an umbrella—it looks like rain. Eat a hearty breakfast. Always wear clean underwear.

And never touch a dead body.

Okay, your mother may have left out the dead body bit unless you grew up playing in a mortuary.

My name is Mercedes McCambridge Harrigan, Sadie to all my friends; and my grandmother is the only female mortician in Portneuf Gap, Idaho: Hence, my mother's advice. I've seen enough dead bodies in my thirty years to know they're nothing to be afraid of . . . at least not the ones lying serenely in their coffins, washed, sterile with hair coiffed and putty-like makeup plastered on to mute death's sting.

But the body sprawled on the kitchen's yellow linoleum, dress hiked up to reveal support hose, was altogether different. Bloated almost beyond recognition, skin a mottled bluish-black, the poor woman looked more like an alien from a 1960's horror flick than one of the tenants in my apartment complex.

In life, on a good day, Thelma Edwards probably tipped the scales at ninety pounds. Now, her inflated body looked like a mini sumo wrestler, the short sleeves of her flowered dress threatening to pop the seams. I put my hand over my mouth and nose, trying not to breathe in the stench, and walked back into the living room, punching 911 as I fled. I was sweating and shaking simultaneously as my fingers fumbled for the right numbers.

After reporting her death, I walked outside into the September sunshine, taking great gulps of air, hoping to cleanse the smell and malodorous taste streaming through my sinuses. Until this morning, I didn't know landlords were required to do welfare checks on tenants if their welfare was in question, but I made a mental note: always carry a tube of mentholated ointment to smear under my nose . . . just in case.

I'd never felt this way after looking at a body. That included my fourth grade year when Rudy Ruckstead and I sneaked a peek at Roosevelt's grade school principal, Mr. Burnett, lying naked on grandma's embalming table with overlapping fat rolls rippling his white hairy body. Rudy screamed and wet himself. I dropped Gram's pilfered key ring, turned, and ran smack into my grandmother.

That day was bad.

This was worse.

Leaning my arms on the top of my car, I lowered my head and tried to think. Which of Thelma's relatives should I contact first? Or would the funeral home handle that call? At this moment my brain wouldn't pull up any info on funeral home procedure or the next steps to take when someone has died. Gram was on a well-deserved two-week-long cruise to the Bahamas and I wouldn't, shouldn't, couldn't disturb her. She'd left her assistant in charge but I'd rather swallow shards of glass than deal with him.

In the early light my vintage apartments looked peaceful, serene with green patches of lawn I'd mowed yesterday matching the green shutters framing each large window. Built in the early forties to house army personal stationed in Portneuf Gap, the three single story units formed a horseshoe around the parking lot. Arched wooden front doors complete with wooden screen doors opened into entry alcoves with tiny coat closets. The rooms were large, sunny and sound didn't carry through the walls.

Each building had four apartments, with white slat wooden siding and wood-framed storm windows that had to be taken down each summer and replaced in the fall. The places were quaint (okay, dated) and required a lot of upkeep but my Aunt Vie had bequeathed them to me and I loved them. I even loved the name: Liberty Apartments.

"Is she . . .?"

I raised my head and looked at Dexter Zoetwilder. He stood between Thelma's porch and his neighboring stoop, rocking back and forth on the balls of his feet. Despite his seventy years, Dexter stood a lean six foot, with forearms that still made his Semper Fi tattoo stand at attention.

"Yes. She's lying on the kitchen floor. Looks like she's been there for a few days."

"I knew it! Dexter ran a hand through his white crew cut. "I told the wife the smell coming through the wall in our bathroom was a dead body smell. I wouldn't have bothered you otherwise. Once you smell it, there's no mistaking it. Kinda like it's branded into your olfactory cells."

Now that was cheery news at eight-thirty on Sunday morning. The sun grew hotter as we stood in the parking lot, and I had to wonder why Thelma had cranked the dial on her thermostat up until her apartment felt like an oven. Indian summer was in full bloom in Portneuf Gap, with nighttime temps starting to cool down, but not enough to require heat. At least I hadn't fiddled with the old oil furnace in my house, but then I'm not a frail seventy-five-year-old with a bad heart.

Never speak ill of the dead was another of my mother's warnings. Did considering someone's last acts stupid count?

"Must've been her heart," Dexter said, his deep-set blue eyes glancing at Thelma's arched wooden doorway as though he expected to see her standing there, everything back to normal. "Wonder why she didn't use the panic button she wears around her neck?"

His question shook me out of my dismal thoughts. Why hadn't she pushed the Life-Alert help button? Did her heart give out so suddenly she didn't have time? I shuddered. If she'd fallen face down wouldn't the button have activated anyway?

How had she landed? Now that I thought about it, all I remembered was a bloated shape, wearing a flowered dress, sprawled on the floor. The kitchen was dark, the blinds over the window above the sink drawn tight. I should go check. I would, just as soon as the paramedics, police, or cavalry arrived.

Right, time to cowgirl-up and march back in. Not only am I responsible for the complex, but I am a writer of thrillers. I took a step toward the apartment and stopped.

Thelma had been my friend. Whenever I came to collect the rent, sharing a cup of tea with her was mandatory, tea and toast from tasty bread she made by hand, no bread machines for Thelma. I didn't want to view her swollen body up close and personal.

"Better go tell the wife," Dexter said. Still, he didn't move. Death has a way of making people do strange things. It paralyzed both Dexter and myself. "Maybe I should stick around in case the officials have any questions," he offered, glancing again at Thelma's shut door.

Violet, Dexter's wife, hobbled out, letting the screen door slam shut behind her, and joined us in the parking lot.

"Is Dex right? Does that awful stench mean . . . .?"

Violet stopped beside Dexter, shoving short, plump hands into the pockets of her navy blue cardigan. Today her Brillo-pad hair was a brilliant autumn red, a startling clash with her vibrant pink lipstick.

"You know how stress affects my arthritis." Out came her hands to wring one another. "And I'm out of my medicine." She sighed and looked up as though trying to find solace in the clear sky.

I caught Dexter's quick eye-roll and smothered a smile. "Not now, Violet." Dexter turned to face me, dropping his voice. "This whole business is funny. She didn't use the button and no one's been around to visit, least not for a couple of days."

"Dexter!" Violet's plaintive whine chafed my nerves.

"Do you suppose someone did Thelma in?" Dexter forged on, ignoring his wife's glare.

Violet snorted. "The way she smoked, it's a wonder she lived this long. Doctor told her to stop, she wouldn't listen. The day my doctor told me to quit, I came home and threw out my cigarettes just like that." She snapped her fingers with no sign of arthritic pain. As if realizing her mistake, her plump fingers sought comfort from each other and her brow furrowed. "Dex, feels like a steam roller is crushing my old bones. I need my medicine!"

"Damn, woman. I'll take you to the pharmacy as soon as I answer any questions the police might have."

As if on cue, a city cruiser pulled into the parking lot. Violet quickly stepped in front of me for a better view of the lone officer parking next to my vintage yellow Karmann Ghia. Wow, the unfolding drama must be a miracle cure.

I started toward the police car to introduce myself but stopped short as the officer emerged from his vehicle. The man had the kind of good looks that could turn heads and give women sinful ideas, all packaged neatly in a tight muscular body. I felt tacky noticing such details—must be the shock of finding Thelma.

The officer nodded to me and adjusted his gun belt. "Someone call 911 from this complex reporting a dead body?"

"I did," I said, Love at first sight is way overrated, but lust at first sight had reduced me to a starry-eyed teen, all clumsy and tongue-tied. Dexter came to my rescue.

"Thelma Edwards is the deceased. Had a bad ticker," he said, thumping his chest. "We've been neighbors for about five years."

"Who discovered the body?" The officer wasn't tall, maybe five-ten, a couple of inches taller than my five foot seven. I felt like an ostrich, all limbs and long neck

"I did. I went into the apartment after Mr. Zoetwilder called to tell me about the funny smell coming through the wall in his bathroom. I'm Mercedes Harrigan. I own this complex." I stuck my hand out.

His handshake was quick, efficient. His hand warm, gentle. "Officer Jack Killian. I'd better go take a look." When he opened the apartment door, he stopped a beat as the smell hit him. Inhaling a deep breath, he stepped inside and was back out in record time.

"You said she had a bad heart?" He looked at Dexter.

"Yeah. Had some kind of heart surgery couple of years ago," Violet replied, sidling closer to lay her hand on Officer Killian's arm. "She was on all kinds of medicine, too. Shame she just kept smoking like a dirty chimney."

"Good to know." Killian's mouth quirked as he nodded and patted Violet's hand before deftly removing it. He murmured cop-speak instructions into the miniature mike attached to his shoulder, then turned to me. "Best guess her heart gave out. Coroner's on his way. Want to help me open the apartment's windows, get some circulation going?"

I nodded and reluctantly followed Officer Killian back into the apartment with Dexter bringing up the rear. I covered my nose and mouth with my hand and Dexter tied a red bandana around his face, making him resemble an old-west robber. We walked down the short hall, Dexter taking one bedroom while I opened the window in the other. Dexter hollered a muffled, "I'll get the bathroom," as I stood staring at Thelma's unmade bed. The sheets and blankets looked as though she'd just crawled from their warmth. The pillow still held her head indentation. I turned away with tears smarting. How many days had she lain on the kitchen floor? Had she struggled, frantic for air or been gone before her head hit the linoleum?

I swiped at the tears and a movement caught my eye. I squealed as the rumpled blanket moved ever so slightly.

Get a grip, Harrigan.

Lifting one corner of the blanket, I stared at slitted, yellow eyes. With a menacing snarl, Thelma's black cat, Spanky, tore past me, ricocheted off the bedroom wall and shot out the door. Dexter's curse told me Spanky was in the bathroom, probably shredding the shower curtain.

"You okay?" Officer Killian's eyes were the most startling green, with dark lashes any female would die for. He stepped into Thelma's bedroom. "I heard a yell."

"I startled Spanky, Thelma's cat. I think he frightened Dexter," I said. "That cat was Thelma's baby." The room began to tilt. Fighting the urge to sit down on the unmade bed, I pinched the bridge of my nose. "Poor Spanky, trapped with a dead body. He's got to be freaking."

Officer Killian took my elbow, leading me into the hall. "Why don't we finish this discussion outside, give the cat a little room."

We started down the narrow hall and a yowling ball of fur shot between us and out the open door. Great. Now I'd never catch the little demon.

A crowd had gathered in the middle of the parking lot, some tenants, and a few neighbors. In their midst stood Violet, arthritis forgotten, arms waving as she fed lurid details to the rapt audience. I felt my stomach roll with anger. Thelma should be remembered for who she was, not what she'd become in her over-heated apartment.

Killian guided me to his squad car. "I need a few more details for my report."

Shade from an oak tree dappled the cruiser, making it look like an oasis in the desert. Dexter followed us, giving his story before Killian could pull out his notebook.

"Name's Dexter Zoetwilder. Like I said, me and the wife have been neighbors with Thelma around five years. We thought she'd gone to stay with . . . well, we thought she'd gone for a couple of days. Didn't see or hear her and no taxi service came by. Thelma didn't drive. Wife was the first one to notice the smell, but once I got a whiff, I called Sadie here right away." He paused and looked around, stepping closer and lowering his voice. "I watch 'Forensic Files'. I know how things are, even if this ain't the big city. Despite Thelma's bad ticker, you think there might'a been foul play?"

Killian struggled not to grin. "I can't say just yet, sir. Thanks for the information. You could help me with one thing." Dexter nodded, straightening his posture, awaiting orders like a good marine. "Go over and make sure the crowd stays away from the apartment while I talk to Ms. Harrigan and inform whomever is talking about the death to not speculate what happened."

Dexter marched off and Killian turned to me. "What can you tell me about Ms. Edwards?"

A faint breeze ruffled the fallen leaves at our feet. I looked at my shoes, trying to gather my thoughts. "Thelma Edwards was one of the tenants living here when I inherited the property. Nice lady. She ran a bookstore on Main Street. Her husband died in a railroad accident I think. She always paid her rent in cash, said she didn't trust banks."

"Heavy smoker, right?"

"Yes. How did . . ."

"There's a long ash in the ashtray by the sink. Lucky for you she put the cigarette down before she died." He shaded his eyes with a hand and looked at the complex. "Old place like this could've burnt down in a matter of minutes."

I felt dizzy again. If the complex had gone up in smoke . . . best not to dwell on that right now. The twelve apartments were my bread and butter. The income wasn't great, but I no longer had to wait tables to support my writing career.

"Ms. Harrigan." Killian's eyes darkened as he peered at me. "You okay?"

"Fine. Peachy." I gestured at the newest graffiti on the side of the four-plex closest to the street. "Someone's been playing gangsta on my buildings, and I have a poor dead tenant who could've burned down the entire complex." I closed my eyes and wished like crazy I'd wake up from this nightmare, or better still, for a glass of water and a large bottle of Excedrin.

Killian scowled at the black symbols. "You report it?"

I shook my head. "Not this time."

"Why don't you sit down?" Killian guided me to the curb where I plopped onto the grass strip between the parking lot and sidewalk. "The coroner's here. I'll let you know his verdict."

Resting my arms across my knees, I watched the circle enlarge around Violet as people stirred from their homes and came to find out what was going on. I thought about trying to convince the crowd to wait until all the facts were known but I knew the gossip train was in full motion and nothing would stop the excited speculation. There's nothing like a crisis to bring people together.

My headache growing, I massaged my temples like I'd seen on YouTube. I think I was supposed to chant something.

"Bad headache?" Agatha Heckathorne, tenant in number nine, drew her finger along the top of my head. Dressed in a white knit shirt, pink levis, and navy tennis shoes with the toe sections cut away to display her ten white piggies. She claimed a stubborn sinus infection had spread to her feet and she had to let air circulate over her toes.

"Both of my brain tumors started with headaches. When all the fuss calms down come over to my place. I have a surefire test that will tell me if you have a tumor. Much more accurate than a brain scan." She patted my head and marched off, probably to look up the purifying qualities of yak urine.

"Damn juvies. Want the same deal as before?"

"What?" Squinting, I looked up into the round face of Justin Pizindki, tenant in number twelve. Justin worked with his uncle painting houses.

"The graffiti." He swept his arm toward the defaced siding. "I cover it and we're square for the rest of the month?"

I nodded.

"That's one bad smell coming from the old lady's place. Gonn'a take an ozonator to get it all out." He sat beside me and shook his head. "Rotted meat is the worst. But I've seen those little ozone machines work wonders. Run one for three, four days, depending, and the next tenant will never know a rotting corpse was in there."

My stomach threatened to do something vile so I eased my head down to my forearms and tried breathing through my mouth. "Where do I get an air cleaner?"

"Ozonator," Justin corrected. "I know a carpet guy who has one. I'll call him if you'd like."

"I'd appreciate that."

Justin harrumphed something and left. I continued staring at the gutter. Ants scurried around the leaves that had collected, no doubt planning for winter. Right now, I wish I had their energy and enthusiasm. A pair of shiny, black wingtip shoes came into my line of sight.

"Ms. Harrigan?" The smooth voice reminded me of thick, chocolate syrup sliding down ice cream. I looked up into the bifocal glasses of our county coroner, James Moneypenny. His bald caramel head glistened in the sun; crinkled white hair formed a neat horseshoe above his ears. He wore a gray-striped suit, white shirt, and a subtle maroon tie. I always thought he belonged on stage speaking lines from Shakespeare; not taking liver temps from a corpse.

"Yes?"

"Near as I can tell right now, Thelma Edwards has been dead approximately three days. From the information Officer Killian gathered, heart attack might be the cause. I'll know more after the autopsy."

I stood to ease the crick in my neck, it didn't help much, I was still looking up. "Who informs her next of kin? She has a sister here in town."

"Before we notify anyone, I'd like to speak to you for a moment." The way he said it I suspected I had only months to live. Swallowing, I followed him to the edge of the property beside a stand of Aspen trees just beginning to turn golden yellow.

"Is there a problem?" I asked.

James Moneypenny took off his glasses and rubbed his dark eyes. "Like I said, I won't be sure until the autopsy is completed, but her aging heart might not be the entire problem." He perched his glasses back on his nose. "The toaster in her apartment has a bare wire, she might not have noticed. Anyway, old as this complex is, well there's no G.F.I. breaker.

"A G.F. what?"

"G.F.I. It's a very sensitive ground fault protector which virtually eliminates the chance of electrocution. G.F.I. breakers are now mandatory. You've probably seen one in a kitchen or bathroom; you know the plugs with the red test buttons? They save lives, might've saved Ms. Edwards. Say, she plugs in her toaster with the bare wire, a G.F.I. would've prevented all of the electricity racing through her."

I must have looked as blank as I felt.

Moneypenny pulled on his top lip and sighed. "With you owning this property, if the wiring was responsible for Ms. Edwards death, the city may want you to rewire the entire complex. Bring everything up to code."

MY TURN TO SIGH. REWIRE THE WHOLE PLACE? Where was I going to come up with the money for that? "Are you positive it was the toaster?" I asked him.

"After the autopsy I'll know more about the exact cause; but her right hand is slightly blackened around the thumb and index finger. And there's two pieces of toast still in the toaster."

Tea and toast. Had the faulty wiring turned Thelma's favorite snack deadly? Two men from the coroner's office pulled a gurney from the van and started toward Thelma's apartment. Time to go home.

TWO

"I HAVE THE ULTIMATE CURE!" Rebbie Russell called through my back screen door. Not waiting for an answer she marched in, followed by my two dachshunds, Bogart and Bacall. So much for ordering the little beggars to keep any and all away from my domicile. I should've assigned guard duty to the barn cats.

I lifted my head from the couch pillow, the better to view the mini-parade marching across the faded blue-checked kitchen tile. Dressed in black leggings, long red sweater, and black cowboy boots, Reb was the perfect majorette. We've been best friends since the sixth grade when we pricked our thumbs, mixed our blood, and pledged our undying friendship forever and ever, amen.

Telling her to leave me alone was out of the question. On the road of good intentions the woman is a bulldozer. Instead, I let inertia plunk my head back onto the pillow. "What time is it?"

"Around four."

"AM or PM?"

Rebbie pulled open the burgundy flowered drapes covering the living room bay window. Sunshine streamed in, sharp and unpleasant. "Time to rise and shine, girlfriend."

Three short hours ago, after all of the officials had finished their gruesome tasks, I'd come home, called Rebbie—a big mistake—and left a message on her voice mail. I'd taken a look at the insurance policy that covered the apartments, decided I needed an expert to decipher it, called and left a message for my insurance agent. Then, after scrubbing myself raw in the shower and pulling on clean clothes, I'd collapsed on the couch with plans to sleep until this nightmare went away. The roof of my mouth felt like it was lined with cotton and my neck complained about my choice of positions. I groaned and struggled upright before Bogart and Bacall decided to use me as a trampoline.

I eyed the paper sack she held in her hands. "What have you got?"

Wiggling her eyebrows, Reb sat on the couch, scooted a pile of books to the side of the coffee table, and reverently placed the sack in the center. "Only manna from heaven." Inserting thin fingers with killer red nails into the sack, she pulled out a bottle of mustard and a loaf of white bread, the kind that shies away from all fiber and can be squashed into a solid dough-ball.

Mustard sandwiches: our answer to every problem since the sixth grade.

"Let the pig-out commence." She began working on the twist-tie holding the white plastic bread sack closed.

I grabbed the bread from her and dropped it back into the paper sack. "No bread. Not now, maybe never again."

Rebbie leaned closer, brown eyes narrowed, as she studied my face. "Another weird diet?"

"No." I sagged back against the couch, trapping Bogart who gave a half-hearted growl. I reached behind me and brought his warm little body to my chest. Stroking his silken ears, I related the coroner's initial verdict: death by toaster.

"Mercedes McCambridge Harrigan! No one dies from making toast. Heavy smoker plus bad ticker equals so sad and too bad. Pure and simple."

I sighed. "How would you feel if you knew you might've inadvertently killed a good woman?"

"Uh-uh. No fair channeling your melodramatic mother," Rebbie shook her head, sending dark curls swishing over her shoulder.

"Stating facts is not melodramatic. The wiring in the apartments isn't up to code."

"So, you going to rewire the whole complex?" She studied her nails. "I'm not in love with this shade. I should've gone with the Cinnamon Candy Red."

"Forget about your stupid nail color. I could be facing financial ruin!" I stood, put Bogart on the floor, and began to pace in front of the fireplace. Bogart took his cue and paced along behind me, his nails clicking on the hardwood floor

"Well, excuse me. Why don't you just sell the complex to your cousins?" She turned cousins into two long syllables.

"Funny." I sent her an eat-dirt-and-die look. She was referring to my Aunt Vie's avaricious twins. My soul and checkbook were still bleeding from the legal battle after their mother left the apartment complex to me. "I'd rather level the place."

"Sounds like Thelma almost did."

"Yeesh, Reb!"

She shrugged. "It's not your fault if a tenant has a decrepit toaster." She went back to studying her nails. "Older people tend to hang onto stuff even if they can afford newer things. You know the Great Depression's influence still marks that generation."

I stopped pacing. Bogart narrowly missed my ankle with one of those artful doggie dodges. "What did you say?"

"Don't get all prissy. I pointed out that older people hang onto . . ."

"No, no. You said something about Thelma's old toaster."

Reb shot me an exasperated "Duh" look.

"That's it! Reb, you're a genius." I plopped down beside Reb and clasped her hands. "Thelma didn't have an old toaster. She got a new one for her birthday from one of the clubs she belonged to. She showed me the wide slots that could accommodate the fat bagels from Bagel Land. It couldn't have been the toaster."

"You're off the hook." Reb reached into the paper sack again. "Let's eat."

"Except the coroner said there was a bare wire, and her hand had black smudge marks, and . . ." I stopped and stared at the ochre rays slanting across the floor. "Come on, we have to look at her kitchen."

"Wait." Reb dropped the sack and jumped to her feet. "It'll be dark soon. We can't burst into a crime scene. Police don't take kindly to anyone crossing their plastic yellow stay-the-hell-out markers."

"It's not a crime scene yet." I said, struggling into a denim jacket. "Where did I put my keys? Doesn't matter, we'll take your car." I felt giddy, light headed. It couldn't have been the toaster. "Bogie, you and Bacall stay here. Play watchdogs and we'll bring you back a treat." I was halfway out the back door before I realized Reb wasn't behind me. I turned and found her rooted in the same spot, eyes wide, face pale. "Reb, you coming?"

She licked dry lips. "I can't go with you."

"What?" I stepped back in and closed the door.

"I don't want to see where Thelma died, or the awful chalk out-line." Her face looked ready to crumple into tears. "Your message said the stench was terrible. I don't want to smell it. I can't go." She sat on the couch, head down, shoulders slumped.

Bacall jumped up and nosed Reb's hand in an effort to comfort.

"There isn't any chalk outline. But, never mind, that's okay. If you're chicken," I slowly enunciated the last word. "I understand."

Reb's head snapped up. Her eyes looked ready to spit lightning and her mouth pinched into a thin line. Bacall, sensing extreme mood change, skittered off the couch.

"I'll just find my keys." I rummaged through my jacket pockets, casting sidelong looks at her angry posture. "Stay here with the dogs and we'll start the pig-out when I get back."

"Very funny, Harrigan," she said between clenched teeth. Scooping her keys off the coffee table, she stood and smoothed her sweater.

My landline rang. We both stared at the cordless sitting upright on its base on the antique table between the kitchen and living room. I know it's weird to have a landline but a couple of elderly tenants like leaving messages on an answering machine instead of my voicemail. A little-known bonus, my landline fields the majority of Robocalls.

"Better get that," Reb said. She looked ready to sink back onto the couch.

"No time." I grabbed her hand and tugged her toward the back door.

"That line is for your seasoned renters. Could be a real crisis." she protested.

I yanked the back door open. "They'll leave a message or if they're really desperate they'll call my cell."

As if on cue, the answering machine repeated my short greeting followed by the beep. A breathless, squeaky voice filled the kitchen. "Hi, my name's Loralee Lish. I work, or, um, worked for Thelma at her bookstore. I just heard. Wow, talk about awful." There was a long pause and then the voice hurried on. "This may sound sort of strange, but it's like fate's stepping in to turn bad into good. See, the apartment I live in has this gross cockroach problem. I've been complaining to Thelma and, well, the way she died, so sudden—it's like she's telling me it was her time to leave this worldly sphere, and like, I should move into her apartment. I'm a great renter with tons of references. Call me as soon as you get this." The voice recited a number and hung up.

Reb looked at me. "Did that person just ask to move into the apartment her boss died in?"

"Sounded like it."

"You know, Harrigan, she might have something with that fate theory. Better call her back."

I pulled Reb out the door and shut it with a bang. "Later."

Reb slid into the driver's seat of her blue Subaru. "Yuck. I wouldn't want to rent a place someone died in." She shoved the key into the starter and stared at me. "What if she's some ghoulish Addams Family wannabe. Into necrophilia or voodoo?"

"I don't care as long as she doesn't bug the other tenants and pays her rent on time." *Call me crass but that's the way the rental business works.*

Once we reached Thelma's door, I wasn't quite as ready to march in as I'd led Reb to believe. The windows had been open most of the day, but the odor was still nauseatingly evident.

"I forgot the Mentholatum ointment for under our noses," I said, as my traitorous hands shook trying to insert the key into the lock.

Reb grimaced. "Too late now. Get on with it, Sherlock," she replied, covering her nose and mouth with one hand and giving me a shove with the other.

I switched on the overhead living room light. The antique fixture banished the shadows, but glared too bright. The room took on a surreal look, like a Picasso painting where couches are not really intended for sitting and the floor seemed to cant slightly to the left. I forced myself into the kitchen and flipped on the overhead fluorescent. Reb was right behind me, heeling like my dogs were supposed to.

"See, no chalk outline. This isn't a crime scene and chalk outlines went out with . . ."

"Whatever. Look at the damn toaster and let's leave before I puke."

I steeled myself and walked across the floor, edging past the dark stain where the body had been, over to the counter beside the fridge. A narrow-slotted, hump-backed toaster, with two pieces of stale toast, sat serenely on the beige Formica. It looked like an appliance right out of *"I Love Lucy."* I picked up the brown cord. Sure enough, it was frayed right next to the plug.

My heart started thrumming in my chest. This was definitely not Thelma's toaster. Weird. Why was she using this relic? Where was the new one?

I opened the cupboard above the counter; nothing but dishes and bowls. The next one held drinking glasses and one lone bottle of Old Granddad Whisky, half-full or half-empty, depending on your outlook.

"What are you doing?" Rebbie's voice was muffled by her hand.

"That is not Thelma's toaster. I'm looking for the new one."

"You gotta look now? Wouldn't it be better in the daylight with a dozen fans running?"

"The guy with the ozonator is coming tomorrow morning and the apartment has to be shut tight while the machine works." I persisted in my search opening the fridge and grabbing a garbage sack from under the kitchen sink.

"What are you doing?" Rebbie asked.

"I need to remove the perishables from the fridge. As a landlord I have to clean out a fridge as it is included in rental of the apartment. Look at this lettuce," I pointed to the crisper bin. "Couple more days and it'll become a ninth-grade science experiment."

Reb wrinkled her nose. "Seriously, Harrigan?"

"Help me toss and it will cut our time here."

We emptied both crispers and tossed anything else that looked debatable.

"Ok, I declare this fridge as good as it's going to get until you invade with your cleaning products." Reb shut the fridge door, washed her hands at the sink and strode out of the kitchen.

I shut off the kitchen light, grabbed the full garbage bag, and followed Reb outside into the crisp night air, throwing the garbage into the complex's shared dumpster as I passed by. A few stars winked overhead in the twilight.

From the inky shadows, a gruff voice asked. "Seen Spanky yet?"

Rebbie squeaked and I whirled, coming face-to-face with Dexter.

"Sorry," he said. "Did I scare you?"

I nodded, hand over my heart, trying to inhale air and exhale fright. Dexter looked out across the gloomy parking lot and shook his head. "Poor cat. Shouldn't have to spend a night out after what he's been through. I been calling him, but no luck."

I'd forgotten all about Spanky. He was an inside cat, only venturing out on the rare occasion to sun himself on the back patio.

"Were you on a friendly basis with Spanky?" I asked.

Dexter shook his head. My heart sank. Spanky adored Thelma. The rest of the world he tolerated . . . barely.

"Do you have any tuna? Maybe if you put an open can by Thelma's back door he'll come." I suggested.

"And have every stray in the neighborhood taking up residence?" Dexter rolled his eyes. "That wouldn't hold too well with Violet. Claims she's allergic." He huffed a sigh.

"Spanky'll come back. This is the only home he's known," I said with more conviction than I felt.

"And when he does?" Rebbie raised an eyebrow. "Who's going to catch the little darling?"

"I could call Animal Control and borrow one of their traps," Dexter said. Rebbie flashed him a look that communicated even in the deepening dusk. "Not that kind of trap," he explained. "A cat trap, very humane. Don't concern yourself, little lady, I'd never hurt an animal."

I stepped between Dexter and Rebbie before she could react to his "little lady" remark. "Let's wait on getting a trap," I said, touching his shoulder. A sudden thought hit me. "What about Claude Phoenix? He and Thelma seemed to enjoy each other's company. She told me he came every Sunday for her world-class meatloaf. Maybe he can handle Spanky."

Dexter frowned at the mention of Claude's name. "Sure, maybe. Or you could talk to the woman across the way."

"Who?" I asked.

"Esther what's-her-bucket." Dexter pointed across the slender Portneuf River which wound through old town, contained by high cement embankments. Five homes of various styles with well-cared-for yards abutted the embankment. "Heavily involved with the Humane Society. Has four dogs and a couple of cats. Spanky may wander over that way to see what's what. She lives in that yellow one-level, can't miss it. Dogs make enough racket she doesn't need a doorbell."

I thanked Dexter and headed for Rebbie's car.

"Uh, Sadie, wait." Dexter came up and took a firm hold of my elbow. With his head he motioned toward his porch, eyes darting around looking for who-knows-what threat.

I glanced back at Rebbie. She glared and pointed at her watch. I held up my index finger then followed Dexter, hoping Reb wouldn't leave if this took over sixty seconds.

"Thought I should warn you, wasn't no love lost between Esther and Thelma," Dexter whispered. "Thelma once called in a nuisance report on Esther's dogs. Said she couldn't stand the racket another minute. You can imagine how that endeared Thelma to Esther."

I thought of my own pets, how I'd feel if someone called the cops on them. Living outside the city limits did have its perks. However, I'd never noticed any abnormal barking while working in or around the apartments. Maybe, like a mother with umpteen kids, I was desensitized to the din coming from the yellow house.

"Wouldn't surprise me none if Esther Clemmens wasn't downright glad to hear Thelma's gone." Dexter gave a curt nod, opened his screen door, and went inside.

FROM THE YELPING AND BRAYING IT SOUNDED more like twenty dogs than a mere four. Bogart and Bacall's threatening barks were nothing compared to the vicious cacophony coming from behind Esther's front door.

A sharp "Enough!" sounded above the uproar and all grew quiet. I was duly impressed. A stately woman dressed in jeans and a blue fisherman's sweater answered the knock and looked at us through the aluminum screen door. She pulled off a pair of heavy, rubber gloves.

"Yes?" She arched a finely drawn eyebrow.

I introduced Rebbie and myself, then told her the reason for our visit.

"Come in, please." She pushed open the screen door.

Four dogs of debatable breeding, ranging from freakin'-huge to ankle-biter in size, sat quietly in the kitchen off to the left of the entryway. Their edgy, watchful posture reminded me of a wolf pack. Good thing I wasn't dressed in a red cape and holding a basket of goodies for granny.

A white cat leaped from the kitchen windowsill and began to twine its body around Esther's legs. Esther bent and scooped the cat up, scratching between its ears while a purr rumbled deep in its throat.

"Please excuse my appearance," she said, tucking a stray lock of champagne-colored hair behind her ear. She put the cat on the floor and threw the green gloves into a basket near the door. "I was out back cleaning up after my babies." From the look she gave the dogs I guessed she considered them as children. "I was sorry to hear about Thelma, even sorrier for her cat. Must be a very scared and confused animal. He's all black, no distinguishing mark? His name is Spanky?"

I nodded. "He's an indoor cat, I'm not sure what he'll do outside without any front claws."

Esther shook her head and clucked her disapproval while the white cat resumed his dance between her feet.

"He's kind of anti-social so he'll be hard to catch," I said.

Esther muttered something that sounded like "just like his owner." I frowned and she favored me with a brilliant smile. "I'll make friends with him. I have a way with cats." She stared past us into the night, then frowned, creasing her smooth forehead. She had a classic face with creamy skin that made guessing her age difficult. My best estimation? Somewhere between forty and fifty.

"Would either of you like something to drink? I was about to fix some tea."

Reb nudged me none too gently with her elbow and did a slight head shake. I glanced at my watch. "Thanks for the offer, but we've got to be going. If you see Spanky will you let Dexter Zoetwilder know?"

"No problem. I'll call the animal shelter and see if any strays have been reported in this area. Chances are, he gets hungry he'll come sneaking around. Isn't that right, Thomas?" She bent down and scratched the silken fur beneath the cat's chin. "This fellow was knocking on death's door when I found him, weren't you my precious?" Thomas answered with another throaty purr and closed his eyes. Esther straightened and opened the door. Reb and I stepped out into the cool night air.

"I've never met an animal I couldn't cozy up to, given enough time. The main thing is to get Spanky off the streets before he runs into trouble. Cars and dogs are bad enough, but we've got kids in this area who delight in torturing small animals. Junior serial-killers in the making." Her blue eyes glinted like fine steel in the glow of the porch light. "If I had my way, I'd tie their hands to a fence post then shove lighted cherry bombs up their little rectums."

With that Esther Clemmens waved and closed the door.

THREE

A FTER A SLEEP-SPOTTED NIGHT, I lay in bed, tangled in a mass of covers and watched dawn color the cracks of the bedroom ceiling. My home is a cozy two-story farmhouse old, rambling, and in some disrepair but it was a unique all-brick style from the nineteen thirties. Classic gables with white gingerbread trim adorn the three large upper windows above the covered front porch. A hexagon tower sits proudly left of the front door with three ample four-paned windows on the ground floor and a similar window sporting a large, beautiful gable on the second floor. Aunt Vie inherited it from an obscure relative and she, in turn, gave it to me. I've adored this house since I first played in the dining room situated on the bottom floor of the hexagon tower. Located about five miles from the outskirts of Portneuf Gap, the house is situated on two acres of cedar trees, wild grass, and sagebrush in an area called Mink Creek Canyon. A person would be hard-pressed to find a single mink, but there are plenty of deer who play alongside cows, horses, and the occasional goat.

My landline shrilled on my nightstand. I eyed the bedside digital clock and groaned. 6:15. *Please, Lord, not a plumbing problem or another dead tenant.*

I snatched the receiver and grumbled hello.

"I'm bereft of family. Truly alone," a woman said. That blunt statement sat me straight up in bed. Bogart emitted a muffled growl at the hasty retreat of my legs from under his body.

"'Scuse me?" My throat felt clogged, unused. I tried clearing it.

"Is this Mercedes Harrigan?" The voice sounded familiar, well-modulated, but I couldn't place it. Maybe a telemarketer in the wrong time zone?

"Yes," I answered, reaching into my nightstand drawer and grabbing the whistle I keep to discourage obscene phone calls. Any telemarketer who calls before 8:00 a.m. is more than obscene. "Do I know you?"

"Judith Kelso. I'm Thelma Edwards' sister. We've met a couple of times."

Judy Kelso: petite lady, a couple of years younger than Thelma. Ash-blonde helmet hair, aquamarine eyes accented with heavy eyeliner and layers of mascara, wide mouth painted pearly-pink; a perfectly-aged Barbie doll.

"What can I do for you, Ms. Kelso?"

"My dear sister is gone and I am truly alone. Do you know how that feels?" There was a plaintive, soap-opera quality to her voice. I half expected dramatic music to follow her question.

"I'm sorry about Thelma," I replied. "She was one of my best tenants. I'll miss her very much."

"Yes, well, everyone who knew my sister will miss her." There was a pregnant pause. "As soon as the coroner releases her body I want to have the funeral as fast as possible. It will be a small, tasteful affair. I'm not sure how many friends and clients from the bookstore will actually want to attend. I originally thought this coming Tuesday or Wednesday would work, but that beastly Mr. Wyco will not budge. For a mortician, he's not very accommodating."

Mr. Wyco had my pity. It would violate an undertaker's decorum to explain the time and amount of ice it takes to cool a hot corpse. "Thank you, I'll let the other tenants know."

"I'm hoping by Friday or Saturday we can send Thelma to her final resting place. As soon as I can make the arrangements. I'll get the paper to run an obit on their website."

Another pause, I couldn't think of a proper response, so I waited for her to continue.

"You know, I tried to convince Thelma to move in with me. I would've welcomed her company. Since my husband died, I just rattle around in this big house," Judy said, her voice dissolving into a sigh. "And my home isn't old, no bare wires to worry about."

Ah ha! There it was. The real reason for this call. I could feel my back molars grinding.

"Thelma was always the stubborn older sister," Judy continued. "Insisted on having her independence and all that hogwash. Didn't want to be treated like an invalid despite her heart problems. But using that antiquated toaster—just shows her senility was taking a toll."

"Thelma was far from senile." I made an effort not to snarl into the receiver. Bacall snuggled beside me and I petted her long ears in an effort to control my blood pressure. "And that was not her toaster!" I plumped my pillow, learned against the headboard, and closed my eyes against the early rays slanting through the blinds. A steaming cup of coffee with plenty of cream and sugar would be nice.

"What do you mean?" Judy's voice lowered a notch, conveying just the right amount of skepticism.

"She got a new one from one of her clubs for her last birthday."

"Oh? Really? Well, Thelma liked to hang onto old things, claimed new stuff might be shiny but didn't have the quality. Take her television for instance . . ."

"She didn't show you her birthday presents?" It was my turn to play the skeptic.

"Of course she did. I don't remember any toaster. Probably took it back and exchanged it for something else."

Then why had Thelma made such a fuss showing me the wide

slots and duel heating controls? Something wasn't right. I hoped I wasn't developing a kitchen appliance fixation.

"I suppose I should come over—collect her things." Judy's voice broke and I could hear discreet sobbing. The lump in my throat erased all thoughts of breakfast, coffee, and cynical remarks.

I hate it when people cry on the phone. Gram could console and finesse her way around extreme sobbing, but I never knew quite what to say. I waited a moment, then plunged ahead. "I'm meeting a fellow with an ozonator at Thelma's apartment this morning."

"Ozonator?" Her voice quavered a little.

"Um, yes, it's a special cleaning machine," I said, wishing I'd kept my mouth shut. There was no need for Judy to know about the awful smell left by her decomposing sibling. "It needs to run with the apartment shut tight for a couple of days." I gave her my landlord-with-authority voice. "I'll let you know when you can go in."

"I'd appreciate it. Not that I'm looking forward to going through everything. When my husband passed away a couple of years ago, Thelma stepped in and took care of dispersing his belongings. Handled all the messy details." A long sigh traveled through the phone. "Now, it all falls on my shoulders."

I could almost feel her shudder and a pang of sympathy made me commiserate. With Gram and Reb's help, I'd cleaned out aunt Vie's closets and sorted through her treasures, which was emotionally draining. Dealing with multiple death certificates, informing all the various government agencies, insurance agencies, banks, even her TV service was the real nightmare.

"My son and his dear, dear girlfriend have offered their help," Judy said. "I don't know what I'd do without Casey. He's a rock. Just a rock." She sighed and was silent.

I clamped my mouth shut before the Good Samaritan in me offered my help. After an uncomfortable few seconds Judy continued, "Please contact me as soon as we can go into the apartment. Let me give you the best numbers to reach me."

"Just a second," I said, sliding out from beneath a warm jumble of blankets and snoring animals. I carried the cordless as I padded downstairs, pawed through the junk drawer, found a gnawed-on pencil and torn envelope. "Okay."

I jotted down her home and cell numbers, promised to call, and she hung up. I added a note under the numbers to remind myself to call C.J.'s Flower Shop and order flowers for the funeral, then stuck the paper under a smiley magnet on the fridge.

I started coffee and I heard my cell phone ring from upstairs. The clock on the stove read 6:45.

What now? I raced upstairs and found the illusive phone tangled in the heap of blankets hanging off the edge of the bed.

"Why didn't you insist Harrigan Funeral Home handle your deceased tenant?" Yancy Candlemass, Gram's assistant mortician, bleated in my ear.

"Good morning to you. FYI I had no choice in the matter. Wyco-Young funeral home was next on the rotation schedule," I answered.

"Where's your sense of pride? Your sense of loyalty? The rotation schedule is rarely adhered to! One word and the money would be in our coffers, not Wyco-Young's"

I pictured Yancy, white-knuckle grip on the phone, pacing his apartment over the funeral home's garage, his patrician features scrunched into a scowl as he dragged his fingers through his thick, golden hair with each step. Gram loved his mad skills for making loved ones look like they were simply sleeping in a satin-lined slumber chamber. I didn't share her view but as long as I wasn't required to help Gram at the funeral home, I could put up with his idiosyncrasies.

"Guess I wasn't thinking straight after seeing Thelma all black and bloated. Trust me, you're lucky you are not dealing with Thelma's sister."

"Mercedes McCambridge Harrigan, I have handled my share of prickly relatives. Thelma's sister wouldn't be a problem."

"Uh-huh. Candlemass, she called me this morning and Wyco-Young will have their hands full."

"Whatever. You'd better not call your grandmother with this trifling matter," he said.

Trifling matter? Now I wish I had pressed Judy Kelso to use Harrigan Funeral Home. I clicked off and turned to find Bogart and Bacall sitting side-by-side on my pillow, tails thumping the headboard.

"Okay, perimeter search." With a single bound the pair raced down the stairs, barking full throttle. Thank heaven for pet doors.

I donned a pair of jeans I'd tossed at the foot of the bed, and a frayed, softer-than-skin sweatshirt, socks and sneakers. With one last longing look at my warm bed, I went back downstairs to wait for the coffee to finish perking.

From the window over the sink, I watched Bogart sniff the left half of my fenced back yard while Bacall sniffed the right. They met in the middle and switched sides. Beyond the six-foot chain-link fence, dew sparkled on clumps of sagebrush and cedar trees, while darkening the poles on my empty corral. An ad I placed in a couple of online papers had produced two measly calls from people in search of a place to board their horse. Neither caller had met my specifications, or vice versa.

I poured a mug of coffee and watched the barn cats, Cagney and Lacey, leap onto the round, metal table in the middle of the patio. With a calico paw, Cagney nudged her bowl and looked at me.

"Coming," I said. Before I could reach the pantry to grab the bag of cat food, the phone rang. Somehow I'd managed to misplace the cordless so had to settle for the ancient wall phone.

"Hello." I tried for a snarl, but it came out more croak.

"Hello, Ms. Harrigan. My name's Casey Kelso. Judy Kelso's son." His voice was soft, almost breathless.

"Mr. Kelso, I'm very sorry about your aunt. But, like I told your mother, there is no way to get into the apartment until the cleaning company is finished."

"That's not the reason I called."

Oh-oh. From his tone, I guessed this was not a social call either.

"My mother wanted to discuss a couple of very important issues, but you hung up so abruptly she didn't have a chance."

I wound the ancient phone cord around my finger and took a deep breath. "Mr. Kelso, your mother ended our conversation."

"Yes, she became . . . flustered."

"She sounded fine."

"Mama has a way of hiding her feelings," he said.

Could've fooled me.

"Truth is Thelma's death is really taking a toll. I had to give her a tranquilizer the doctor ordered. After talking with you, she fell apart."

For a moment I had a vivid image of a Judy Kelso mannequin collapsing into a heap while her son tried to put her right again. I wondered if he'd placed a call to all the king's horses and men. Cagney jumped onto the window ledge and pawed at the window pane.

"Can you hang on one second? I need to switch phones." I laid the kitchen phone down on the counter and raced up the stairs. The cordless was on the bed, just where I'd dropped it. "Are you still there?"

"Yes, Ms. Harrigan, but I don't have all day."

Like I did? "What did your mother want to discuss, Mr. Kelso?" I hung up the antique kitchen wall phone, grabbed the bag of cat food from the pantry and went outside onto the patio. While I poured fish-shaped morsels into two bowls, the cats purred and Kelso launched into a lengthy narration about what a tremendous influence his aunt had been in his life. Wonderful, but why tell me?

"We were close. Lately I was more or less in charge of the bookstore. Her death has created a real void."

"You have my sympathy, Mr. Kelso. Your aunt was a fine woman. I'll miss her, too." I opened the screen door, intending to warm up my coffee and end this conversation. Kelso was rambling, not explaining any more than his mother had. If I let him continue, I'd be late meeting the ozone commando.

"Then you'll agree that something must be done to compensate the family for our loss?"

"What?"

"I've been in touch with our lawyer. He thinks we have a good case against you for renting out apartments with substandard wiring."

The plastic mug slipped from my fingers, landing next to Bacall and sloshing her with lukewarm coffee. Wedging the phone between my shoulder and ear, I grabbed a handful of paper towels and began blotting my bewildered dog.

"It's okay, baby. You're okay." I whispered.

"Excuse me?" Kelso's voice boomed in my ear.

I handed both dogs a doggie biscuit and started mopping the floor with more paper towels. "Mr. Kelso, are you telling me you intend to sue me?"

"No. Of course not. Lawsuits are expensive. I'm sure we can come to an agreement that would satisfy both parties without ever stepping inside a courtroom."

Lawsuit?

Settlement?

All Kelso's nice-nice talk had thrown me off-guard. The man was lower than snake dung in a wagon rut. I wanted to scream or kick something. Instead, I gritted my teeth and said, "I'll have my lawyer contact your lawyer." Then I slammed down the phone—not a smart move with a cordless. Good thing neither Kelso had my cell number. Slamming it would've added another crack to the screen.

I poured another mug of coffee, added the proper amount of cream and sugar for my stress level, and slumped into the nearest kitchen chair.

Me and my mouth—I didn't have a lawyer. The only attorney I knew was Gram's friend, and he was on the same cruise as Gram. I couldn't ask him any questions without alerting Gram to the situation. She'd cancel her trip, race home, and I'd feel guilty forever.

Would legal aid take my case?

Did Kelso have a case? Or was the pompous jerk testing the ol' proverbial waters? If so, he'd find my waters were nothing more than a small, muddy puddle.

Moneypenny had said he wouldn't have the autopsy results until later today. I didn't know whether my wiring or Thelma's heart was the cause of death. Where had Kelso gotten his information? Did he have a source inside the coroner's office?

"Buzzards are quick to smell money after a death," Gram always said.

My cell shrilled, and I eyed it warily. The caller I.D. read A-1 Cleaning. This could not be good. I answered and learned Seeley, the ozone commando, had been called out on an emergency. His wife apologized and said he'd get back to me ASAP. I thanked her and hung up, wondering if it wouldn't be prudent for me to go back to bed and forget the rest of the day.

While I poured Bogart and Bacall their food, my mind kept picturing the old toaster on Thelma's counter. I'd eaten plenty of toast in her kitchen, but not toasted by that nifty-fifties model.

Yesterday, Dexter's comment about "someone doing Thelma in" seemed comical. Now I wasn't so sure.

I leaned against the tile countertop, sipped my coffee, and stared at the fridge magnets. Say I wanted to murder an older person with a bad heart. Electricity shooting from a bare wire ought to stop an old ticker and make the death seem accidental. The idea was nefarious, brilliant. A shiver ran through me and I gulped more coffee.

Who would want to murder a sweet, elderly bookstore owner? And why? I fished a notebook from under a pile of catalogues and junk mail stacked on the counter, sat down at the table and began listing Thelma's acquaintances: her sister, nephew, the other tenants and neighbors, her flower club, bridge club, people from the bookstore, and her boyfriend, Claude Phoenix.

I sighed and laid down my pencil: too many people, too many unknowns. This wasn't one of my fictitious stories I could mold and shape, it was real life. Thelma's death was an accident. Even if it wasn't, what could I, a wet-behind-the-ears-landlord and thriller writer, do about it?

My cell phone rang and the name W. Harrigan popped into the little square. Wilma Harrigan, a.k.a. my mother. I groaned, laid my head on the table and hoped she was busy explaining her latest drama to my voicemail. Or she could hang up and try again later; her choice. I knew I'd have to talk to her before the day was over.

Don't get me wrong. I love Willie for bringing me into this world, but she's missing the mothering gene. At age twenty, she landed a couple of walk-on parts in B-grade horror films. After that, she turned her back on the hippie generation and reinvented herself with classic Hollywood style: choosing to stuff her bras instead of burn them, and naming me Mercedes McCambridge and my brother, Cary Grant, after her favorite actors. She lives in L.A. and gives true meaning to the catch phrase Drama Queen. Aunt Vie always called her a pip. I can't repeat what Gram calls her.

So far, every phone call had played havoc with my morning. I wanted to call Gram just to hear her reassuring voice, her sound logic to quell this slight crisis; since that wasn't an option I decided it was time to spread a little ruin of my own. I ran upstairs, washed my face, brushed my teeth, and stuffed my hair under a Cardinals baseball cap.

Making sure the latch on the backyard gate was secure, I left Bogart and Bacall barking their annoyance, while I tromped up the hill to the barn and into the tack room where I store all my garden paraphernalia. I shrugged into a tank sprayer backpack filled with Weed-Be-Dead and began coating the legions of dandelions, milkweeds, and morning glory around the corral. Possibly a waste of time since a hard freeze could hit and turn lively green stalks barren black. But annihilating weeds made me feel powerful—like Bill Murray in *Ghostbusters*—extremely therapeutic.

The sprayer was nearly empty when I heard the dogs launch themselves at the fence and bark in frenzied guard mode. Wiping the sweat trickling along my hairline, I shielded my eyes against the sun and scanned the horizon. A dark horse and rider were loping along the ridge on the hill behind my barn. The horse halted beside a copse of golden aspen trees and began picking its way down the boulder-strewn path heading straight for my corral.

A swallow caught in my throat. My favorite childhood fantasy involved seeking adventure on the back of a magnificent black horse with long, glossy mane and tail. Now, Lord have mercy, that horse was wending its way toward me.

The rider, dressed all in black from boots to well-worn hat, was a perfect complement to the steed of this girl's dreams. The pair stopped beside the corral and the man dismounted. I blinked a couple of times to make sure it wasn't a mirage, then walked toward the pair, anxious to touch the horse's soft muzzle.

"Nice area. Is this the place advertised on the fairground notice board?" the rider asked.

"Yes," I said. This morning from hell was looking better. "You need a place to board your horse?"

"If the terms meet my budget." He dismounted and secured the reins to the middle fence pole; then turned, tilted his hat up, and I realized why his voice sounded familiar. I was looking into the green eyes of Officer Jack Killian.

FOUR

"**H**EY, WE MEET AGAIN," KILLIAN SAID.

He flashed a dimpled smile that made my insides go all tingly.

"Officer Killian, right?" I said.

Refusing to grimace and dive for cover, I straightened my shoulders and lifted my chin. Forcing a smile, I wiped my hand on my pant leg then extended it. His hand clasped mine, sending an electrical twinge through my already nervous stomach.

Control, Harrigan! Control.

Shrugging off the weed sprayer into the tall grass, I took a few steps past Killian toward his horse. "What a beautiful animal. Is he friendly?"

"Eclipse is one of the best horses around. Loves attention, especially from the ladies," he said, giving me a broad wink.

Hokey, yet part of me found the wink charming. I held my hand out for the stallion to smell before skimming a finger down his dark muzzle. His bright, black eyes sized me up, and he blew softly into my palm as though he sensed the battle raging between my brain and hormones.

Bogart and Bacall added a jealous yip to their barking. Eclipse gave a quick ear flick and snort, which I guessed was horse for "chill-your-yapping."

"My dogs don't seem to bother him," I said, scratching between his ears. I gave the shush command to my canines and for once they obeyed.

"Dogs don't trouble this guy. His current boarding place has five or six Rhodesian Ridgebacks. Dinnertime is chaos." Killian leaned against the fence and shoved a hand into the front pocket of his jeans. "You own all this?" he asked, sweeping his free arm in a wide arc.

"Most of four acres, from the road in front of the house to the ridge above."

He nodded. "Great place, but a little isolated. Must get kind of lonely."

He glanced sideways at me, and his full lips parted in a grin.

I gave him my best deadpan, get-over-yourself expression and answered, "Sometimes isolation is a great reprieve from picky tenant demands."

He took his hat off and raked a hand through thick, tawny hair, strong biceps showing beneath the short sleeves of his tee shirt. No telltale wedding ring but that didn't mean much.

Replacing his hat, he climbed between the rails of the fence. "What would it cost me a month to board Eclipse if I furnished his feed?" He paced off the length of the corral and glanced back, waiting for my answer.

"If you provide his feed? How does $150.00 a month sound?"

The price was lower than I'd had in mind, but it could work.

He paused, looked at the dust on his boots, and I could almost hear his mental calculator tallying expenses.

"Great. You've got yourself a new boarder." We shook on it.

He led Eclipse along the perimeter of the pole fence and into the barn. After surveying the three stalls he led Eclipse into the closest one. "Think I'll take this one, looks a little wider than the other two."

"First come, first choice," I said. I had goose bumps on top of goose bumps watching this magnificent horse move. "As soon as I can afford the upkeep, I plan on getting a horse of my own."

"I hear you about the money part. This guy nearly breaks me at times." He tightened the cinch strap while Eclipse stood placid, tail twitching. Killian looked at me and pushed his hat back a notch. "I thought owning apartments was a real moneymaker."

"Can be, but I'm trying to renovate the whole complex. And don't get me started on property taxes. Two or more vacancies and I start searching for part-time jobs."

He thunked the heel of his hand against his forehead. "I meant to talk to you yesterday after the coroner finished but got called out on a fender-bender. A good friend of mine owns a cleaning business. She can help you get rid of the smell in that apartment."

According to Dexter, the stench would linger in my memory for eternity. Terrific!

"Thanks, I've already contacted a cleaning service." I paused. Here was an opportunity to confide my switched toaster theory to a trained professional—a trained professional who might label me crazy. He might change his mind about keeping his beautiful horse in my barn. It was best to keep quiet and not stick my size eight boot in my mouth.

"Okay. But, if you ever need help, this woman knows her stuff. Guess I better head back. I'll bring Eclipse over in the morning around seven and get him settled before I report for work," he said, swinging smoothly up into the saddle. "If that's okay?"

"Seven's great." I gave Eclipse a final pat on the rump. "I'll have fresh straw in his stall by then."

Killian tipped his hat. He nudged Eclipse into a canter and rode back up the trail he'd come down. The two of them made a fine sight—coming or going.

I stored the weed sprayer and hurried back to the house. The blinking light on my answering machine drew my eye. I pressed play, heard Willie's voice, and pressed skip. I checked my cell and found two voice mails from her. Calling both of my phones meant something big was happening, at least in the world according to Willie. I should call her. I would when I had more time. Right now, I needed to purchase some straw for the stall, call Rebbie, and give myself and my dogs a shower, in that order.

As I passed the fridge, pulling off my damp sweatshirt and tossing it into the laundry alcove off the back porch, I saw the note under the smiley magnet reminding me to call C.J.'s Flower Shop.

I hit speed dial, then sat and pulled off my sneakers. I was picking cheat-grass out of my socks when C.J. answered, breathing hard.

"Hey, C.J., sounds like you're running a marathon."

"You have no idea, Doll. Had two workers up and run off with each other a couple of days ago. Now I'm stuck unloading the latest flower shipment by my lonesome."

C.J. Grissom is the primo florist in Portneuf Gap. All the mortuaries know and love his work. I could imagine him perched on the tall stool he keeps next to the phone, his long legs wrapped around the lowest rung, while he reached for a pad to take my order.

"What can I do you for?"

"I want to order a small arrangement for Thelma Edwards' funeral this Friday."

"Poor, dear Thelma. Bet finding her in that condition gave you a shock."

"You got that right. Looking at dead people doesn't usually bother me, but Thelma . . ." I shuddered, remembering her bloated body.

"Such a dear woman. I'll really miss her. As V.P. of the flower club, she was all set to step into the president's shoes come January."

"Still hard to think of her as gone." I shucked off my jeans, adding them to the pile of dirty clothes. I thought about starting a load in the washer but decided to wait until I got off the phone.

"Did the old wiring in your complex cause her heart failure?"

My eyebrows tried to crawl together while I stared at the phone.

"Sadie, you still there?"

"Where did you hear about the wiring?" My tone was sharper than intended. I took a moment and tried to unknot the muscles in my shoulders, doing a couple of shrugs and messaging my neck.

"Violet Zoetwilder. She called last night."

Of course, Violet was steering the gossip train. "I'd appreciate it if you didn't let that information out until the coroner is sure."

"Won't say a word, girlfriend. If it was the wiring, you looking at any kind of liability?"

"I don't know yet. The city might want me to bring everything up to code. Hell, C.J., I don't know where I'll get the money. Suppose all the renters have to find another place to live until . . ." I left that thought unfinished as I pictured my bank account draining like a sieve.

"Fellow in our club is a retired electrician. Name's Kennis O'Connor. His wife drags him to the meetings when she can. Nice guy. Why don't you give him a call and see what he thinks? I know he'd rather look at your wiring than discuss the best fertilizer for hothouse roses."

Outside, the day was growing warmer, but inside, dressed only in bra and panties, my arms and legs sprouted a field of goose bumps. I quickly took O'Connor's phone number and told C.J. I'd leave the type of flowers for Thelma's funeral up to him. "Just try to keep within my pitiful price range."

"Will do. Say, what about a nice plant instead? I have a couple of beyond beautiful Jade plants."

"A plant? Is Judy into plants?"

"Whoops, forgot. She hates plants. One look from that Stepford woman and all the leaves would wilt. She's one scary broad."

C.J. stood six-foot-four, solid muscle from the top of his shaved head to his big feet. "You're afraid of an aging Barbie Doll?" I laughed.

"Better believe it. You should be, too," he said and hung up.

After a long, hot shower with my pups (Bogart hates showers, Bacall revels in one) I dressed in a fresh tee and jeans and began calling the list of people I needed to get in touch with. Kennis O'Conner, the electrician, wasn't home. I left a message. I called Rebbie's cell, got her voice-mail and told her to call me ASAP.

I decided to call Seeley, the ozone commando again. As I searched for A-1 Cleaning's number, I wondered if C.J. might provide some insight into Thelma's death. The antique toaster and its implication continued to skip through my mind like a scratched vintage record. I couldn't shake the idea that something wasn't right. If I confided in C.J. would he give me the horse laugh? Maybe, maybe not. Reb was the only person I could run my idea past and not be ridiculed for eternity.

Neither Seeley nor his wife was in but a mechanical voice assured me I'd reached A-1 Cleaning and gave a short resume of what jobs they'd do. The voice then asked me to state my name and number and guaranteed someone would get back to me. I did as asked, hoping the mechanical voice wasn't prone to giving out false promises.

I placed a call to the farmer Aunt Vie bought straw from. Again, I was invited to leave a brief message on voicemail. I complied and hung up, wondering if a neutron bomb had been dropped while I was in the shower. Was I the only person left on earth with scores of eager answering machines patiently awaiting my message?

FIVE

THURSDAY NIGHT, OVER DING DONGS AND apple cider, I'd explained the switched toaster hypothesis to Rebbie. I finally had the autopsy report from the coroner's office, for now, it was inconclusive enough to exonerate my complex from a civil lawsuit due to substandard wiring. My mind wouldn't give up about the strange circumstances. Thelma's accident seemed a little too coincidental, too convenient. She smoked. She had a bad heart. That should be the end of it. But I couldn't shake the feeling something was wrong. As I explained things to Rebbie, my theory appeared solid. However, the longer I talked, the more inept each suspicion sounded, until I ran out of energy and stopped mid-sentence.

Reb frowned, doubt lines creasing the smooth skin between her brown eyes. "Sadie, who would want to kill little old Thelma? No, wait. Why? There's always a why."

"I don't know. But once we discover the "why," the "who" is only a logical deduction or two away. Right?"

"Sure thing, Nancy Drew. Okay, girlfriend, truth or consequence time." Reb deftly split a Ding Dong in half to better invade the gooey center with her tongue. "This is one of your practical jokes, right? And the cute cop you told me about is in on it."

"No joke, no way. I really think Thelma was murdered."

Reb put down the Ding Dong, folded her hands on the table, and stared hard at me, one perfectly waxed eyebrow disappearing beneath her bangs. "But why? You still haven't explained why."

How could I make Reb understand when I didn't have a handle on my reasoning? It would be easy to walk away and let the police stamp accidental or whatever under cause of death and tie it all up with a big bow marked "Rest in Peace." That would be the logical thing to do. But, like the last piece of a jigsaw puzzle that should fit but just misses, something was off. I couldn't give that *something* a name. I only knew I felt pressed to dig deeper, ask questions.

"I have a gut feeling. A very powerful gut feeling." I shrugged. Maybe there wasn't anything to my suspicions except an overactive imagination and a born inclination to snoop.

Reb continued to stare at me for what seemed eons before licking the last chocolate crumb from her fingers. "Okay, I'm in. What do we do?"

It was my gut feeling that sold her. My cause had become her cause. We brainstormed, looking for motives, clues, anything we could take to the police.

NINE O'CLOCK FRIDAY MORNING, WITH HER feet rooted firmly to the edge of the living room carpet, Rebbie stuck her nose into Thelma's kitchen and sniffed. "Smells . . . clean. Hot damn, that little machine really works."

"Not a foul whiff left. Thank you so much, Mr. Seeley." I handed the plump, middle-aged cleaner his payment.

"Anytime you need to 'quench the stench,' just give us a call." He folded the check and put it in his shirt pocket.

Reb favored Seeley with a killer smile. "Mr. Seeley, you are a savior."

I watched the man's chubby face melt into an aw-shucks grin. Damn, I should've let Reb handle the payment. Might've gotten something knocked off the bill.

We'd stopped to check out the apartment on our way to Thelma's funeral. Dressed appropriately in a black dress, I was ready to pay my last respects, whereas Reb had chosen an unconventional layered gray skirt, black lace shirt with matching gloves, and a tight, leather corset. She claimed her outfit would enhance her intuitive vibes.

For our first goal of figuring out who murdered Thelma was to arrive at the mortuary early enough to observe the crowd of mourners, just in case someone up and confessed. Trite, I know, but at two in the morning and hyped on sugar, that was our best plan.

As I helped Seeley maneuver his machine onto the sidewalk, Reb locked the apartment's front door, and we sprinted for her Subaru.

A Jeep Cherokee rumbled into the parking lot and stopped beside us. The driver's door opened and a blonde with short, corkscrew curls hopped out. Dressed in a black peasant skirt and black poet's blouse, she bounced onto the front step and pressed Thelma's doorbell, gnawing on a thumbnail while she scanned the area.

"Who's that?" Reb asked, revving her car's cold engine.

I stuck my head out the passenger window and yelled, "Can I help you?"

The blonde's ankle-high black boots beat a staccato rhythm on the asphalt as she hurried over. "I'm looking for Mercedes Harrigan. Do you know her?" Her voice was high-pitched with a nasal quality like a pebble skittering down a tin roof.

"I'm Mercedes."

"Oh, wow." She clapped her hands and grinned, showing perfect white teeth. "I'm Loralee Lish. I called, left a message about renting Thelma's apartment. The bookstore's been in total chaos since her death. I'm talking grueling hours, haven't had a moment to myself, then, I'm driving by and it hits me—why not take a couple of seconds, bang on some doors, see if the apartment is still for rent. And what do I find? The actual landlord, right here, right now. Talk about great Karma."

Reb leaned forward, pushing her face next to mine. "You want to live in the apartment where your boss died?"

Loralee shrugged. "Sure. Why not? It's not like she was murdered and her ghost will haunt me."

Reb cast me a sidelong glance.

I made a production of looking at my watch. "Ms. Lish, can we discuss this after the funeral?"

"Absolutely. I'd planned on doing the whole funeral and farewell bit, except last night, Casey, Thelma's nephew called and asked me to open the bookstore—you know, for folks that are allergic to funerals but might want to stop by and pay their condolences."

"Or spend a little money," Reb murmured, putting the car in gear.

"I'll get in touch with you later," I said.

Loralee took a step back. "You've got my number?"

"Yes. I do."

Reb turned out of the complex parking lot and stomped on the accelerator. "Man-oh-man do you have her number!" Reb snorted. "That Loralee looks normal, who'd ever suspect she'd want to live at Ghost Gables?"

I braced myself as Reb wrenched the steering wheel and took a sharp left onto Garfield. "My apartments *are not* haunted. I don't want that kind of talk getting around!"

"Okay. Don't get your panties in a bunch. But tell me, truth now, would you want to move into Thelma's?"

The truth? I wasn't about to confess that the area where her bloated body had lain still gave me pause and sometimes goose bumps.

"I'm very comfortable in my house, thank you."

Reb gave me a yeah-right look. "That's not an answer."

"Just shut up and drive."

We screeched into the funeral home parking lot, drawing open-mouthed stares from a few mourners gathered outside for a quick smoke before the service began. From the outside, the Wyco-Young funeral home looked like a small reproduction of Tara in *Gone With the Wind*. Four huge white pillars bordered a wide-planked veranda. Ornate black shutters and window boxes filled with pink carnations graced each window.

I missed the old Wyco mortuary, a three-story, Victorian masterpiece with turrets and a massive wraparound porch. On Halloween, some prankster would change the "C" to a "G" making the white sign out front read: Wygo Funeral Home. After old man Wyco's only child married Stephen Young, the Victorian building was bulldozed, and a new antebellum building erected in its place. Plus, a new hyphenated sign now towered above the mortuary making adding graffiti next to impossible. However, waxing nostalgic wasn't what I'd come here to do.

I pulled open the double front doors and stopped. Reb's sharp inhale echoed my own astonishment. Everything; walls, carpet, upholstered chairs, even the ornately carved banister winding along the stairs to the upper level screamed pink. From deep Pepto-Bismol to the lightest pearl, the entire entry was a monochromatic nightmare. No wonder Judy Kelso had chosen this particular mortuary. It looked like Mattel's version of a Barbie funeral parlor.

"Good Lord, who turned the Easter Bunny loose with a paint brush?" Reb hissed.

"Yancy said old man Wyco gave his daughter carte blanche on a supreme makeover. Probably thinks this pink onslaught is supposed to mute the sting of death, make the patron feel at ease."

"Not working for me. I'm getting queasy."

A large group of mourners milled about, some looking for seats inside two mirror-image chapels, others seeking comfort among small groups of familiar faces. My fingers sought my phone, but I dropped it back in my bag. Probably be in bad taste to take pictures even if I was itching to show this disaster to Gram. I'd wait until the crowd thinned and maybe sneak down a hallway.

Two funerals were planned for the afternoon. We turned toward the right chapel with a discreet black sign that spelled out Thelma's name in white letters.

"Wait." Reb tugged at my sleeve and pointed to a group of people. "There's Vince Broam. Ol' deep pockets called the other day, wants me to list his townhouse. We keep playing phone tag. Be right back." She smoothed her skirt, fluffed her hair, put on her realtor face and sauntered off.

All this pink was giving me a headache. I fumbled in my purse for some aspirin, poured a couple into my palm, and headed down the hall in search of a drinking fountain. Loud voices drew my attention. I sidled up to the corner and peered around the etched-glass water cooler. In an alcove off to the left, Claude Phoenix, Thelma's boyfriend, stood almost nose-to-nose with another man. Handsome face mottled red, Claude growled something I couldn't make out and gestured to the ceiling. His leonine white hair flopped about in disheveled disarray.

The other man, younger and a couple of inches shorter than Claude's six-three, stood with his feet wide apart, arms folded over his chest. His chocolate-brown hair was tied in a stubby ponytail. Without the scowl, his face might be nice looking, even studious, given the black-rimmed glasses perched on his long nose. Both were dressed in black suits, but appeared ready to shed their coats and take the argument out into the alley.

The aspirin clutched in my hand turned sticky slick. I plucked a tissue from one of the boxes placed at convenient intervals and caught movement in my peripheral vision. Stephen Young, Wyco's son-in-law, came hurrying down the chapel aisle. In two strides, he reached the men and put a hand on each of their shoulders.

Wiping my palm, I crept within hearing range a little too late. All I caught was, "We'll just see about that!" from Claude as he brushed away a lock of hair and stormed out a door at the rear of the room.

"Unfortunate." Stephen commented to the heavens in an unctuous voice. He inclined his head, folded his arms, and murmured something to the young man. I turned to make my escape.

"Mercedes? Mercedes Harrigan, is that you? How's your li'l ol' Granmama doin'?"

Gram was neither little nor that old, but, by the snide overtones, I guessed Stephen was smarting over Yancy taking a position at Harrigan Funeral Home. I hoped the grimace didn't show as I turned and bit back my own snarky reply.

"Hi, Stephen. Cass is great, she's on a cruise. Thanks for asking."

Stephen's hairline had receded even further since the last time I'd seen him, giving the top of his head a prominent blonde M. His impeccable suit spoke of success but, decked out or not, he still reminded me of a tall, gangly scarecrow with watery blue eyes. We'd gone to the same high school where he led the basketball team in clobbering the competition. He surprised everyone when he married Sunny Wyco and enrolled in Mortuary College instead of pursuing a basketball career.

Stephen wrapped my hand with his long, cool fingers and nodded to the man at his side. "Have you met Thelma's nephew, Casey Kelso?"

Casey Kelso, Mama Kelso's little swamp slime?

I wanted to have words with Mr. Kelso, yes indeedy. But this wasn't the time or place. Judy Kelso saved me from replying. At least I assumed it was Judy. The woman who wobbled through the door Claude had exited was the correct size and shape, but her features were obscured by a chin-length veil attached to the top of a little black hat. Waving a hanky and sobbing Casey's name, she flung her arms around his neck, weeping and muttering against his shirtfront.

"What's up?" Reb whispered in my ear. I looked around and realized a small group had gathered in the hall.

"Set up bleachers and we can sell popcorn," I murmured.

Before anyone could speculate further, Stephen and Casey each grabbed one of Judy's arms and ushered her out of the room.

A pipe-organ dirge sounded. Stephen's assistant materialized and began quietly directing people into the chapel. Reb and I selected a tufted, dusky-rose bench in the rear to better keep an eye on the rows in front. The second row held tenants from the complex. C.J. was squeezed into the third row next to Dexter and Violet Zoetwielder. By the slow swivel of his bald head, I guessed C.J. was checking out the competition's floral arrangements. Several women seated on either side of the Zoetwielders were doing the same rubbernecking, Thelma's flower club was present and accounted for.

The next row back, I recognized two women from her bridge group sitting beside my resident hypochondriac Agatha Heckathorne.

"Look," Reb whispered, pointing to the first pew on the right-hand side. Claude Phoenix sat ramrod straight, his classic features in profile as he stared at the flower-draped, closed casket. "The poor man's all alone. He owns the Subaru dealership; bet he knows half the people in town. Isn't that strange?"

"Sometimes grief is so overwhelming, people put up invisible barriers."

"His barrier must be flashing leave me be in capital letters."

I nodded. "Emotions are running high. Claude and Casey Kelso had a disagreement earlier in the room where Judy Kelso had her melt-down."

"Disagreement?" Reb's eyes widened. "About?"

"Not sure. That's something we should look into." I settled back against the bench to watch the proceedings.

The chapel was nearly full. The organ music quieted, and the congregation watched in silence as Stephen and Casey maneuvered a sobbing Judy down the aisle. A pencil-thin young woman wearing a long, black sweater-dress walked behind the trio. Midway, Judy either collapsed or tripped, ending up in Stephen's arms. A collective gasp filled the room. Before anyone could leap up and begin CPR, Casey grabbed his mother from Stephen and hauled her unceremoniously to the front pew.

The young woman helped Casey propel Judy from behind.

Judith's daughter? It was hard to make out her features, hidden by the voluminous waves of golden hair hanging in her face.

The two maneuvered Judy into the front row reserved for family, and the golden-haired woman nudged Judy over with a well-placed hip. With everyone seated, the music stopped, and the minister walked to the pulpit.

I'd grown up listening to Gram critique eulogies and had learned they pretty much fall into three categories: good, mediocre, and pretty darn poor. Thelma's fell into the latter. It was obvious the minister had never met Thelma and was covering by spouting scripture. I tuned out and began to study the crowd.

Did Claude Phoenix choose to sit alone out of grief or guilt? Had Dexter Zoetwielder known what I'd find before I'd opened Thelma's door? And what about animal-loving Esther Clemmens, sitting serene and regal beside the stained-glass window? Had she decided to retaliate after Thelma made the nuisance report against her dogs? Had I gone over the edge thinking such macabre thoughts?

The preacher finished. An elderly couple stood to the right of the podium and played a shaky "Shall We Gather at the River" on violins. Stephen rose and instructed the pallbearers to come to their post, then closed by inviting all who wished to join the family for concluding remarks at Mt. Summit cemetery. As Thelma exited the chapel for the final time, Stephen followed behind the casket and family, a signal for the ushers to begin dismissing the congregation by rows. The flower club rose and filed out en masse. As C.J. passed, he bent and whispered that we should join him in the foyer.

"Hitch a ride in my van," he said, clasping my hand as I entered the crowded foyer. "We'll have time to talk on the way to the cemetery. Kennis and Nancy O'Conner are riding with me."

"Who?" Reb asked.

"The O'Conner's. Kennis is an electrician." C.J. enunciated the last word as though speaking to a slow child. He patted Reb's head then turned and threaded his way through the crush of people. I rolled my eyes and sighed. C.J. needed to stifle that attitude.

"Ask a simple question . . ." Reb folded her arms. "I'm not riding with Mr. Jolly Green Jerk."

"Reb, talking to the O'Conner's might be important." I grabbed her elbow and guided her down the hall. "Don't have a hissy-fit."

She snatched her arm from my grasp and looked at me. I swear I saw steam rising from her bouncing curls as she pivoted and headed in the opposite direction.

Faced with either riding with Reb and listening to her rant or riding with C.J. and quizzing Kennis and Nancy on my own, I sighed. Columbo and Jessica Fletcher never faced such decisions. By now the headache that had threatened earlier was building strength. I snatched a drink from the water cooler, gulped down three aspirin, and sprinted for C.J.'s van.

Kennis O'Conner reminded me of an aging Poppin' Fresh Doughboy; bright-eyed and passionate about conduit and cables. He spoke in clipped, rapid sentences, explaining all about the electrical wiring of today versus yesterday. Not much of it made sense to me, but if I wanted an expert he'd be the first one I'd call.

His wife Nancy, seated beside me, remained silent for three blocks, until C.J. turned right onto South Fourth.

"Kennis," she said, interrupting him mid-sentence. "You can bore this young woman with your consummate knowledge later. Right now, there are more pressing issues to discuss." She turned and gave me a long appraising look before reaching into her purse and pulling out a gold compact mirror.

"I suppose you know that Violet Zoetwielder and Thelma never got along." She dotted bright pink lipstick along her lips, smoothed the dots with her pinkie and inspected the results in the mirror. Satisfied, she slipped the compact back into her purse. A statuesque woman compared to her short hubby, Gram would pronounce Nancy a "handsome woman" if she'd use a little more discretion in the makeup department.

"About a year ago, after a very intense club meeting, they nearly got into a slugging match! Right in the parking lot," Nancy continued.

"Over flowers?"

"It began with flowers and ended with Violet accusing Thelma of trying to seduce her hubby, Dexter. I believe she called Thelma a 'brazen hussy.' Something along those lines. Isn't that right, Kennis?"

He shrugged. C.J. nodded his agreement and winked in the rearview mirror.

I couldn't picture Thelma fighting with anyone. "You're joking."

"Do I look like I'm joking? No, Violet was serious. Of course, the problem really started a few months earlier when Thelma accused Violet of poisoning her prize tea roses. Right, Kennis?"

"If you say so, dear." With his thunder stolen, he turned nonverbal.

Poisoned roses? Thelma and Violet going at it like aging alley cats? The whole idea was ludicrous. I felt like I'd slipped down Alice in Wonderland's rabbit hole; wouldn't surprise me to find The Mad Hatter serving tea at the grave site.

Nancy reached over and patted my hand. "I'm only telling you this so you can be careful who you rent Thelma's apartment to. If you rented to, say, a couple instead of a single woman, Violet may feel, well, more secure."

No single women? What would Violet think of Loralee Lish, Thelma's bookstore clerk?

C.J. made the turn into the cemetery and Nancy sighed, loud and long. "Thank God, this is almost over. I really detest funerals. I'm attending more every year." She grasped my hand once more, face somber, fake eyelashes weighing down her lids. "You know, youth really is wasted on the young."

She shook her head, hand on the door handle. "Before I forget . . ." She pointed out the van's back window at a white Volkswagen pulling up behind. "That's Floydean Mollicker in her cute little car.

I'll introduce you after this is over. Floydean has access to a big truck, and she said she'd be happy to help move Thelma's plants if no one else has offered. I'd love to have the Asparagus Fern hanging in the kitchen, but I just haven't any room."

Thelma's plants! How could I have forgotten? They were like family to her. Each one had a name, and she played appropriate music for different growth seasons. With my knowledge of flora, it would be a death sentence if I hauled them home. From what C.J. had said, Judy Kelso would not welcome the various plants decorating Thelma's apartment. I'd have to check and see. If she agreed to come and get the plants, great! One less hassle for me. If she didn't want any of them, I'd have to appeal to everyone in her club to please have mercy and find homes for the multitude of plants.

We climbed out of the van. Nancy took C.J.'s arm and wobbled unsteadily, spiked heels aerating the lawn as they walked to the awning-covered grave. Too bad she didn't know Gram's rule: always wear flats to a funeral. Lush cemetery lawns are murder on Bianni Binis.

The crowd surrounding the grave shifted uneasily as the pall-bearers unloaded the casket. Standing beside Kennis, I scanned the crowd, looking for Reb. No sign of her, but I was happy to see Claude Phoenix was no longer alone. A young man, with a strong family resemblance, stood by his side. Claude's grandson?

The guy's sun-bleached, wavy hair accented a generous mouth, chiseled chin, and eyes the color of dark chocolate. The gray sports coat and black shirt looked like they'd been custom tailored. Thelma had tried numerous times to set me up on a blind date with Claude's grandson. She always described him as "An excellent dude, ready to step into the big bucks with his graduate degree in electrical engineering." I gave myself a mental slap for turning her down.

"Still can't understand," Kennis whispered.

"Understand what?"

"Thelma's toaster shorting out like that. The club gave her the dang thing couple of months ago. Must'a been a lemon. Guess a body can't be too careful nowadays." He shook his head at the sorry state of the world and eased his way through the crowd to join C.J. and Nancy.

I took a step forward and stopped. The distinct powerful smell of fresh toasted bread swirled past my nose, dotting my arms with goose bumps. I closed my eyes and the smell transported me back to Thelma's kitchen and the many conversations we'd had about different authors, world events, everyday life.

"Thelma?" I whispered. My heart tapped a staccato cadence, and my mouth went dry as cleansing powder. I forgot about joining C.J. and the O'Conner's, and turned, head swiveling, expecting . . . what? A ghostly apparition floating above the freshly dug grave? *Yeah, right!*

Gram and Yancy loved to recount the times they'd felt the spirit of a deceased person reaching out from beyond; nothing horrid or earthshaking, usually just a subtle goodbye or to leave a lingering thought. Even though I loved a good ghost story, I'd dismissed their paranormal experiences as the side effect of working with so many embalming chemicals.

Until now.

A sensation shimmied through me so strong and I'm no more psychic than the average person, but at that moment, I understood completely: Thelma's death was no accident.

Thelma had been murdered.

Murdered . . . somehow the word felt exactly right.

However, I couldn't march into the police station with details of my supernatural experience.

I needed facts, hard facts.

And I needed names.

A strong motive would help.

The killer thought he'd gotten away with murder.

I knew better. Now I just had to prove it.

Six

DRESSING UP TO ATTEND A STATEWIDE AWARDS dinner when the theme is real estate and stock markets, prime lending rates, and blah, blah, blah is not at the top of my entertainment list. I'm not a realtor. I've never had a strong desire to join their ranks. And attending a dinner to celebrate top realtors ranked just above double root canal on my list of things to do.

So why was I seated next to Reb at a round table with ten chatty, animated people expounding recent sales and the fluctuation in interest rates? Sometimes I make prior promises with the best of intentions, especially if the cause sounds good and the event is in the *distant* future. I usually shelve the commitment in some dark recess of my mind, secure in the thought that said future is at least several weeks away. I'll have plenty of time to prepare to attend . . . or prepare an excuse . . . or Armageddon will happen, and I won't have to do anything. But, always at the most inopportune time, the promise sneaks up on me . . . like now.

Of course, I wanted to support Reb at this dinner. It was important and she was very excited to be nominated for something pretty darn exciting. When she invited me, I was all onboard. Then Thelma died, I was looking at a possible lawsuit, and my hunch that her death wasn't accidental had me a little distracted. Eating rubbery chicken and listening to people gush about the amazing houses they'd either sold or listed wasn't where I wanted to be.

Reb was seated to my right, dressed for beyond success in a Michael Korr knockoff. She'd introduced me to everyone at our table and I'd smiled and made the obligatory comments as their names slid into a "forgettable" file in my mind. A young woman stood at the podium explaining the latest, greatest new tech tool that was sure to help create listings. Reb was leaning forward, arms crossed neatly on the table, giving the gentleman across the table a peek at her cleavage. Her eyes were fever bright as she absorbed what sounded like gobble-gook to me. Not feeling the excitement, I tried to pinpoint the dessert cart which should be making an appearance soon according to Robert's Rules or whatever dictates the ebb and flow of banquets. My gaze landed on two people I'd seen a couple of days ago at Thelma's funeral: Casey Kelso and Mama Kelso. The duo was seated at the table closest to the podium and stage—interesting. At the head of their table sat one of the top realtors in Portneuf Gap, Marci Seamons. Marci might be an extremely voracious reader and frequent customer at the bookstore. Still, it struck me as odd. I wasn't sure Thelma's bookstore carried books on real estate and Marci didn't seem the type to curl up with a book at the end of the day. But stranger things . . .

I spied Agatha Heckathorn at a table in the far corner by the exit door. Her attendance didn't surprise me much, my resident hypochondriac tends to get around: funerals, viewings, ribbon cuttings, you name it. I think she invented the art of photo bombing. She was in an animated conversation with a woman who looked like she'd rather be somewhere else. If the woman only knew the secret to listening to Agatha; she didn't need an attentive audience, just a person willing to nod at the appropriate time as she touted the latest "natural" cure.

Claude Phoenix was seated at a table near the center of the room. I watched him push his food around his plate and felt a sorrowful pang zing my heart. I suppose this was as good a place to sell cars, realtors practically live in their vehicles, either driving potential buyers all around looking at homes or meeting to show the buyer a listing from one of the many websites. Sadly, Claude's usual robust personality was lacking tonight, no trouble guessing why.

"What are you looking at?" Reb asked.

"Looking at?"

"Yes, your head is swiveling like you're in need of an exorcism."

"I'm scouting for the dessert cart, I need chocolate. Haven't seen the cart yet but a few mourners from the funeral are here." I pointed to the table in front of the stage.

Reb gasped. "Mama Kelso and sonny boy? And sitting at the head table! Is that Marci Seamons? Why would they be with her? What is that vile woman up to now?"

"Maybe they're looking to join the ranks of successful realtors and wanted to rub shoulders with the crème de la crème."

Reb gave me her "how can you be so clueless" look. "Seamons is more snake de la snake."

"Uh-huh."

"Google cutthroat and you'll find her picture. It's rumored she sold a used cemetery plot for a fat commission!" Reb tapped a staccato with her nails against the tablecloth.

The realtor on Reb's left, Carolyn Tusch according to her name tag, touched Reb's arm. "It's also rumored Ms. Kelso is in the market to sell her home and that prime block of storage units on Philbin Road. She's thinking of downsizing!" Tusch sat back and folded her arms across her beanpole body. "Watching the feeding frenzy to see which company lands *that* listing will be better than *Shark Week.*" With her shock of short red hair, bright gold hoop earrings, and blue eyes like the carnival glass candy dish on Gram's beside table, I wondered what type of realtor Carolyn was. Her wide predatory smile erased any doubts.

She extracted a vintage cigarette case from her purse, flipped the catch and handed me one of her business cards: Carolyn Tusch in bold black letters stood out against a cream background and underneath the words, *I'll Work My Tusch Off For You*, underscored her commitment.

Clever . . . and she scored points for using vintage instead of plastic.

Reb snatched the card and handed it back to Carolyn. "If Mercedes needs a topnotch realtor she has my number."

"Mercedes?" Carolyn frowned, tilted her head and gave me a long look. "Is your last name Harrigan?"

I nodded waiting for the usual 'are you related to the funeral home Harrigans' question.

"So you're the landlord that Ms Kelso is bringing a lawsuit against, right? Or is it a lawsuit against your apartment complex?"

Reb choked on a sip of water and the gentle buzz of conversation quieted around our table as each person assumed the unmistakable posture of dropper of eves.

I felt my face heat and dabbed my lips with a linen napkin. "I'm afraid I cannot comment at this time." *Lame! Lame! Lame!* I need to take some type of course that taught *Fast Thinking on Your Feet or Best Come-backs For Awkward Situations!*

The gentleman across from Reb blinked a couple of times behind thick glasses and stroked his goatee with his soft fingers. "Something to do with outdated wiring, right? A bare wire might've triggered a heart attack in Ms. Kelso's elderly sister?"

I drew in a sharp breath. Tension shot up my neck muscles. It seemed our table had pronounced sentence against my apartments without getting all of the facts. Was it too late to run away and join the circus? I pushed aside thoughts of sparkly tights, hearing the excited roar of the crowd with zero apartment problems attached, and forced myself to take a deep breath.

"Ms. Kelso's sister, Thelma, was a heavy smoker. The coroner's verdict was inconclusive." I said.

"Smoking? Wiring? Either way, once your heart stops that's pretty much all she wrote," the bespectacled fellow murmured. "But

I'm not telling you anything. Aren't you related to the Harrigan Funeral Home folks?"

There it was the recognition I was familiar with.

"I'll have you all know that my friend is a responsible landlord. She goes the extra mile to make sure her tenants are well taken care of." Rebbie put her arm around me and dared anyone to contradict her.

"Might not be in your best interest to let the Kelso's know you're BFF's," Carolyn said. "It could skew your chance to list any of their multiple properties." She excused herself, stood and took her skinny, hard-working derriere toward the doors leading to the restrooms.

Waiters in tailored, gray-striped pants, white shirt and crisp red bowties began placing luscious-looking seven layer chocolate cake on tiny plates to each attendee.

Reb elbowed me and whispered, "Those guys beat a wobbly dessert cart any day."

Gorgeous waiters aside, I looked down at the delectable treat and sighed. My appetite had deserted me just when I needed it most. Chocolate was my go-to friend in times of trouble, but right now this heavenly confection looked wretched. Unable to eat, I picked at the gooey center as my thoughts wandered like the new baby ducks around my neighbor's pond; impossible to catch or contain.

"Chocolate can be very restorative in the right circumstances." Agatha slipped into the seat vacated by Carolyn Tusch, picked up a fork and took a sample bite of my cake.

"I thought you decided to ban all sugar from your diet," Reb said, scooting her plate away from Agatha's reach.

"I am able to indulge only when my biorhythms and the phasing of the moon is exactly copacetic. For the next week I shall revel in all types of chocolate."

"Or when a free dessert is available," our myopic tablemate stage whispered.

Agatha's head jerked around so fast I wondered if she'd be sporting a whiplash collar tomorrow. "I'll have you know young Whippersnapper . . ."

I was about to grab Reb's hand and exit the table, but she pulled me to my feet first. "Time to mingle."

I couldn't decide which was the worst option—listening to Agatha berate the young Whippersnapper or trailing behind Reb like a lost dog as she schmoozed the room. I caught a snippet of Agatha's rant from our table and quickly joined Reb, except she was headed toward the restrooms. Hey if nature calls . . .

She burst into the Lady's Room making the swinging door rico-chet off the wall. I caught the door and let it ease shut. The room appeared empty. Reb bent double and started looking under each closed stall door. I folded my arms and watched, both intrigued and amused.

She stood and glared at me. "What are you smiling at?"

"Nothing. Nothing whatsoever."

"Where did she go?"

"Who?"

"*I'll Work My Tusch Off For You.* That's who!"

"Sorry. Didn't know it was my day to watch her."

"Oh, shut up!" Reb marched over to the gilded mirror above the sinks and plunked her tiny bag on the beautiful mosaic tile counter in shades of peach and green. Two antique ice cream parlor chairs, upholstered to match the countertop were tucked sedately underneath.

Did I mention the awards dinner was being held at one of the poshest hotels in Portneuf Gap. Yancy would've swooned.

I watched her apply more mascara and lipstick and fluff her hair with a manic air.

I rubbed my stiff neck muscles. "A little hint? A tiny clue? Help me out. I'm actually clueless here."

"Mama Kelso has multiple properties. How did I not know this?" Reb tapped the mascara tube against her palm. "I need to up my game! Damn *I'll Work My Tusch Off For You* cards! Damn, damn, damn!"

Probably not a good time to point out that we were both clever repartee-challenged. I went over and put my arm around her shoulders. "Hey, you're great at what you do. You're always hustling. So Tusch has a gimmick card. Sure, at first it's fun but the fun wears off if she can't deliver the goods. You just got an award. She didn't."

Reb swiped at a tear and stood straighter. "She didn't, did she?"

I shook my head.

A slow quirky smile appeared from her freshly colored lips. "Let's go schmooze."

As we exited the ladies room, the banquet seemed to be winding down. All the awards had been handed out. All the speeches had been given and I could see the vendors for the event discreetly packing away their merchandise.

"Looks like they're calling it a night." I laughed as I caught site of Agatha Heckathorn hugging three takeout boxes to her chest. Strike one for moon phasing and biorhythms.

Reb effusively thanked the trio that I guessed was responsible for hosting the event while I wandered over to the indoor pool to suck in the chlorinated air. In the corner, beside the portable bar stood Mama Kelso, Sonny Kelso, and Claude Phoenix. Each had a drink and at first, I thought they were having a civil conversation. Then Mama Kelso slammed her drink onto the bar and marched out. Sonny followed. His goodbye was brief, two words. The first started with the letter "F."

SEVEN

Floydean Mollicker's infectious laugh jingled like a wind chime in the crisp afternoon air. Part Cherokee, with to-die-for cheekbones and glossy black hair, she also sported blue eyes, a smattering of freckles across the bridge of her nose, and a bawdy sense of humor, compliments of her Irish ancestors. Married with a couple of kids, she worked as a dispatcher for the police department and had come straight from a grueling day at work to my complex.

I'd gleaned this info while we gathered Thelma's plants to divide among her friends as Thelma's family did not want them. So much for chitchat, it was time to delve into some serious questions. Thelma had been in the ground for nearly three days, and I wasn't any closer to finding the one responsible.

According to Thelma, Floydean fancied herself as a cop-in-training. She loved to drop small tidbits of the everyday drama from the station.

Hoping she was in the mood to share some knowledge; I began my interrogation with the perfect icebreaker: Officer Jack Killian.

"You want to know if I'm acquainted with cute-buns Killian?" She grinned and rolled her eyes. "Honey, every woman at the station knows that man. Age doesn't matter. He's an equal opportunity flirt."

Dressed in a plain white blouse with a Peter Pan collar, slim navy skirt, and plastic I.D. tag glinting in the sun's rays, Floydean trudged to the truck, bearing the weight of a beautiful Ficus tree. "I'm telling you; the man should get a raise. He's the best ego-booster around."

Uh-huh. My intuition was dead on. Killian might not be married, but he was a big flirt. No need to waste time or energy on the man.

Right, my libido chortled as I shuffled behind Floydean, trying not to inhale the ruffled foliage of a giant Boston fern clutched against my chest.

Floydean gave me a sidelong glance as she set the tree on the pavement near the rear wheel well. "How do you know our stud in blue?"

I put the fern down, untangled a couple of tenacious fronds from my hair, and dusted my dirty hands on my jeans. "He stables his horse at my place."

"Yeah?" Floydean raised a wicked eyebrow. "Is that all he stables?"

"Yes." I folded my arms and gave her a steady look. "He's not my type."

"Better watch yourself. He's been known to wear a girl down until he becomes her type." Her skirt hiked up as she hoisted herself into the pickup bed. She stood, tugged the skirt back in place, and began arranging various sized packing boxes in a neat circle. "Hand me the plants, one at a time, so I can judge where to stash them."

I looked at the mini jungle circling the truck, cursed Thelma's green thumb, and began lifting pots. By the time Floydean arranged the last large plant, my shoulders were starting to complain, and the truck looked decidedly lower. She jumped down, dusted off her palms, and shut the tailgate. "Good thing I came today. Some of those babies wouldn't have lasted another twenty-four without water. Thelma had a real gift, especially with exotics."

That was an understatement. The pickup's bed smelled like a tropical rain forest. In the bathroom, next to the tub, we'd discovered a lemon tree sporting two shiny fruits among the dark leaves.

"Are you going to keep any of this?" I asked, swiping at the sweat on my forehead and picking up the last remaining plant.

"Maybe one or two. I stick with what I know. African Violets and the succulent family are—dang girl, where did you find that?" She seized the plant from me and held it at eye level, turning it slowly.

I peered at the green shoots sprouting from the water-stained clay pot nestled inside a yellow and black striped basket. "Is it illegal?"

Floydean shook her head, plucked the pot out and handed it to me. "Hold this." She turned the basket over, ran her hand lovingly across the braided surface, and muttered, "Damn fool."

I stepped closer. "Something special about this basket?"

"Better believe it. If I'm right, this is an antique from her bookstore."

"Thelma was in the antique business?" That was news to me.

"She'd just started. Casey turned her onto a source that provides the store with these incredible ancient Indian baskets. Some go for two hundred a pop."

I whistled and stared at the woven basket. It didn't look special, in fact it looked like it needed a good cleaning.

"You have any use for it?" Floydean asked.

I shrugged and shook my head.

"Well, you know the law. Finders Keepers." She flashed me a grin and put the basket reverently on the blanket-covered front seat of her pickup. "If this is antique, my husband's going to crap his chaps."

"Great." I stretched, yawned, and asked ever so casually, "Is there a lot of competition among different flower clubs?"

"You wouldn't believe it." Leaning against the truck's rust-pocked fender, she rolled her eyes. "Horticulturists are not the mild-mannered, soft-spoken type I thought they'd be. In our own small club, some members act as though you've screwed their husband if you encroach on their particular floral territory.

"The rose and iris growers are the worst. Very hush-hush. Always trying to come up with a new, improved breed to outdo last year's state fair winner."

"I heard there was trouble between the Zoetweilders and Thelma. Something about tea roses?"

"Whew, you got that right. Bad feelings were brewing between those two for months. Then one night, Violet starts accusing Thelma of this and that and Thelma leaps in with more accusations. All of us, especially Dexter, stayed low, hoping they'd settle the mess between them." Floydean looked at Violet and Dexter's apartment and lowered her voice, "The two did make up. Eventually."

"Would Violet purposely poison a plant?" As a bona fide animal lover, I'd rather eat broken glass than harm some creature. I assumed the same would go for plant enthusiasts.

Floydean gnawed her lower lip, eyes down, thinking. "Being Violet's landlord, you might know Violet better than I do. But from what I've seen, if revenge was the motive I'd have to say yes."

I was surprised and it must've shown. She immediately began back-pedaling. "'Course, I couldn't say for sure. The variety of tea rose Thelma chose is very delicate. She started the rose slips in her bathroom, iffy move. She might have moved the plants outside too soon." She checked her watch, pushed away from the fender and started around the front of the truck. "Think I'll grab some Chinese take-out before I pick the kiddos up."

Damn, I'd blown it. She was making a hasty retreat.

I had questions, so I blurted the first thing that came to mind. "Would Violet kill someone for revenge?"

"Lord love a duck! Killing flowers is one thing, but . . ." Hands on her hips, she narrowed her eyes and looked at me like she was glad we had the pickup between us. At least she wasn't climbing behind the wheel and peeling out of the parking lot. "What makes you ask?"

"Well, you work in law enforcement," I hedged. "Bet you've seen some nasty stuff."

She remained silent. I'd come this far, might as well jump in all the way. I leaned back against my car, folded my arms to show how harmless I really am, and explained my murder by toaster suspicion. Floydean listened, hands relaxing, eyes slowly returning to their normal almond shape. When I finished, she again sucked in her lower lip and studied the toes of her black shoes with interest.

"The club bought her a new toaster. Maybe she took it in for repairs. Probably borrowed the faulty one." She chewed that lip a little more, looked off into the distance and frowned. "No. To murder Thelma with a faulty toaster the culprit would've had to be there to keep Thelma's hand pressed against the bare wire. That would mean watching Thelma flop around until her heart stopped."

Yuck! I started to protest, but she held up her hand. "Murder involves a strong motive. I can't see anyone, even Violet, working up that kind of anger at Thelma. Her poor ol' heart simply up and quit. Guess you know she smoked like crazy. If electricity was the culprit, then I'd say fate lent a helping hand."

I shrugged, powerless to counter her logic. I wasn't about to tell her about my paranormal experience at the cemetery. Instead, I thanked her for her help.

"Why don't you pick out a plant?" She waved a hand at the foliage-filled truck bed. "Thelma would want you to have one."

I eyed the multitude, trying to find one I wouldn't kill outright in the first week. A red geranium hunkered by the tailgate looked like a hearty one. Before I could reach over the side, screeching tires snagged my attention. A Domino's Pizza delivery truck shot into the parking lot, jerked twice, then stalled. The driver sat inside, scanning a yellow slip of paper.

I walked over, ready to read this idiot the riot act. Floydean came up beside me—to lend moral support, I suppose.

A slim girl in skinny jeans pushed the door open and hopped out of the truck. She sported purple and black striped hair held in a loose topknot by a number two yellow pencil. Her eye shadow was retro 'bride-of-Frankenstein.' "Hey, either of you know a guy named Arlis? He lives in either nine or seven?"

"Nine," I replied. "Came in a little fast, didn't you?"

"Oh, yeah, sorry. Not real great with a stick yet." She bent and pulled a red-zippered thermal bag from the front seat. Glancing over at Thelma's apartment, she nodded at the loaded truck. "Don't tell me the old lady in number four is moving?"

"She died," Floydean said.

"No shit? There goes a great customer." The girl sighed. "Shame she passed on. I liked her. We talked about books and stuff, and she always tipped, sometimes high as five bucks. This side of town is loaded with tightwads who think I love driving all over, delivering their freakin' order for nothing."

She sighed again, then brightened. "You guys get hungry for pizza, call Domino's. I can have it here in twenty or less."

The mention of pizza, coupled with the aroma coming from the bag, had my stomach making all kinds of demands. Wouldn't be a bad idea to call Reb and see if she'd meet me somewhere. I'd even spring for dinner as sort of a peace offering for the fiasco after the funeral.

"Sorry," I told the girl. "I don't live here, and nobody delivers up Mink Creek."

Her heavily lined eyes narrowed. "You don't live here? Then how'd you know where Arlis lives?"

"I'm the landlord," I explained.

"Yeah? Like you own all these?" she asked.

"Yeah. Like I do."

"Then I guess you know about the funny place the old lady stashed her money. She told me it was better than any bank. I mean,

I've read about people keeping wads of bills in their mattress, but I never saw it until I delivered to her."

Floydean's eyes widened. As if on unspoken command, we turned and walked together to Thelma's apartment, through the living room and into the back bedroom. On my knees, I flipped the edge of the yellow chenille bedspread and purple wool blanket onto the top of the bed. Peeling off the flowered bottom sheet and mattress pad, I looked up at Floydean then back at the two-foot long line of buttons dotting the side of the mattress.

My hands shook as I unfastened the first metal orb. Floydean joined me and soon eager green bills poked through the slit as we unbuttoned our way to the center. I reached in and grabbed a twenty, then another and another.

Floydean let out a low whistle. "Girl, if you're still thinking of murder, you're holding a pretty good motive."

"Murder? My sister was murdered?" Startled, I turned to find Judy Kelso in the bedroom doorway, eyes wide, right hand splayed across her heart.

Behind her, Casey Kelso and the young woman with the fantastic blonde hair I'd seen at the funeral, peered over Judy's shoulder. Neither looked pleased to find me on my knees clutching a wad of bills. A couple of Viking-sized men wearing gray-striped coveralls with a moving company insignia stitched across the breast pocket, brought up the rear. Judy had arranged to pick up Thelma's belongings today. According to my watch they were an hour early.

I closed my eyes and prayed for strength as all hell broke loose.

Eight

"**C**OME ON, HARRIGAN. YOU WEREN'T TEMPTED to slide a couple of twenties up your sleeve? Help pay for repainting the apartment?" Seated at my kitchen table, Rebbie frowned as she concentrated on removing all the black olives from her pizza slice.

"It's not my money." I took a bite and let the melted cheese, onions, and smoked chicken dance across my taste buds. I simply wanted to wallow in the moment, indulge my growling stomach, and forget about Judy Kelso and the multiple gallons of paint Thelma's smoke-yellowed walls would require returning to normal.

"Considering all of the grief Mama Kelso and Sonny Boy have caused, I'd have grabbed a fistful." Reb tilted her head and gave me a look as she chewed. "You thought about it though."

Rebbie's my blood sister and knows me well. For one nanosecond I had been tempted to get even with the duo. A handful of twenties would help ease the sleepless nights and multiple ulcers I was cultivating due to their threatened lawsuit.

"Okay. I thought about it. But I didn't."

"Good thing. You'd have been caught, your poker face sucks, big time." She bent down to give Bogart, sitting up, front paws quivering, a slice of mozzarella-covered chicken.

"You gonna clean up after he gets sick?" I asked.

"One little piece won't hurt him." Bogart took the morsel like a gentleman and gulped it whole. Tail dusting the floor, he looked back and forth between me and Reb with beseeching brown eyes. "How can you ignore that face?" She reached down and scratched under his chin.

"Too much human food equals another vet go-around. His stomach is not as cast-iron as he thinks. You want to foot the next bill?"

"The Kelsos have made your mama grumpy," Rebbie cooed, rubbing Bogart's chest. "She'll get over herself." Bacall chose that moment to slip in through the pet door carrying a dirt-crusted chew bone, and Bogart bounded after her, no doubt thinking she'd unearthed his winter stash. Maybe she had. "How much money was shoved in that mattress?"

"Don't know, don't want to know. Sometimes I wonder if Aunt Vie left me the apartments in a moment of madness." I laid down the slice of pizza, my appetite waning. "I should've let Justine and Jared have the damn property. Then this mess would be on their heads."

Reb rolled her eyes. "If your covetous cousins owned the complex, it would be in shambles, and you'd still be waiting tables. Geesh, what's your problem?"

"Being accused of robbery *and* murder by Mama Kelso makes me a little crazy."

"Ignore that aging Barbie doll."

"Kinda hard when the woman's ranting in my face. She could give my mother drama lessons. In the middle of our screaming match, Casey's girlfriend jumps in calling my apartments 'scummy' and making me out to be a cross between Jeffery Dahmer and Charles Manson. I'm just glad Floydean Mollicker was there. She remained cool. Got everyone calmed down."

I took a deep breath and sipped some water, wishing for something stronger . . . maybe arsenic. "When I left, I told Mama

Kelso to leave the extra key on the table. If I never see that woman again it'll be too soon."

"So that's it!" Reb slapped the table and beamed as though she'd just answered the ten-million-dollar question. "Judy Kelso reminds you of Willy."

"What?"

She held up her hand like a traffic cop. "Just hear me out. Since this whole business started, I've been trying to figure out what's making you so crazy? Finding Thelma was traumatic. Okay. The Kelso's lawsuit threat has you worried. But, Sadie, you remind me of a whipped pup, slinking low, ready to leap out of your skin. And I keep asking myself why?"

"And what do you answer yourself?"

"Judy Kelso intimidates the hell out of you. Just like your mom."

I snorted. Reb ignored me and forged on. "In a way, she's exactly like your mother, only smaller, possibly meaner. Your inner child is running in circles, trying to figure out how to please the little Gestapo maven."

Heaven help me, Reb had morphed into *Wonder Psychologist.* I clenched my fists until my palms hurt. I would not stick my tongue out—or call her names. Even though she was bound to babble on about my inner child's dysfunctional this and that until my teeth hurt. All this grief, thanks to a six-week Community-Ed psych course she'd taken over a year ago.

I opened my mouth to tell her she was wrong, but no sound came out. Instead, I found myself suddenly lightheaded. My heart started thumping like a mean drum solo for some heavy metal band. There wasn't enough air in the kitchen.

I pushed away from the table, went to the sink, and turned on the kitchen faucet. Letting cold water run over my fingertips, I stared out the window at the expanding evening shadows. In the background, I heard Reb's voice, distant and indistinct, asking if I was all right.

Okay, I get panic attacks.

They're handed down from my mother's side, sort of like brown eyes or stubby toes. The attacks started in my teens, a couple of years after my dad disappeared. Older mystery novels would call his absence "taking a powder." It's been a long powder. He vanished when I was fourteen, going out the door to work and never coming home.

I take medication if the anxiety is severe. However, this whopper had blind-sided me but good. Maybe Reb's amateur mumbo-jumbo wasn't so farfetched.

"Sadie, you with me, woman?" Reb put her arm around my shoulders.

"Yes." I swallowed and patted Reb's hand, concentrating on the water swirling down the drain and taking slow, deep breaths.

"Need your pills? I'll get 'em."

I shook my head, gulped air into my lungs, then let it out slowly. "Let's talk about something, anything besides Willy and Mama Kelso."

"Right. Hey, I almost forgot." Reb reached for her purse beneath the table. "I picked this up before coming over." She pulled out a thick photo envelope and began shuffling through the colored pictures. "Most of these are houses I'm showing, but remember last June? The apartment picnic?" She handed me a group of photos.

I sat at the table and thumbed through the small stack, concentrating on the images instead of my pounding heart.

Feeling flush after selling a story, I'd decided an ice breaker for the whole complex was in order. With Reb's help, I'd hosted a parking lot barbeque to get to know my tenants and vice versa. While hotdogs and hamburgers sizzled, neighbors chatted and feasted on potluck dishes.

I grinned at a close-up of one of my tenants chugging a Mountain Dew, yellow liquid streaming down his neck, streaking a white tank top.

"Reb, these are great. Mind if I keep them?"

"Hey, scrapbook away. Except, I want a copy of this one." She held up a picture of the Dorseys, a retired couple in number eight, standing beside their daughter-in-law and newest grandbaby. The young mother gazed down at the sleeping newborn cradled in her arms, her smile was so ethereal it made my heart ache.

Reb sighed. "Right here is the makings of a country song waiting to be twanged. Makes me want to hunt down Mr. Right and start my own little bundle of joy."

I took the photo from her. Just looking at the picture kickstarted my nurturing urges. To hold something so small and feel such a glow, the thought was heady.

Bogart and Bacall raced through the kitchen and out the pet door at full bark about the time I heard a familiar whinny.

Reb's eyes grew round, and I swear her nostrils flared ever so slightly as she parted the curtain over the sink for a better view in the deepening dusk. Pushing away from the sink, she stood straighter, chest thrust forward, and gave her hair a quick fluff.

"Sounds like Killian and Eclipse are back. Want to go say hi?" I asked, trying for nonchalance. Killian might not be my type, but for Reb he was perfect. The only question was who would notch whom on their bedpost.

Reb shrugged. "Okay."

She sauntered out the door, and I couldn't help but grin. Her lips might speak indifference, but her strut was talking a whole 'nother dialect.

We found Killian in the barn, his back to us, as he hefted the black leather saddle and pad from Eclipse and placed it temporarily on the stall's top rail.

"Hey, Jack, how was the ride?"

I went into the stall and began rubbing down Eclipse with my hands. The sweet tang of a horse after a workout is such an aphrodisiac, it's a good thing cologne makers haven't bottled the scent. I'd make a fool of myself around any man who slapped it on. *Whoa, deep breath. Stop with the sensual thoughts! The man was a known ultimate heartbreaker.* I gave myself a firm mental shake.

"I love this time of year," Jack said, working his way down Eclipse's other side with a curry brush. "Spotted seven doe, and a big ol' five-point buck, just over the rise." He turned, brush in hand, eyes focusing on Rebbie for the first time.

Framed against the aging stall gate, her red plaid flannel shirt was suddenly opened to a tantalizing depth. Black jeans accentuated her tiny waist, and she stood with one booted heel hooked over the bottom rail—a great photo if Victoria's Secret started selling western clothes.

"Hello." Killian's grin grew wider, creasing his dimples.

"Hello yourself." Reb said.

I made the proper introductions while the two stood eyeing each other like opposing gladiators.

Jack tipped his hat. "Ms. Russell."

"Rebbie, please." She pushed away from the gate and held her hand out for Eclipse to sniff. Lowering her lashes, she gave Jack an appraising look. "What a beautiful animal."

"He is that." Jack began brushing the horses' long neck, glancing every so often in Rebbie's direction.

They continued to chat in a slow, blasé warm-up. An "Animal Planet" British voiceover added commentary in my head: *"Notice the two Homosapien Extrovertis executing the beginning of the flirtatious ritual."*

Leaning against the gatepost, I folded my arms and waited for the fun to begin.

And I waited.

Instead of witty repartee, which I expected, their banter became inane, bordering on sophomoric, sprinkled with enough cutesy comments to make me want to gag.

Eclipse seemed to sense the building tension and let out a loud knicker, shaking his head and pawing the straw. Not to be left out, Bogart and Bacall began to howl in unison from the backyard. I excused myself on the pretext of checking on the singing duo.

"Catch you later," Reb said, waving me away with a flick of her fingers as though dismissing a faithful servant.

Stomping back to the house, my mood darker than the encroaching night, I stopped outside my back porch and sat on the wooden steps. I took a couple of deep breaths and scooped both dogs onto my lap, holding them close, muttering sweet nothings into their fur. What was wrong with me?

"Jealous," my inner voice whispered.

"Am not!" I countered. Bogart and Bacall looked at me. "Well, I'm not."

Jealousy wasn't a factor. My mood was a culmination of weird events: the money in Thelma's mattress, the hostile confrontation with Judy Kelso ending with the ever-fun grand mal panic blitz. Food was the answer . . . food and a Cherry Pepsi with lots of ice. Did I have any soda? God save the world if I didn't.

"Let's just go have a look-see," I told the dogs, putting them down and opening the back door.

The kitchen light revealed butter-yellow walls and painted red cabinets designed to brighten gloomy moods. In the fridge a lone Cherry Pepsi sat way back on the bottom shelf. I snatched it, twisted off the cap, grabbed a large slice of cold pizza and prepared to make my world right once again. Standing at the counter, I munched and slurped, sharing tidbits of crust with Bogart and Bacall. Okay, their stomachs weren't as touchy as I'd told Reb. I'd been plain grouchy, and it was time to get over it.

I scooted the pile of pictures over and looked through them again. Reb occasionally uses her cell phone to capture photos, but she prefers her Canon DSLR that takes a billion shots a minute and can either do auto focus or manual. She picked it up at a pawn shop, along with enough wide-angle and zoom lenses to impress a seasoned photographer, which was exactly what she was trying to do; impress the teacher of a photography class. The romance didn't last long, but Reb's skill with a camera did.

The piece-de-resistance picture was of the Dorseys with their daughter-in-law and granddaughter. I looked closer at the baby, a blonde angel with round pink cheeks, bow mouth, and plump fists. As I studied the picture, I noticed three people in the far background, standing off to the right, near the chain link fence which borders the river: Judy Kelso, Thelma, and Casey Kelso.

Hmm . . . the Kelsos were guests at the barbeque? My mind said no. The picture proved otherwise. I clearly remembered meeting Judy at Thelma's a couple of weeks after the party. The difference between the two sisters was so blatant, at the time I'd wondered if they were biological siblings. And although Thelma had talked about Casey, it wasn't until the funeral that I'd met Mr. Charm.

I thought back to the picnic. I'd been busy grilling hamburgers, hotdogs, and getting to know all the tenants. But I was positive I hadn't talked to the Kelsos or served them anything from the grill.

Had they eaten? When did they arrive? How long did they stay?

I rummaged through my junk drawer until I found a tiny magnifying glass. Viewing the threesome under the magnifier, I understood why Thelma had been reluctant to make introductions that night. Their body language was not a happy sight. Both women looked as though they were ready to scratch the other's eyes out. Thelma's face was suffused with naked hatred. Judy's eyes looked ready to spit lightning. But it was Casey's expression that held my interest. He lounged against the fence, arms folded, lips curled in a sardonic sneer.

The screen door banged open, and Reb stepped into the kitchen, face flushed, eyes bright, feet barely touching the linoleum as she twirled in a circle. "Jack Killian is capital "G" gorgeous. We have a date on Monday. We might go dancing. Imagine a gorgeous man who loves to dance!"

"That's nice." I returned to the picture.

"Nice? Nice! Ms. Bibliophile and the only word you come up with is nice? Girl, where's your brain?"

"Thinking," I said. I handed Reb the picture and the magnifier. "Look close. See the three unhappy campers in the background?"

Reb studied the picture and whistled. "Talk about a poster for anger management."

"Judy claims she and Thelma were close, hardly ever had a disagreement."

"Wonder why she's trying to paint such happy-home garbage?" Reb frowned. "Wait a minute, Sherlock, you missed one. There are four people." She handed the photo back to me. "Look closer, beyond the giant Clematis climbing the telephone pole, there's a person leaning against the fence on the opposite side of the river."

Reb was right. There was someone in a white shirt hiding behind the climbing vine. I moved the magnifier up and down until I could just make out Esther Clemmens, the Humane Society neighbor.

"That's Ester, and I think she's smiling," I said.

Reb folded her arms and leaned against the counter. "Not sure if she's smiling but, I know she's listening. She's clinging to the fence just like the climbing vine. We need to revisit Ms. Clemmens and jog her memory, get her to do a little walking down memory lane.

NINE

I'D JUST CLOSED MY EYES when the phone woke me with a start. I snatched it from my bedside table and mumbled hello.

"I got 'em Sadie. Shot the little hoodlums square in their baggy-assed pants. They won't be spraying anymore graffiti tonight."

"Dexter?" I looked at my bedside clock. Two friggin' a.m. and my tenant was shooting up the neighborhood. Tucking the phone between my shoulder and chin, I threw on a pair of sweatpants and shoved my feet into worn slippers.

"It was priceless, the three bastards crawling on the ground, crying like babies. Pizinski's doing guard duty. Hustle over and you can help us smack some sense into the idjits before the cops get here."

"Dexter no! No smacking, no nothing. Just hang tight, I'm on my way." I pushed end, instructed Bogart and Bacall to keep the bed warm and raced downstairs. What had gotten into Dexter, shooting kids? Shooting kids! I grabbed my coat and keys and hauled my tired butt out the door.

Racing down the mountain road, I prayed I wouldn't hit a deer and that the graffiti artists wouldn't sue Dexter . . . or me. How serious was a shot to the ol' gluteus anyway? And what kind of gun had he used? A shotgun would only pattern one's buttock, but a twenty-two?

Fifteen minutes later, I skidded to a stop in the middle of the complex's parking lot, kicking up a cloud of dust that added to the surreal looking landscape colored by red, blue, and yellow lights flashing atop two cop cars. I climbed from my car and jogged to the sidewalk where tenants in various styles of pajamas formed a semi-circle.

Agatha, in a quilted, pink robe, eyes fever bright, grabbed my arm. "Sadie, Dexter said he'd get the punks and he did. He did!" She squeezed my hand and giggled.

"Right." I pulled away and noted all the smiling faces. Who were these bloodthirsty people and where were my normal tenants?

Dexter, clad in camouflage with a pair of night vision goggles pushed up on his head, stood away from the group talking to a police officer. In his right hand, barrel pointed at the ground, Dexter held a funny looking shotgun. Was the officer a rookie? Didn't he know enough to disarm a shooter, even if the shooter was in his seventies?

I hurried over and touched Dexter's arm. "Dex, why? Why take the law into your own hands?"

He grinned and patted my hand. "I can't take all the credit. I managed to fell two, then Pizinski tackled the third one." He pointed to the corner of the building where Justin Pizinski, dressed all in black, stood talking with the second officer. On the ground, handcuffed and looking miserable sat three boys. It was hard to tell their ages with the globs of paint splashed on their heads and bodies.

A paint-ball gun?

Dexter's weapon was a paint-ball gun?

I let out the breath I'd been holding and started to laugh.

"You think this is a laughing matter?" Violet appeared at my side, arms folded, a scowl wrinkling her face.

"I thought Dexter had used a real gun."

"Might as well have, damned old fart thinks he's back in the Marines, planning strategy with that knuckleheaded punk Pizinski.

He's doing your bidding, out here lying on the cold ground, waiting for those gang bangers who could be armed with who knows what. He could catch his death."

I swallowed a sigh. "Violet, I didn't know Dexter was planning this."

"And another thing, what makes you think Thelma was murdered? Damn woman died from abusing her body with nicotine and sins of the flesh!" Violet gave a curt nod to emphasize her point.

"What?"

"Don't act coy with me, missy. I know you've been asking questions. That will only bring you trouble. Mark my words. Trouble!" She turned on her heel and threaded her way through the crowd.

The woman's gossip connections were amazing—either that or she'd been eavesdropping when I questioned Floydean earlier that day.

EIGHT THE NEXT MORNING FOUND ME staring at my computer monitor, rereading the measly three pages of my latest story. Talk about stink on ice. The prose that had seemed magical when I first began was now pathetic with a capital 'P'.

Fatigued, yet wired from last night, I swiveled in my chair and gazed out the window, watching the mid-morning sun tenaciously erase the first frost from the cedar trees and scrub brush.

The second-story turret room had originally been Aunt Vie's bedroom but I'd turned it into my office, hoping the panoramic view would inspire my muse. Uh-huh.

I swiveled away from the window and stared at the opposite wall where light and dust motes bathed movie posters of *Dracula*, *The Bride of Frankenstein*, and *Aliens*. No inspiration there, either. Only one thing left to do. I took a sip of coffee and thunked my head a couple of times on the mouse pad. That ought to shake up the little gray cells.

It should've been easy to get into my character's shoes since both of us were facing a dilemma. A week had passed since Thelma's murder. I'd spent four days painting and scrubbing every inch of her apartment, while letting my mind wander along insidious paths, hoping to ferret out a motive behind her death. My hands were raw, my shoulders ached, and I was stymied with the investigation.

After dragging myself home from the paint-ball caper, I'd drifted off for a couple of hours only to jolt awake, certain that the snapshot I'd scrutinized with Reb last night held the key. While sipping my first cup of coffee, I'd taken another look at the incriminating picture and called Esther Clemmens. She'd answered, as most perpetually cheery morning people do, coming damn close to chirping as she told me about a new cat that had been visiting her backyard food pans. She was ninety-eight percent sure it was Thelma's cat, Spanky, and would I come over and check the cat out? I'd agreed to drop by later tonight and wait with her to make an identification.

"Great. Maybe you can help entice him onto my back porch. It's enclosed. I'll detain him, and you can make a positive I.D."

Oh yeah, cornering Spanky while he went ballistic was my idea of a good time. I told her I'd be at her house by seven—plenty of time to check the date of my last tetanus shot, in case Spanky and I had a close encounter of the worst kind, and come up with a subtle way to get Esther talking about the argument she'd eavesdropped on last June.

I shut down the computer and stretched. While writer's block had my poor muse in a choke-hold, I might as well do something productive like clean Eclipse's stall. I shrugged out of my sweats and into jeans, flannel shirt, and worn boots. Outside the air was brisk and smelled of sage and damp leaves. The sky was a cloudless, intense blue, and the sun promised balmy warmth.

Opening the backyard gate, I watched Bogart and Bacall bound up the hill, barking after some imaginary varmint. "Don't piss off any skunks," I warned.

In the barn, Eclipse stuck his head over the stall as I gathered shovel, wheelbarrow, and rake from the tack room.

"Okay, big guy, play time. Try not to step on the mutts." I opened the gate, caught his halter, and hung on as he led me out into the corral.

He stopped and nudged my right hip pocket. I stuck my hand in, rummaging around until I found a lone sugar cube. "Spoiling you rotten I am," I croaked in a fair Yoda impersonation. Eclipse took the cube and blew softly against my cheek. He loves when I talk Yoda. I patted his rump and watched as he galloped the length of the corral. Securing the gate, I returned to his stall.

While I shoveled and raked, my mind roamed over possible ways to approach different people with dicey questions. Despite Violet's warning, I still needed to talk with Claude Phoenix, Casey Kelso, Judith Kelso, and Ellie with-the-great-hair. A phone call should do it for Claude, but the rest would take some finessing.

Dumping the last wheelbarrow load, I hooked my arms over the corral's weathered top rail and whistled. Eclipse trotted to me and nudged at my pocket, searching for another cube.

"Sorry, big guy. All out." I scratched under his forelock. He twitched his ears and snorted. "Look, I have places to go, people to press, and sugar cubes to buy."

I stepped down from the fence and went to check out the water trough beside the corral gate. It was low.

"Been entertaining the neighborhood deer?" I asked, uncurling the hose beside the barn and turning on the water spigot. Eclipse watched, fascinated, while the tank filled.

"The Kelsos will be the hardest to crack. What do you favor, straightforward grilling like *Law and Order* Lennie Brisco or round-about like *Columbo*?

"Don't forget the good cop, bad cop approach."

I squealed and whirled, hose in hand, soaking Jack Killian's black jeans from the knees down.

"Only a suggestion," he cried, stepping back out of range.

"Scare me half to death," I said, patting my chest to get my heart back where it belonged. Bogart and Bacall rounded the barn, barking their greeting.

"Sorry. Thought you heard me pull up." He grinned, brushed at his wet jeans and patted the dogs. "Still jumpy from last night?"

I shrugged. The cop grapevine was faster than Violet's . . . good thing to remember.

"So who are you grilling and why? Can't be the three graffiti artists tucked away at Juvie hall."

Okay, did I spill my hunch or not? What did I have to lose? He'd caught me asking his horse's opinion. I was glad he hadn't heard me ask the cats.

"I'm trying to find out who killed Thelma Edwards."

Killian's smile dissolved. His face turned cop-serious, and he straightened. "The coroner's verdict was heart failure. What makes you think she was murdered?"

"You'll laugh or call for backup and a straitjacket." I walked back to the barn and turned the faucet off.

He shook his head. "Why don't you try me? I might surprise you."

I took a deep breath, blew it out, and told him about the old toaster, the money in the mattress, and Judy Kelso's behavior. I ended with my gut feeling. If he smirked, I'd die of embarrassment right here. Killian's face remained neutral, and I vowed never to play cards with him.

"What's the motive?" he asked.

"I'm not sure, yet."

He nodded, ducked his head to study his boots and no doubt hide a smirk.

"Have a nice ride," I said, grabbing the wheelbarrow and heading back to the barn. It didn't matter if he laughed his fool head off. I was still going to find out the truth.

"Sadie, wait." He caught up to me and helped me store my tools. "I'm not saying you're wrong. I just can't see using a toaster to murder someone."

"Exactly!"

He frowned, folded his arms, and leaned back against the tack room wall. "I'm not following here . . ."

"Floydean Mollicker said the same thing, no one would use a toaster. But what if the killer used a common household appliance just to throw everyone off? It would be the perfect crime, right?"

His look told me he considered me in the same class as Dexter the apartment commando and "Forensic Files" authority.

"Sadie, you want to be careful. The Kelsos could cry harassment and drag you into court."

I opened my mouth, clamped it shut, and tried to look chastised. "I won't harass anyone. I just have a couple of questions that need answers."

"Remember what curiosity did to the cat." He pushed away from the wall and headed for the tack room. I stuck my tongue out at the back of his head, called my dogs and started for the house.

"Sadie."

I turned, and he pointed a hoof pick at me. "Just be careful. Okay?"

I gave him a salute and hurried for the back door before his concern had my libido doing things my mind would later regret. In my bedroom, I selected some hard-rock, attitude adjustment music on my Bluetooth and turned the volume up. I exchanged my grungy clothes for tight black jeans, red silk blouse, and red leather ankle boots with stacked two-inch heels.

In the bathroom, I plugged in my curling iron. While it heated, I carefully applied makeup, adding a couple of extra passes with the mascara brush for good measure and emerged from the bathroom, hair curled, sprayed into obedience. A little cologne spritzed on appropriate pulse points, and Sadie Super Sleuth Harrigan was ready to take on whatever came my way.

In the kitchen, I snatched my shoulder bag and keys from the table and instructed the dogs to do their watchdog bit.

I might live in the sticks, but the drive to town only takes fifteen minutes. I hadn't quite formulated a plan before I reached Thelma's store and spent agonizing minutes jockeying my Karmann Ghia into a parallel parking space in front of The Bookmark.

Inside, I took a moment to inhale the heady fragrance of old leather-bound books mixed with new paperbacks while surveying the place. To my right, I saw Casey Kelso behind the counter ringing up a customer. Best wait until he's free, I decided, looking over the rest of the store. In the near left corner, a floor-to-ceiling bookshelf held various sized baskets similar to the one Floydean had claimed. I wondered how well they were selling considering the hefty price tag.

Claude Phoenix and Dexter Zoetwilder stood beside the baskets, sipping steaming mugs of coffee and talking like old friends.

Interesting.

Stacked heels striking hardwood drew their attention as I walked toward them. Mouths open, they looked ready to drop their dentures. Either I was looking hotter than the sun or their meeting was meant to be a secret. I hoped for the first but was betting on the latter.

"Dexter. Mr. Phoenix. What a pleasant surprise," I said, making my way around three overstuffed chintz chairs surrounding a table littered with magazines.

Dexter nodded and looked ready to bolt for the door. Claude Phoenix, ever the car salesman, beamed and offered his hand.

"Ms. Harrigan. Ready to trade in that little car for something more dependable in the snow?"

I'd inherited my vintage yellow Karmann Ghia Coupe from aunt Vie shortly before she passed away. It might've been made in 1972 but she looked nearly as good as the day she rolled off the assembly line in Germany.

"Get rid of a classic? Not likely." I shook Claude's hand but kept my eye on Dexter, who was looking everywhere but at me. His gaze settled on his wrist, and he stared at his watch like it might suddenly sprout wings and fly away.

"Hey, Sadie, would you look at the time. Gotta' run. Can't keep Violet waiting." In his haste to leave, he nearly collided with a mother and two children entering the store. I looked at Claude. He lifted his right shoulder in a semi-shrug and started to follow Dexter. Before he could make his escape, I grabbed his hand with both of mine.

"I haven't had a chance to tell you how sorry I am about Thelma." Not a great conversation starter but better than, "*Read any good books lately?*"

All animation left his face. Even his abundant white hair seemed to lose its shine. "Funny, reality hasn't hit me yet. Whenever my cell phone rings, I expect to hear her voice. She always called to see how my day was going. Still seems like a bad dream." Stepping closer, he lowered his voice. "Then holding her funeral in that hellish pink palace . . . I tried to steer Judy to Harrigan's, but . . ." He snorted and shook his head. "Dexter was just telling me the bridge club pitched a fit when they found out Judy had chosen Wayco-Young."

So, I wasn't the only one turned off by the color scheme. "I'm surprised to find you and Dexter, uh, together. Talking?"

"Oh, that." Claude waved his hand as though chasing away a fly. "Dex is all bluff and bluster for Violet's sake. He's never had a quarrel with the relationship Thelma and I had. But you know Violet. Everything is black and white with that woman." He cleared his throat and pitched his voice falsetto. "Living together in sin is a one-way ticket to H-E-double-toothpicks."

His Violet imitation wasn't bad. I smiled. "Claude, why was Thelma using that old toaster?"

Claude pulled his hand free from mine and stared at me as though I'd grown a third eye. "Old toaster?"

So much for finessing, the question had popped past my lips before my brain could react. I gave him the condensed version of my toaster suspicion. He pursed his lips and looked at the ceiling. Was he praying for strength or wondering about my mental health?

"Hard to keep a secret in this town." His face sagged and he shook his head. "Guess by now everyone knows about our little squabble. And Thelma could be very stubborn: course, so am I.

Two old stubborn fools." He pulled out one of the overstuffed chairs, sank down into the button-tufted center, and seemed to diminish right before my eyes.

Interesting, mention toasters and the man starts telling me about some lover's quarrel? Whatever, I sat in the chair nearest his and bit my tongue. Leaping in with kind words might stifle his explanation. So I clamped my lips together and waited. Then waited some more. I was about to dive in any way when he finally raised his head: and, though his eyes were dry, his voice was choked with tears.

"We hadn't spoken for a week. Seven days of pure willfulness! Now it's too late for apologies. Or goodbyes." He swallowed, and I imagined the taste of his grief was pretty bitter.

"But life goes on, or so people say." He reached into his coat pocket and pulled out a key ring with a solitary gold key. "Thelma gave this to me. Glad I ran into you, saves me the trouble of returning it."

I took the key and put it in my pocket.

"The day you found her; Dexter called me after all the fuss had died down. I drove over and went into the apartment, guess it must've been around one a.m. Needed to get my things out before sister Judy raided the place. I didn't stay long, the smell was . . ." He winced and scrubbed his face with both hands. "But I did check out the damn toaster, nearly picked the thing up and smashed it against the floor." His sigh seemed to come from the soles of his polished shoes. "I have no idea why she was using that relic."

"The new one conked out?" I ventured. "So she was using her old one?"

"Wasn't hers, at least I'd never seen it before. Who knows where she got it? But, Sadie, the idea of someone coming to Thelma's door, antique toaster in hand, to do her harm . . ." He shook his head.

It was my turn to sigh. My theory was beginning to look like a used sponge with everyone poking holes in it. Claude's cell phone rang, saving me from a reply. I stood, pulled Thelma's key from my pocket, held it up and whispered "Thanks." He nodded, pushed himself to his feet and walked to the door, voice booming, back in salesman mode.

Looking for Casey Kelso I walked to the counter area. It was empty. Damn.

"I've decided not to rent Thelma's apartment, but it has nothing to do with your complex being haunted."

I turned and stared into the magnified blue eyes of Loralee Lish. The large, square-framed glasses perched on her short nose looked at odds with her abundant blonde ringlets.

"My apartments are not haunted," I snapped.

She patted my shoulder. "Don't take offense. Older places have quirks. Take my apartment, the former cockroach hotel. My land-lord has finally caved in and agreed to have the place fumigated so I can stay put. I hate moving."

Yuck! Good thing roach infestation isn't transferred by a pat on the shoulder. I took a step back anyway. "Fine." I took another step. "Is Casey around?"

"He just slipped out to do some banking. Are you here to discuss the lawsuit?"

That halted my retreat. "Lawsuit?"

"I keep telling Casey he's wasting his time and money if he tries to sue you."

"Casey told you he wants to sue me?" My anxiety meter roared into the red zone. Two vacant apartments and Kelso still planning on dragging me into court?

"Yeah. But I think he's going to take my advice. Yesterday, he was talking to his girlfriend, Ellie, and they mostly agreed to, you know, keep the peace."

"Ellie?"

"Ellie Stromberg." She took a step closer and lowered her voice. "If you want to know, I think she's the one who came up with the lawsuit idea. She is one high-maintenance girl, very expensive taste."

"Really?"

Loralee nodded and took her glasses off, chewing on the stem. "Thelma told me you're a writer, and like you've had stories published in lots of magazines." She stated this with such awe, eyes bright, cheeks flushed, I was afraid she might drop to her knees and genuflect. "I've written a little poetry and I'm working on a novel, and, like, meeting you is just . . . serendipitous!"

I did a mental eye roll and sighed. She was going to ask me to read her stuff. I could feel my antiperspirant beginning to fail.

She checked her watch. "I close the shop for lunch in half an hour. We could meet at the deli around the corner, my treat, and, if you have time you could read my first chapter."

She looked so hopeful I wanted to cringe. But, I also needed information. "Okay, I'll see you in about thirty minutes."

I left and sat in my car, time to put an ad on Zillow for Thelma's apartment. After talking to Loralee, I thought about including 'guaranteed roach free.' Envisioning an invasion of the vile bugs didn't help my appetite and pumping Loralee for info while I ate off her tab had me feeling all creepy. I'd rather chew tinfoil than critique her novel, but, now was not the time to wimp out.

TEN

LORALEE WAS AMAZING. If her chatty personality was an indication, it could take weeks to plow through the first chapter of her novel. I'd learned that Claude Phoenix had dated Judy Kelso before he became involved with Thelma. The two sisters didn't speak for several months after he dropped Judy. Dexter Zoetweilder read strictly Louis L'Amour and Thelma had promised Dexter the bronze John Wayne bust which overlooked the western section; but it was only a verbal agreement and Casey wasn't about to part with *that* bust. All of this info came between the time the waitress took our order and then delivered our sandwiches.

"Not that I'm blaming Casey. He tends to be blown around by the whims of different women in his life," she said, eyes glazing over as she took a big bite from her Ruben pita. Either her sandwich was to die for or she had it bad for Casey.

"Sounds pretty serious between Casey and Ellie," I said. "Funny, Thelma never mentioned her to me." Fact was Thelma and I discussed different authors, but we rarely talked about the store or her relatives.

"Thelma and Ellie didn't get along. Thelma got major pissed whenever Ellie stopped by to talk with Casey. A couple of months ago, Thelma told Casey he'd better pay attention to business and stop playing the lovesick ass or he'd be standing in the unemployment line. Casey quit and stormed out." Eyes narrowed, Loralee stuffed the remainder of her dill pickle in her mouth and crunched away. "Next thing I know, Judy Kelso shows up and she and Thelma go into the back office and squabble for a while."

I mentally crossed my fingers. "Did you happen to hear the argument?"

"No. Thelma slammed the door. Even though their voices were pretty loud, I only caught a word or two. But, the next day, Casey's back at work, and it's like the fight never happened. He doesn't mention Ellie, and she doesn't come near the store. It was that way until the day before Thelma died. I remember because Thelma had just left to make a bank deposit and in walks Ellie. She and Casey head into the office. After a couple of minutes she leaves, and Casey's happy as a clam for the rest of the day."

Hmm. Interesting. If I were Nancy Drew or Hercule Poirot, I'd take this glut of info, times it by the square root of three and come up with the culprit. "Any idea what will happen to The Bookmark now?"

Loralee frowned and pushed at her glasses. "Hard to guess. Thelma's will is beyond pitiful. She wrote it herself, and the language is vague to the point of being useless. Claude claims the store is his because of the money he invested when the place was remodeled. He'd probably sell it to the highest bidder." Loralee sighed. "The man's only interested in a fast buck. But Casey . . ." Awe colored her face. She nibbled on her lower lip and some of her mauve-colored lipstick stuck to her front teeth. "He has awesome plans to turn The Bookmark into much more than a little hole-in-the-wall bookstore."

I toyed with the fat-free potato chips on my plate. Loralee swore they tasted like the real thing . . . but wrong. I was beginning to wonder if I should trust anything else she'd told me. "What kinds of plans?"

"He wants to, you know, turn it into a more eclectic place, entice the college crowd and John Q. Public to mingle, have insightful discussions over coffee."

"Sort of a mini Barnes and Noble?"

She narrowed her eyes. "There would be nothing mini about it!"

"What about the baskets? Was that Casey's idea?"

Loralee smiled and pushed at her glasses. "Yes, Casey discovered the best website with authentic Indian baskets. Thelma was against selling them until Casey turned tenacious and wore her down. She clears out one shelf, one meager shelf for display. After a couple of weeks, she gets a look at the profit margin, and wham-bam, she relegates a whole section."

"The baskets are selling well?"

Loralee stirred her ice tea and nodded. "Better believe it. After the success with the baskets, you'd think she'd be willing to try other ideas. Like open mike Friday. But, hell no. She wouldn't budge. Sometimes she could be such a bitch."

"Open mike Fridays?"

"For a small cover charge, people could come to the store, nosh on hors d'oeuvres, sip a little wine or coffee, and read their stuff. Imagine all that artistic energy, mixing, growing, the experience would be beyond awesome! Casey's plans include bringing in different authors to do book signings; really put the store out there, you know. The man's a real visionary, with the right woman by his side . . ." She stopped and stared down at her empty plate then brightened. "I'll let you know when he gets the Friday thing going. You could drop in and read a story, or just talk about your publishing experience."

I tried not to openly shudder. I'd rather stand barefoot in a bathtub filled with piranhas than share my work with a roomful of artsy-fartsy types.

Loralee tossed back the last of her tea and dabbed a napkin across her lips. "Back to the grind." She pushed her plate aside, bent down and hefted a plastic shopping bag onto the table. A half-ream of paper looked ready to spill out. "I decided to give you a hard copy so you can make notes. Here are a couple of chapters. Take your time. There's no rush. And don't be afraid to be honest. In fact, be brutal. I can take it." Her bright eyes and hopeful smile said otherwise. She'd just handed me her baby . . . handle with care.

I shook her outstretched hand and watched as she nearly skipped out the door. Gathering up her manuscript and my purse, I left the deli with the abundant chapters weighing me down, physically, and mentally. Halfway down the block, I spotted my car and all thoughts about Loralee vanished. Something wasn't right. The Ghia seemed to slump against the curb. I jogged to the rear bumper, stopped, and stared. Both left-side tires were flat, their rims kissing asphalt.

This couldn't be my car. My car wouldn't betray me like this. I looked up and down the block of parked vehicles, hoping to find another yellow Karman Ghia.

"Son-of-a . . ." I dumped Loralee's sack into the passenger seat. How could I have two flats? One, maybe. But two?

I scrambled through my purse, pulled out my phone and dialed Reb's number. The low battery signal beeped once and the phone went dead. I thought of tossing the ancient thing into the gutter and stomping its intricate guts out. Instead, I jammed it in my purse.

Yanking the trunk open, I wished I'd listened to Reb and gotten a new, improved cell, wished I had two spares instead of a measly one. And while I was at it, I wished for a tire-changing Fairy Godmother. I was phoneless, clueless, but not hopeless. I'd borrow the deli owner's phone and call for a tow-truck to take my car to the nearest tire place; good thing I'd listened, for once, to Harvey Stevens, my insurance guy, and bought the policy that included free towing

I'D USED UP ONE STAIN-STICK on my grime-spotted blouse plus my entire repertoire of cuss words before I left the laundry room and padded upstairs to find comfort in my favorite sweats. I exchanged my red attitude boots—I'd had enough attitude, thank you very much—for fluffy slippers.

Back downstairs I fixed a big cup of hot chocolate, added a handful of petite marshmallows, and while I waited for the marshmallows to go gooey, I grabbed a jar of chunky peanut butter and a spoon. Solace was but a couple of bites away. I went to my CD library and snatched *Silver Bullet*. I plopped down on the couch, prepared to eat peanut butter and slurp hot chocolate while a werewolf ravaged some make-believe town in Maine. Bogart and Bacall snuggled next to me, ready to provide comfort and help should I spill anything.

This was *not* a pity party. I was regrouping. I'd ruined my blouse attempting to help hook up my poor car, and depleted my savings account down to fifty dollars. What did I have to show for my efforts? Two shiny new tires from Les Schwab and a burning desire to strangle the tire-shredding culprit.

Casey Kelso seemed like a reasonable suspect. He was in the area, and he'd taken an early lunch. Was he weasel enough to slash and run? A conversation with Kelso now headed my list of things to do—but I needed to prepare.

I looked at my dachshunds. "How would you two like a big brother, say a hungry Rottweiler with razor-sharp fangs?" They looked back at me with soft, trusting eyes. "Trained to eat only mean people." I added.

I wasn't sure the Humane Society adopted out that type of animal, but I bet Esther Clemmens had connections. I could drop a few hints tonight while we waited for Spanky to slink by.

The phone rang. I muted the movie, saw Willie's name on the cordless. Guessing she was tired of leaving messages on my cell and she knew I usually picked up the landline, I took a deep breath and answered.

"I hear you're stabling two studs. That's my girl!"

I groaned and closed my eyes; just what I needed, a call from Mommy Dearest.

"Hi, Willie."

"Is this guy hung like his horse?"

"Can't say," I said, opening my eyes to watch the werewolf stalk a wheelchair bound young lad.

"Can't or won't? Hell's bells, Mercedes, you gotta use those perky breasts God gave you for something other than holding out sweaters. Let the man know you're a real woman."

I remained silent and prayed for strength.

"All right, Ms. not-getting-any-younger. When you're ready for expert love advice, you know where to come. When was the last time you talked to Cary?"

"A couple of weeks." If I thought having the name Mercedes McCambridge Harrigan was bad, I couldn't imagine being stuck with Cary Grant Harrigan like my brother. Had Willie joined the hippie movement, we probably would've answered to Moonbean and Rainbow.

"My dear girl, amour is in the air. Your brother's got a new squeeze, a skinny little thing according to wagging tongues, but he refuses to bring her around." Willie sniffed like a pouting three-year-old.

"Maybe he's busy," I offered.

"Busy, my butt." She sighed deep and long. "Guess he doesn't want to intimidate the poor waif."

"Intimidate?"

"Rumor has it she's a real Plain Jane. Naturally, she'd pale next to me."

I did a pantomime finger gag for Bogart and Bacall. Bogart wagged his tail. He appreciates my humor. "Why don't you call Cary?"

"I have! Cary," she made his name into two distinct syllables, "is ignoring my messages. Can you believe it?"

My cell trilled Reb's tone. "Sorry, got another call. Don't worry, Cary will be in touch." I clicked off the cordless before Willie could protest and answered my cell.

"Heard about the excitement you had last night. Why didn't you call me?"

"It was over by the time I got to the complex. I owe Dexter for nailing those graffiti artists."

"I love a feisty senior. By the way, Ellie with-the-great-hair's last name is . . ."

"Stromberg, right?"

"How'd you know?"

"Loralee, the chatty clerk at the Bookmark. We had lunch, and she filled me in on all sorts of interesting things," I said. "Which reminds me, has your mom been discussing my love-life with Willie?"

"Huh?"

"Willie called all stoked cause she thinks I'm stabling two studs."

"I did *not* tell Mama that!"

"Doesn't matter, life is a sexual innuendo to Willie. Reb, what else do you know about Ms. Hair?"

"She just left the office. Came in here dressed to strut her stuff, wanted to speak to the head broker. She recently stuck her granny in a rest home and needs to sell granny's humble abode."

"Really?"

"The woman is a real greedy gut, wants to ego-price the house right out of the market. It's a go-nowhere listing, bet my broker will let me have it if I ask nicely. While I'm doing the inspection of granny's home, I can ask Ms. Stromberg a few subtle questions."

"Great."

"Any new info on your end?"

"Someone slashed two of my tires while I was lunching with Loralee."

"Damn, girlfriend, you're a magnet for disaster. Maybe the gangsta boys did a payback."

"Don't think so. They're tucked in Juvenile Hall. My guess would be Casey Kelso."

"We could hunt Mama Kelso's baby boy down and play good detective/bad detective."

"No time. I have an appointment with Esther Clemmens in about an hour. I'll be asking her a few subtle questions while we wait to make a positive ID on Spanky."

"Hey, Subtle-R-Us, right? How do you plan to work Esther's eavesdropping into the conversation?"

"I'll be too cunning for words. Want to come along?"

"Can't. Got a hot date with Jack Killian," Reb said.

A date with Killian? I couldn't breathe or speak.

"Right. Guess I forgot," I managed to squeak.

"You sound funny. You okay?" Was that concern or suspicion in Reb's voice?

"Fine," I answered. *Liar, liar pants on fire!* "Have a good time. Call me later."

"Uh-huh."

I hung up, turned off *Silver Bullet*, and stared at the late afternoon sun slanting through the picture window, puddling on the floor. I was not jealous! Nope—not me—I had plans for tonight. Trapping a manic cat and weaseling info from the president of the Humane Society would keep me busy. So what if I wasn't out with a gorgeous hunk? My life, unlike Willie dearest's, did not revolve around hunkdom. How could I obsess about dating when I had a killer to track down?

ESTHER CLEMMENS STOOD ON HER PORCH dressed in navy wool slacks and a white knit sweater. This was her chosen armor for catching Spanky? Before I could say anything, she put a finger to her lips, opened her front door, and motioned for me to follow. Tiptoeing through the entry and into her kitchen, past the various dogs lying in front of the stove, we stopped before the sliding glass door. She pointed out onto the darkened patio and mouthed, "Careful."

I pressed my forehead to the glass and squinted into the night. As my eyes adjusted, I saw three cats eating from a rectangular plastic box placed near the end of the sparsely-lighted cement patio. I started to tell Esther I couldn't be sure if Spanky was one of the felines, but she shook her head, grabbed my arm, and pulled me into the living room.

"He spooks easy when he's eating. If he hears sounds coming from the house he bolts." Esther said her voice low.

"How am I supposed to make sure it's Spanky?" I whispered.

"Just wait about fifteen minutes. When they're all finished eating, he might come and sit by the door with the other two."

I sat on the edge of the sofa, suddenly conscious of my ratty jeans, stained sweatshirt and threadbare tennis shoes. I'd come prepared for battle.

"Guess you won't have to worry about people spray painting your places anymore," she said, taking a seat in a chair across from me. "The whole neighborhood's buzzing about the arrest last night. Dexter's quite the hero."

"Yes, he's an amazing guy."

She smiled. "He is that. It's time to take back our neighborhoods, use force if we have to." She smoothed back a stray hair and checked her watch. "Would you like something to drink while we wait?"

"No thanks." I looked around her living room. It was done in tones of beige and white, and not a single dog hair in sight. Maybe she trained her motley crew not to shed—neat trick. I'd have to learn how, but first, I had more pressing questions.

"I take it Thelma wasn't much of a dog person?" The direct approach had worked well with Claude Phoenix, I was hoping it would work with Esther.

She tilted her head slightly and looked hard at me before answering. "I don't think dogs were the issue. I think it was more a battle of wills."

"A battle of wills?"

"Thelma was versed in every subject, or so she thought. Her opinions were set in stone. Soon after I moved in, she informed me that too many animals living together was not a healthy situation—for the animals or their owner. I explained I had literature that proved otherwise, and I would be glad to show it to her."

Surprised, I nodded. Thelma knew I had a menagerie, yet she'd never said a word to me.

"She was nice enough, but she didn't want to read anything I offered. I thought we'd agreed to disagree on that subject. I'd forgotten about it until she called the police to report my dogs as a nuisance—claimed they barked day and night."

"What happened?"

"The officer who took the call knew me; he's adopted a couple of dogs from the Society. I told him I didn't know what she was complaining about, my dogs are very well-behaved. He gave me a warning." She sighed and looked at the ceiling. "But the next call brought a real Barney Fife type to my door. Wrote me a ticket to the tune of fifty dollars and said one more call and I'd have to get rid of a couple of the dogs or apply for a kennel license."

"You're kidding!"

"I wish." She looked at her watch, stood and motioned for me to follow her back into the kitchen.

Just as she'd predicted, three cats—a big yellow tabby, little calico, and one black as coal—sat on the doormat, looking through the glass door. I told her the black one looked like Spanky.

"I thought he might be Thelma's scared fellow. I'm making progress. He's let me pet him a couple of times when he's come into the yard. With the two of us standing here, he's not disappearing. That's a good sign."

I was willing to stand there all night, as long as I didn't have to physically catch the little devil. "He seems okay with your cats." No hissing. No fur flying. Maybe this docile creature wasn't Spanky after all.

"That's Mother Teresa and her kitten Boo Radley. They can tame the most feral cat."

Interesting. "Will you keep Spanky?"

"No. He really prefers to be an only cat. I've got a woman who wants him. She lost her big male six months ago and is now ready to get another one. She'd baby him just the way Thelma did."

"Good. He's a big old grouch, but I want him to go to a nice home."

"Oh, he will. Let's hope he picks up his new owner's attitude," she said, placing special emphasis on the last three words.

Translation: Thelma was a holy terror and I, the new landlord, was clueless. Okay, so according to Esther's theory, my personality had turned my dachshunds into fun loving, curious—no make that nosey and rambunctious—creatures. Here I'd always thought that was the nature of the breed.

Esther seemed comfortable talking about Thelma's quirks, so I crossed my fingers behind my back and forged on. "Guess I didn't know Thelma as well as I thought. I've learned she didn't get along very well with her sister, either." I tried a dismayed look and held my breath, hoping she'd jump in. Esther pursed her lips and nodded.

Okay, time for plan B. Too bad I didn't have one.

Esther pulled on her right earlobe. "You know, Thelma had her favorites, and if you weren't on that list, watch out. Violet Zoetwilder probably felt her wrath more than anyone else, not that Violet is the easiest person to get along with. But she and Thelma seemed to always be pushing each other's buttons, real oil-and-water neighbors."

"Really?" I raised my eyebrows. Just color me naïve.

"You can ask anyone in your complex. Their shouting matches were legendary. One particular argument, I was working in my yard and heard Violet accuse Thelma of poisoning a couple of her prize plants. For a minute it looked like they might start trading punches. I nearly called the police."

"What stopped you?"

"I wasn't about to stick my nose into Thelma's business. I didn't want her reporting my animals again." She looked at her seven dogs. "Isn't that right, babies?" Seven tails thumped against the floor in agreement."

"Did you witness any other disturbances?" I crossed my fingers, again, and muttered a silent please-please-please.

Her forehead wrinkled, and she gazed at the far wall. "No, nothing comes to mind. But if I had, I'd learned it wasn't any of my business." Esther bent down to pet the largest dog, and the rest mobbed her in one huge, furry mass. It was time for me to leave before I got sucked into the hairy vortex.

Driving home, I thought about Thelma. I really hadn't known the darker side of her personality, but Judy, Esther, and Violet had. And according to Loralee Lish, Casey and his girlfriend Ellie Stromberg had also stumbled into her line of ire.

Had any of them been angry enough to kill her? It didn't seem likely. I drummed the steering wheel. Esther was mum about the night of the picnic, maybe with the incriminating picture in hand she'd talk. *Yeah, right. Get real, Harrigan.* I wasn't a cop—or a P.I. I was a nosey landlord, poking around in something that Esther would think was *none of my business. I was also hoping to find out what happened to stop the lawsuit.*

Frustrated, I stopped at the end of my driveway, rolled my window down, and opened my mailbox. On top of a stack of envelopes and magazines lay an object wrapped in white paper. I reached in and picked it up. It felt like a rock. I turned on the overhead light and removed the blue rubber band securing the paper. It was a rock, a dirty fist-sized one.

I tossed the rock out of the open window into the nearest sagebrush and smoothed the paper out. Scrawled in red were the words: I KNOW WHERE YOU LIVE!

ELEVEN

A THREATENING NOTE AROUND A ROCK; HOW quaint, how juvenile, how psychotic. Whatever, I was ready: Phone in one hand, .38 special in the other, wooden cross from the barn's tack room tucked into the waistband of my jeans. Hey, I've seen enough vampire movies to know that the only people who survive a blood-sucking invasion are the ones willing to admit night stalkers might exist.

Armed and nervous, I went between the kitchen and living room, checking and rechecking deadbolts, making sure drapes were tightly drawn, listening for odd sounds. The state I was in, every creak of my old house sounded ominous.

Bogart and Bacall lay side by side on the couch, snoring and twitching. I took this as a good sign until I considered that they may have been drugged to lull me into complacency. Living in the country was supposed to be soothing— ha!

Isolated, nobody-will-hear-you-scream frightening, yes.

Soothing? In a pig's eye!

I SLUMPED INTO THE ROCKING CHAIR BY the fireplace and tried not to think about horror movies where monsters slithered down unguarded chimneys. Chances were good the note was a stupid prank concocted by a couple of stupid punks—in which case, they'd had their laugh watching me race, trip, and crawl from the car to the back door.

Reb and I had annoyed enough people back in our teen years. Maybe the god of paybacks decided it was my turn. I was the perfect target: single female living alone with nothing for protection but two snoring dachshunds and a couple of outside cats—plus, my Aunt Vie's 38 Special. I was a fair shot if the object I was aiming at stood perfectly still and allowed me time to sight down the barrel then shoot until I ran out of bullets. Empty cans on stumps feared me.

The phone shrilled. I screamed and dropped it. Bacall and Bogart raised their heads and looked at me like I was deranged.

"Sorry, guys," I said, picking up the phone and looking at the caller ID window: unavailable—probably someone selling aluminum siding or checking to see the status of my windshield.

I punched the talk button and croaked, "Hello."

Nothing; no heavy breathing, just dead air. The *X-Files* theme reverberated in my head, and I jerked around, expecting to see agent Mulder coming down the staircase, telling me the answer was out there. I pressed the off button and went into the kitchen in search of fortifying refreshment.

In the fridge, a lone bottle of Heineken kept a six pack of Cherry Pepsi company. A hard-boiled super sleuth would take the Heineken and chase it with some fine whisky. I opted for Cherry Pepsi on the rocks.

I took a big gulp, wiped the foam from my mouth with the back of my hand, and sat at the kitchen table. Okay, if this was the work of the graffiti gang who'd decorated my apartments, I'd simply show no fear; but I felt that writing notes wasn't their M.O.

Floydean Mollicker would be privy to any serial-type killings reported at police headquarters, however, she already thought my killed-by-toaster hypothesis odd. If I called whining about the note, she'd file me under complete weirdo—or worse: wimp!

I really wanted to run this past Reb and toyed with calling her. But that smacked of checking up on her and officer "Killian. Use his name and not a nickname.

Think, Harrigan. Think. Okay, if this wasn't a prank or a psycho, there was another possibility. Reb and I had been asking questions about Thelma's death. Had we stepped on someone's toes? Would this someone try to scare us, or rather *moi*, with slashed tires and cryptic notes?

Warming to the idea, I went back into the kitchen for pencil and paper. I sat at the table and divided the paper into two columns. One I titled suspect, the other motive. Under suspect I jotted Casey Kelso. The man had grated on me from the get-go. Loralee claimed he was an entrepreneur with grandiose plans for the bookstore. Had Thelma shot down one too many of his ideas?

What about the girlfriend, Ellie Stromberg? Thelma had forbidden Casey to see Ellie at work. Could that have set him off? Or was Ellie the real mastermind and Casey her puppet? I wrote Ellie's name next to Casey's and put a question mark under motive.

I closed my eyes and sniffed the air, hoping for a whiff of toast, a scent of Earl Gray tea. *Come on, Thelma, a little help would be nice. Nothing.*

I shrugged and wrote Claude Phoenix on the list. He'd admitted they'd had a lover's quarrel. What started the fight? Jealousy, perhaps? Money? I put down fight with a question mark.

Violet Zoetweilder: Enemy in capital letters.

Judy Kelso: Sibling rivalry? Claude had dated Judy before Thelma, causing a rift between the two sisters. That was something worth checking on.

Esther Clemmens: Thelma had turned her "babies" in twice on a nuisance violation. She'd talked about shoving cherry bombs up a couple of neighborhood delinquents' little butts. That didn't mean she'd do the deed. But just how far would she go to get even?

I chewed on the eraser and reviewed what I had so far. The motive section seemed weak. I got another Cherry Pepsi from the fridge and wondered what could make me kill another person.

Self-defense? Yes. A toaster, however, wouldn't be my weapon of choice unless I used it to pop someone over the head.

Maybe it would be to protect someone, I loved? You bet.

While in the grip of a passionate rage? Hard to tell since it had been a while since I experienced much passion. And how could I? Here I sat alone in my kitchen with pseudo-murderous thoughts spinning in my head—talk about pitiful.

The phone rang, but this time I remained cool and didn't chuck it across the room.

"Heard you went to Waygo for the funeral? Tell me the rumors are *not* true!"

Yancy Candlemass: Gram's right-hand man at Harrigan's Funeral Home. Any conversation with the man was a total concentration-breaker, guaranteed.

"Are you talking about the pink on pink-on-pink color scheme?"

"OMG. Tone on tone is so passé. I tried to tell them before I quit. Wait until Cassandra hears about this big blunder." Yancy's nasal giggle echoed through the phone.

"Yancy do not, I repeat Do Not bug her! She gets away so seldom . . ."

"Chill out, Mercedes. I've only called her with a couple of questions about funeral details. What do you take me for?"

He'd handed me the perfect straight line for a witty come-back, the fact I didn't take the bait showed my low state of mind. I thought about running the strong smell of toast I'd experienced in the cemetery past him but decided to wait until Gram got home.

"So everything is going okay?" I asked.

"Like you need to ask. Just wanted to verify the Young's horrid decorating blunder."

"It's even worse than you can imagine," I said and hung up.

The phone rang again: the caller, ID Sagebrush Inn, a rent-by-the week motel in a seen-better-days part of town. Hmmm. I barked a no-nonsense hello.

"Yes, you have apartment for rent?" The guy asked.

"That's right." I answered.

"Two bedroom. No smoking, right?"

"Right."

"I can come see it, maybe now? Bring a friend?"

I checked my watch. Eight-thirty. Not that late to show an apartment but leaving the safety of my house and braving the dark all alone didn't thrill me. Yet, I couldn't let some note-writing nut turn me into a prisoner. The caller and I arranged to meet in half an hour.

I hung up and asked Bogart and Bacall if they wanted to go. They went into their ritual bark-and-dance routine while I shoved the rental lease folder and gun into my purse, then unlocked the back door. The porch light did little to illuminate the back steps as I relocked the deadbolt. Too bad I couldn't magically zap Bogart and Bacall into snarling Dobermans. The night had turned frosty, my breath made frantic smoke signals as we hotfooted it to the car.

Driving into town, I wondered if the phone call was a ploy to lure me from the safety of my house. The caller with an accent sounded genuine, but recognizing accents is not my forte. My dashboard clock read nine when I pulled into the apartment's parking lot. A lone streetlight cast a puddle of weak illumination on the asphalt near the entrance. A few cars hunkered against the sharp wind.

Monday night, where was everyone on the fall evening? In the entire complex only three windows glowed behind closed blinds. I had counted on Violet and Dexter being home. No lights, not even a flickering TV, shone through their half-open blinds.

Two figures climbed from a compact car at the far end of the lot and started walking toward me. Show no fear, show no fear, I chanted, slinging my purse over my right shoulder, and shoving my hand inside to grip the gun.

"Remember, if I scream, aim for their kneecaps," I instructed my dogs.

I stepped out and leaned back against the car, a smile plastered on my face. No one here, folks, but us confident landlords, ready to show property or foil would-be killers, whichever came first.

"My name is Kim Kasai, are you the landlady I spoke with?"

The couple turned out to be dressed in matching tan pants and olive down jackets. I felt relieved and foolish, and released my death grip on the gun while Kim introduced me to his fiancée. Students at Portneuf Valley College, they owned only one car so a place close to school and work was high on their list. My complex fit their needs.

I showed them Thelma's apartment and explained she'd recently passed away. They seemed okay with it. Of course, I didn't go into great detail; I knew Violet would handle that part. They filled out the rental application, and I assured them I'd do a fast credit check and get back to them tomorrow.

Driving home, with Kim's security deposit and credit petition tucked away in my purse, I had a revelation that nearly caused me to drive off the road. Why not run a credit check on my list of suspects? All sorts of skeletons can pop up in a credit report. It's a simple procedure and, best of all, anonymous.

I pulled into my driveway, let the dogs out, and shouted, "Eureka!" Living in the country did have its perks: I might not get a response if I screamed for help, but I could celebrate at the top of my lungs and not worry the neighbors.

My night had done a one-eighty turn and euphoria replaced fear—until I saw a pair of headlights crawling up my road, dragging a mid-size car behind. I wasn't expecting visitors, and the way the lights hunted over unfamiliar ground told me it wasn't anyone I knew. But wait, hadn't the note stated the culprit knew where I lived?

Oh get a grip, Harrigan. The car turning into my drive was probably someone lost, in need of direction. I stuck my hand into my bag and touched the gun for reassurance. I grabbed a barking Bogart and Bacall by their collars, shoved them into the backyard, and slammed the gate. I didn't want my "hounds from hell" rushing under tires, just close by should I need a quick distraction.

The motion-activated light mounted on the side of the house made the car look mud-brown in color. A medium-sized sedan, maybe American, with tinted windows that made the occupant all but invisible. It stopped. I held my breath. The driver-side door opened. A slender woman with gorgeous blonde hair emerged.

Ellie Stromberg? At my house?

"Are you Mercedes Harrigan?" Sexy hair and a voice to match, life was definitely not fair.

"Yes," I said.

"I'm Ellie Stromberg. I'm here to talk to you about Casey Kelso. Wow, but you live in the boonies." She shook her wonderful mane. "Can I come in?" Model-tall, model-thin, wearing one of those sand-washed silk pantsuits that cost enough to give me hives, she strutted toward my front door.

This was the new millennium. Hating her for being drop-dead gorgeous was taboo, I had to find another reason. Maybe she'd turn out to be a vampire, and I'd have to stake her with the cross from the tack room. One could always hope.

TWELVE

BOGART AND BACALL LAY BESIDE ME on the couch uttering soft growls. I had brought them in the house from the backyard. My tiny dogs were ready to defend me, body and soul, should Stromberg make a wrong move.

Ellie didn't seem to notice as she paced in front of the fireplace, then stopped to pose, head down, right arm resting on the mantel. Pace. Pose. Pace. Pose. I grew exhausted just watching.

While pacing, she told a convoluted tale about good ol' Casey, the great idea man. She stopped mid-sentence and stared across the room. "You've no idea how frustrating it is to love a spineless mama's boy. Casey has a great mind in business matters but runs from any type of confrontation with his mother. Or Thelma."

"You've chosen to stay in this relationship because . . . ?"

"Because he has potential! Some of his ideas are close to genius. If his mama would cut those damn apron strings, we could leave this dump and never look back."

Uh-huh. Loralee Lish's take on Kelso was the same as Ellie's. The man sounded like a pliable lump of clay pressed into different molds by the strong women in his life. It wasn't the impression I got from ol' Casey, but that was beside the point. Why would Stromberg drive to my house and explain their pitiful relationship to me?

Did Casey know she was here?

Had he sent her?

Ellie settled upon the hassock in front of the couch. She crossed her long legs, leaned forward, and stared at me. "Casey did not kill his aunt."

"What?" My mouth fell open; I couldn't seem to shut it.

"Don't look so surprised, Ms. Harrigan. I know you've been asking questions."

"Um . . . um." My brain went into lock and freeze.

"Loralee told Casey you grilled her about Thelma and her relationship with Casey during lunch."

Yeesh! I'd asked a few simple questions; Loralee had turned into a Mt. St. Helens of information all on her own.

"Wait a minute. Are you suggesting Thelma's death was *not* an accident?" I leaned closer to Ellie, hoping the best defense really was a good offense.

"I'm not saying anything like that. You're the one asking questions." Ellie folded her arms and gave me a smug smile that begged for a reply—or a slap. Lucky for her I'm no longer ten years old, so slapping was out.

I clamped my teeth against any reply and stared back at her. If she wanted to play "who blinks first," bring it on. Keeping quiet also seemed safer while I collected my thoughts.

I stared.

She stared.

The phone rang. I snatched it and barked, "Hello."

Silence. Black silence.

I punched the off button and glared at Ellie. "I will not be intimidated by infantile games!"

Ellie didn't move, but the smug smile disappeared. "Excuse me?"

"First Casey threatens me with a lawsuit. Then my tires get slashed, next the ominous message in my mailbox—not very original, by the way. Now the silent phone calls start. All this to creep me out, right? Well, Missy, I'm not scared. I'm pissed!" Bogart and Bacall stood, hackles up, ready to mangle her kneecaps.

"What are you talking about?" She rose to her feet, worry lines pleating her smooth forehead.

Good question; I didn't know exactly where my anger was headed, but I felt like a tea kettle ready to spout. I stood and tried pacing. "Me thinks the lady protests too much."

"What?" Ellie's forehead scrunched higher, pulling her nose and eyes along for effect.

"Okay, the quote wasn't perfect. I'm not the first to slaughter Shakespeare." I stopped beside the mantel but resisted resting my arm along its smooth surface like Stromberg had. "Why did you really make the trip out to the boonies tonight? To gauge my anxiety? See if the lets-terrorize-Mercedes-plan is working?"

"You're crazy!"

"Not yet. But keep up your scare tactics and who knows?"

"I don't have to listen to this."

Ellie started for the front door, but I beat her to it. Using my body as a barrier, I said. "I want answers. You're not leaving until I get some."

Ellie folded her arms and looked at the floor. The way her shoulders slumped, I hoped she was ready to reveal the real reason for her visit.

She raised her head and shook her golden locks. "Being completely alone and bored must be hard."

My mouth fell open as Ellie pushed past me and disappeared into the night. The sound of her revving engine kick-started my brain a little too late for any type of snappy comeback. If I could only think of one.

I uttered a few choice words and kicked the wall for emphasis while Bogart and Bacall watched from the safety of the couch. Was I so transparent a stranger could see past my bravado and right into my pitiful love life? I slid down the wall, wrapped my arms around my knees, and sighed a long sigh that threatened to turn into a moan.

In unison, the dogs leapt from the couch and came over to nuzzle my hands. That's the best thing about dogs, no matter how crappy the day went, no matter what stupid choices you'd made and crawled home looking like death warmed over, dogs always loved you. Who needed a guy to cuddle with when I had Bogart and Bacall.

"We're making people nervous," I said, stroking their silky heads. "And nervous people make mistakes. That's good. Right?" Bogart looked up at me and thumped his tail.

The phone rang.

I chose to ignore it.

The ringing stopped. Fine; whoever it was would either leave a voice mail or they wouldn't.

My cell started bleating again. I remained on the floor, counting ways dogs are better than men. My cell phone gave up and I decided to change the ringtone to something less annoying. I settled against the wall. A little later, a banging on the door startled me to my feet.

"Who is it?" I managed to squeak before my heart blocked my throat.

"It's me, silly. Open up."

The person sounded like Reb, and my dogs were wagging instead of barking. I grabbed my purse and scrabbled through it in search of the gun.

"Door's open," I called, hiding the .38 behind my back.

"Don't be obtuse, Harrigan. Open the damn door, my hands are full."

I cracked the door and Reb waved two hot fudge sundaes before my eyes. "Eat up, girlfriend."

Tucking the gun into the back of my waistband, I opened the door all the way and followed Reb into the kitchen. "Why are you here?"

"That's a fine hello after all the trouble I went to, bringing this decadent offering. I called, but you didn't answer. Is your phone dead again?" She reverently placed the sundaes on the table. "I just took a chance you'd be home." She held up long plastic spoons and grinned. "Let the celebration begin."

"Celebrate what?"

"I'm pretty sure I've found my soul mate."

"Killian?" Either the whipped cream and chocolate had her grinning, or her date with Mr. C.B. had gone very well. Then again, if the date was such a success, why was she sitting in my kitchen at eleven?

"Eat up." She motioned with her spoon to my sundae. "It's going to be a long night. I have so much to tell you."

I looked at the rich concoction, and my inner voice whispered, "Sure. Eat it all." I ignored the sundae and remained standing.

"What's with you?"

"Just not hungry," I said.

"Hell's bells, Harrigan. What's your problem?" she asked, spoon poised halfway to her mouth.

"One of us had a great evening. And one of us didn't." I took the gun from my waistband, placed it on the counter by the stove and sat opposite her.

She laid the spoon down, melting ice cream oozing onto the table. "Is that thing loaded?"

I nodded.

Reb grimaced. "You didn't shoot anyone, did you?"

"Not yet."

"Wanna talk about it?"

"Talking would be good."

"But first, I gotta tell you about Jack. Please, please, or I'll burst."

I sighed. "Okay, talk."

"We have so many things in common. He loves music from the Eighties, especially Bon Jovi's *Slippery When Wet*. Finally, a man who appreciates their raw, naïve exuberance compared to their later introspective, homogenized stuff. He loves lemon cream pie. Favorite tongue-in-cheek sci-fi film: *Tremors* . . ."

Tremors? I adore that movie.

With the exception of his favorite pie, Reb could've been describing my soul mate while I sat in abject silence.

"Earth to Harrigan. Come in, please."

I blinked. "Sorry. Go on."

"It's no fun if you don't ooh and ah in the right places. What's with you?" Reb asked.

I'd rather dive into a pool filled with razor blades than admit I might be suffering from a twinge of jealousy. "This was in my mailbox, wrapped around a rock." I pulled the eerie note from my pocket.

She took the paper, read it, then held it up to the light. "Probably friends of the graffiti artists."

"Or it could mean we've stepped on some toes with the investigation. Maybe the killer's toes."

"That's a stretch." Reb laid the paper on the table. "Feels more like a prank."

"Then what do you make of Ellie Stromberg paying me a visit?"

"Ms. Hair?" Reb glanced around as though Ellie had left behind some of her presence.

"You just missed her."

"What did she want?"

"To inform me that Casey didn't kill Thelma."

Rebbie stared at me. "You're joking, right?"

I shook my head and gave her the high points of my conversation with Ms. Stromberg, leaving out Ellie's assessment of my love life.

"Let me see if I have this right? Loralee tells Casey you're asking questions, he adds B to C, then Ellie comes up to confront you with D?" Reb tapped her bright red nails on the table. "This is getting weird."

There's weird and then there's weird. "Why are you here instead of with Jack?" I asked, as nonchalantly as you please.

"He went into work."

"I thought he had the night off."

"Right. We were at his house watching a movie."

I bit my tongue to keep from inquiring: romantic chick-flick or gut-wrenching action?

"His police scanner squawked out code ten something or other. It's the code for possible dead body. Jack decided he'd better go check it out."

"A body? Where was it found?" Thelma's bloated corpse came to mind. I shuddered and looked at Reb.

"Jack wouldn't say." Reb frowned and scraped the last chocolate drizzle from the bottom of her cup. Pushing the empty sundae dish aside, she started eyeballing mine. I knew she was upset, and I smiled inwardly. The real reason behind the sundaes: she'd been dumped for a corpse.

"He said he'd call me later—I'll ask him then. Are you going to eat that?"

I pushed the tall plastic cup to her. "Have it. You need it more than I do."

She glared at me and scooped out a spoonful. "Ha, ha," she said around the whipped cream.

The phone rang.

We booth stared at it.

"Jack will call my cell," Reb said, and took another bite of sundae, eyes glazing from the experience.

I snatched the receiver. "Hello."

"Mercedes?"

It was Agatha Heckathorn, my hypochondriac renter. *Perfect.* Reb got calls from Killian. I got Agatha. "Yes, Agatha. Is there a problem?"

"I want another deadbolt on my front and back doors. And security locks on all windows!"

I mouthed Agatha's name to Reb and crossed my eyes. "Are you having trouble with your locks?"

"There's a homicidal maniac loose! The police found a dead guy stuffed behind a dumpster, not two blocks from my front door. I don't feel safe living here all alone."

"I'm sorry, Agatha. I'll see about getting better locks installed tomorrow."

"The night is shot. I won't sleep, not one wink. I can't believe it. It's just awful. This maniac is targeting the elderly! Not that I'm—"

"Agatha, lock your doors," I said, cutting off her tirade. "You'll be safe enough."

"Wait, there's more. Dexter went to see what was up with all the lights and commotion." Her emotional pitch was reaching a level only bats could hear. "Oh gawd, Mercedes. I can't believe this . . . the dead guy is Thelma's ex beau, Claude Phoenix!"

Thirteen

*C*LAUDE PHOENIX?

I told Agatha I'd get back to her and hung up. The woman was mistaken. Dexter was mistaken. Someone had to be mistaken. I'd just talked to Claude. He'd told me about the argument he'd had with Thelma. Now his body was discovered behind a dumpster.

A dumpster? The man was a successful car salesman. People like that don't end up stuffed behind enormous garbage bins—not in Portneuf Gap, thank you very much.

I closed my eyes and inhaled as much air as I could and blew it out. I was no longer jealous of Reb and Killian. I was cold—very cold. I hugged my chest and looked at Reb.

"What?" Reb asked.

"Hang on, girlfriend." I walked to the sink and looked out into the ink-black, ominous night. Blinking back tears, I turned and blurted the awful fact fast. "Claude Phoenix is dead."

"Shut up!" Reb paled and her eyes widened. She drummed her fingers against the table. "That's impossible. Agatha's exaggerating. Again. It's what she does best."

"Yeah? I'm going to find out." I picked up my cell and hunted for the text Floydean Mollicker had sent.

"Who are you texting?"

"Floydean Mollicker."

We waited in silence for a response: nothing. I checked to make sure I'd actually sent the text to Floydean. My phone read delivered under the text. Fifteen gruesome minutes passed and my phone didn't beep.

I looked at Reb. "Call her. Desperate times, desperate measures," she said.

A sleepy sounding male answered, and I cringed. "I'm looking for Floydean."

"Ok, hang on."

In the background I heard Floydean say, "Why are you answering my cell?"

"Dun'no. I'm going to bed."

"Hello." Floydean didn't sound sleepy. Maybe she woke up easier than her husband.

"Hi, Floydean. This is Mercedes Harrigan. I apologize for calling so late."

"No problem. Patrick fell asleep watching this stupid movie, but I'm sticking with it until the bitter end. What's up?"

I hesitated.

Where to begin?

"A body was found in an alley by a dumpster. Close to my apartments. It's Thelma's boyfriend, Claude Phoenix."

Floydean's voice dropped a notch. "How did you find out?" Uh-oh. Either she didn't believe me, or I was in some kind of trouble.

I told her about the call that came over Killian's scanner. "Dexter Zoetwilder went to check out the lights and commotion and came back to my complex with the news."

"Let me call the station. I'll get back to you."

Reb was at the window peering into the darkness when I hung up.

"Kinda isolated up here, Harrigan. Ever think of moving? I just listed a couple of houses, both are in great neighborhoods, close to schools and shopping."

"Schools? My dogs are smart but . . ."

She ignored my feeble humor attempt. "You've been complaining about not getting any trick-or-treaters here in the boonies." She turned; her forehead pleated with concern.

Earlier, my out-of-the-way location had seemed ominous, but hearing the anxiety in Reb's voice made me defensive. "I love my house. I'm fine."

"Uh-huh. You're toting a gun because it goes with your outfit?"

"All right, the note freaked me, and I admit I overreacted. But if someone really wanted to get me, living in town wouldn't guarantee safety. What about you?"

Her eyebrows disappeared into her bangs, and she mouthed, "Moi?"

"You've been asking questions too, you know."

Reb pondered this. "We might be getting our panties in a bunch for nothing. Agatha's probably wrong. If the woman told me it was raining *and* I heard water pelting the roof, I'd still step outside to check."

She did have a point.

"Now maybe you'll hustle your butt and get yourself a new cell phone to replace the piece of crap that you never carry." She gave me a no-nonsense glare.

My cell is old but it does have a certain charm: it's a master when it comes to play hide-and-go-seek! Half the time I can't find it and the other half I forget to throw it in my purse. Plus, to be honest, I'm like the Bermuda Triangle of Technology, the new phone would probably punk out a week after I got it.

"I'll get one tomorrow."

"Damn straight, girl. I know this cute guy down at the Cell-phones-cheap, a total pleasure to do business with. He has refurbished phones you can try, totally guaranteed. But a new one isn't that much. Mention me and he'll give you a great deal."

The phone rang, and we both jumped.

"Claude Phoenix has been taken to Portneuf Memorial Hospital.

Report isn't complete, word is he was the victim of a mugging. He has a head injury which rendered him unconscious, but he's still breathing," Floydean reported.

I felt like crying and laughing. "Unconscious, but breathing," I repeated for Reb's ears. "That's great! Well, not great about the mugging but . . ."

"No explanation needed," Floydean cut in. "Oh, and while I have you on the phone, remember that basket Thelma had the plant in?"

"The expensive antique?"

"Unfortunately, no. It's a great reproduction that could fool most people."

"Thelma's selling knock-off baskets?"

"Doubt it. Thelma wouldn't sell something advertised as an original if it wasn't," Floydean said. "Maybe she had the knock-off at her house because she didn't want to spring for the real article."

Last week I would've agreed. But since then I'd learned things about Thelma that had me wondering, and I thought I detected a layer of suspicion in Floydean's voice. I made a mental note to pay another visit to the bookstore and check out the baskets.

Reb's cell played its annoying little ditty from inside her cavernous purse. She answered with a throaty, "Hello."

"Sounds like you're busy," Floydean said. "You can check on Claude tomorrow. Have a good night."

"Wait!" I cried before she could hang up. I motioned for Reb to go into the other room with her call. "Floydean, don't you find this whole thing just a little suspicious?"

"Do you?"

"Yes. I do. I've been asking questions about Thelma . . ."

"For heaven's sake, Mercedes . . ."

"Now, Claude gets mugged on the same night I find a threatening note wrapped around a rock in my mailbox."

"Threatening note? What does it say?" Floydean's voice dropped, I could tell she'd slipped into professional mode.

"I know where you live." Repeating the sentence out loud suddenly made the whole incident seem juvenile. I resisted telling her the words were in red ink. "I know it sounds like a prank, but . . ." I stopped when a quavering whine crept into my voice.

"Okay. Listen up. Most likely you're the victim of a prankster. If it were me, I'd forget about it. If it happens again, then we'll regroup. Claude tangled with a mugger. Things like that happen. Portneuf Gap has its share of crime, you know that. Plus, not all crimes get reported. Were you going to call and report the note?"

"No." I'd inserted my foot, might as well swallow the rest of my leg. "But I think the two are somehow connected."

Silence. If Floydean laughed, I'd pack up and move to Australia.

She cleared her throat before speaking. "I'd call it a coincidence. Tell you what, if anything else happens, no matter how trivial it might seem, let me know. Okay?"

I agreed and hung up. At least now if Reb and I joined the growing list of victims, Floydean would be curious.

Reb came in from the living room with a seductive smile on her face. She re-glossed her lips and gave her hair a fluff. "Jack wants me to come back over and finish watching the movie. Until Claude wakes up, there's not much the police can do. I'll call you tomorrow. Don't forget to lock the doors!"

I hunched over, twisted my head at an angle, rubbed my hands and cackled, "Walking out into the dark alone, are you?"

Reb stopped, turned and gave me her best get-over-yourself-look. "Stop with the *Walking Dead* impression. I hate it. You always slaughter Zombiehood. Now get your butt over here and stand watch until I'm in the car."

In three-inch heels and a tight leather skirt, Reb couldn't quite run, but her power-walk ate up the short distance. A honk and a flash from her headlights and she was gone. I locked both doors, cleaned up the kitchen, and trudged upstairs to bed.

My body felt like I'd spent the night digging a mile-long trench. My mind, however, was on alert: listening, waiting, and thinking. I didn't care what Floydean said. Take Thelma's death, add the note, my slashed tires, plus the attack on Claude and it all equaled something. Trouble was, I didn't know what and I didn't have any proof.

Gut instinct, yes.

Logical, tangible proof, no.

The wind moaned through the trees and the surrounding hillside. My house picked up the chorus, loose shingles tapping, weathered shutters whistling. Every creak became a menacing presence. Despite my tossing and turning, Bogart and Bacall slept. Reb was back snuggling close with Killian while I entertained the monsters in my imagination. The night would end just like it began.

THE NEXT MORNING, VIOLET WOKE ME with the horrible news of a plugged toilet. *Oh joy.*

I fed and watered my menagerie, snatched my car keys off the hook by the backdoor, and caught Eclipse's excited whinny. Killian was here.

Killian was here? I looked at the clock, 8:15. Well, well. Either his date with Reb ended earlier than I'd imagined—and sad to say, my fevered brain had imagined quite the hot scenario—or Reb was still at his place, and he'd slipped away to be with his horse.

No. Killian wouldn't leave Reb just to ride Eclipse—unless? Gulping the last swallow of orange juice, I stuffed a handful of chocolate kisses into my sweatshirt pocket for moral support and headed out into the crisp morning air.

Killian came out of the barn carrying his saddle. "Hey, Sadie. Beautiful morning."

"Beautiful," I called back, nonchalance dripping off every syllable.

"You're out the door early." His breath plumed in the cold.

I could say the same for you, buddy. "Yeah, duty calls." I held up my plumber's helper (toilet plunger, for the unenlightened.)

Killian whistled. "There's something intriguing about a woman who can use one of those."

"You should see me in action."

"Uh-huh." The look he gave me made my heart and tonsils trade places.

Not trusting my voice, I gave him a wave and sauntered to my car. As I drove down the road, I chanted *he's Reb's new boyfriend* four hundred or so times. Killian is a flirt, just like Floydean said.

I pulled into the apartment parking lot and noticed all the geraniums drooping under a coat of frost. Add prep flower beds for winter to my growing list of things to do. Dressed in a pink quilted bathrobe, Violet stood in front of her apartment hunched over like the flowers. This week her coal-black hair color matched the scowl on her face. *Uh-oh!*

"Morning, Violet," I called swiveling out from behind the steering wheel.

"Maybe for you. Dexter takes off early, doesn't tell where he's headed, the toilet's stopped up . . ."

"Here to fix that," I said, walking into her living room, hoping to do my plumber-thing fast and leave before she sucked me into her pit of despair.

Violet shuffled behind me, the plastic flip-flops on her feet underscoring her annoyance. "Dexter said he'd get us some of those lovely, sticky buns from Geraldine's Bakery for breakfast. After all the excitement last night, I need something sweet to sink my teeth into. I wake up and what do I find? No sticky buns. A plugged toilet. And not a soul around to help."

I pushed up my sleeves, mentally crossed my fingers and lifted the toilet lid. If my plunger didn't solve the problem, I'd have to call a real plumber. Pricey numbers danced in my head.

Violet leaned against the door jam and looked on.

I prayed the phone would ring, the doorbell chimes, her stove implodes—anything to distract her from the bathroom.

"You know," she said. "God works in mysterious ways."

"Huh?" I positioned the red toilet plunger and pushed down. Was Violet about to pray for divine intervention on behalf of her troubled toilet? What the heck, couldn't hurt.

"Thelma and Claude found out exactly how *His* justice works."

She began quoting dire consequences found in scripture should one partake of sex outside the bonds of marriage. I stopped working and looked at her. Violet stands around five feet—give or take an inch. How could such a large river of piousness seethe through such a tiny vessel?

"I tried talking to Thelma." She said and looked at the ceiling. "Lord knows, I tried."

I followed her gaze, half expecting to find a mini-hallelujah chorus of angels forming in the corner.

"Now it's too late for both of them!" She placed her right hand over her heart and intoned the words like a zealous preacher reaching his peak. The only thing missing was a pulpit and a Bible to thump. The hair on the back of my neck began to wiggle and goose bumps peppered my arms.

I drew a deep breath and let it out. Slowly. "Violet, Claude is not dead."

"Yes, he is." We both turned to find Dexter standing in the hall. In one hand he clutched a white paper bag, grease marks staining the bottom.

"Ooh, are those sticky buns?" Violet grabbed the bag. She opened it and peered in. "You only got three?"

"Already had one—wish I hadn't. You can have the rest," Dexter said. He slouched against the wall; perfect posture forgotten. A gray tinge replaced his normal ruddy skin tone.

"No, Dexter, Claude isn't dead." I wanted to wrap my arms around his shoulders, but I didn't want Violet getting any twisted ideas. I kept working the plunger, waiting for the water to begin a lovely swirl. "I called Floydean Mollicker last night. She said he's in the hospital. I'm going to call as soon as I'm done here."

"Don't bother. I went to the hospital first thing and I ran into

Claude's sister and brother in law. Claude died early this morning." Dexter said.

Little white dots whirled before my eyes. I dropped the plunger, turned and gripped the sink as loud ringing clanged through my head. Unfortunately, the noise wasn't enough to drown out Violet's voice. She yammered away at Dexter for rushing to check on Claude, leaving her alone with a bathroom crisis.

My heart lodged in my throat, but this time Killian wasn't the cause.

FOURTEEN

CALL ME CALLOUS. CALL ME INSENSITIVE. After the reality of Claude's demise sank in, *thank heavens he's not one of my tenants,* was my first thought. I'm not proud, but that's how it is.

Had he been living in my complex; I would've had two apartments attached to a death stigma like a red slash across their doors. Pretty soon normal tenants would leave. It would be great fodder for horror stories, not so good for cash flow.

Dexter and Violet continued their heated argument as I made my exit. With their toilet working, I decided to head back home and run the credit check on Kim Kasai, the possible new renter from the night before. As I drove through early morning empty streets, I thought about Claude: so vital, so vibrant; now, so dead.

His personality matched his body-type: big, booming, and boisterous. Only a strong assailant could do him real harm. Or, maybe the assailant was someone Claude knew and had caught him off guard. But who would bash his head in and leave him for dead? A random mugging didn't feel right. Yet, a disgruntled customer stuck with a lemon of a car didn't ring true, either.

I passed a Krispy Kreme shop, flipped a U-turn, and parked between two big-wheeled behemoth trucks. A doughnut or two might help my thinking process, and if Killian was around when

I got home some tasty pastries might loosen his tongue when it came to questions about Claude's murder.

I grabbed six assorted doughnuts, paid the clerk and sat at a table near the window to enjoy the fat-laden concoction and call Reb.

She answered with a cheery, "Yel-low." I could hear traffic noise in the background. She must have a hot prospect, probably showing homes to a family with two-point-five kids.

"Hey, got some bad news." I explained about Claude.

"No way!"

"'Fraid so."

"Shame. Such a nice man." She was silent for a minute. "You realize your circle of elderly friends are being terminated one by one, just like the people in that Agatha Christie novel."

"The death rate hasn't reached *Ten Little Indians* yet. But, I agree . . . weird. You working?"

"Showing a couple of houses to a family."

"How many kids do they have?"

"Two with one due in January. Why?"

"Just curious." *Can I call em or what?* "We need to reconnoiter. Want to meet for lunch? Johnny-B-Goode's around twelve?"

"Home fries? You're on. My treat if I close this deal. See you at noon."

Outside, the sun had risen high enough in the cobalt sky to banish the mid-October morning haze. The air felt like it might turn shirt-sleeve warm by noon. I reached my car and watched, amazed, as a petite woman with apricot-colored hair and a slim cigar clamped between her red lips hoisted herself into the driver's seat of the giant black truck to my right. Looking at her stick-thin arms and dried-apple face, I judged her to be somewhere between eighty and a hundred.

"Nice truck," I said.

She removed the cigar and gave me a missing tooth jack-o-lantern grin. "Thanks. Bought it from my nephew. Used to drive one of them little compacts," she pointed to my Ghia. "But people kept backing into it. Now I'm the one who does the backing."

She winked, slammed the door shut, gunned the engine and hauled out of the parking lot. I followed in her wake of dust, turned right, changed my mind and flipped another u-turn in the middle of the street. This close to the Old Town district, I might as well visit The Bookmark, take a closer look at the questionable baskets, and talk to Casey Kelso—see if he knew about Claude—do a little backing up of my own.

Still paranoid about someone vandalizing my car, I parked behind an antique store and jogged one block over then one block up to reach Thelma's store. The front door had an old-fashioned pull-down shade covering the frosted window and a closed sign hanging slightly askew. Red lettering on the window stated the store hours were 10:00-5:00 Tuesday through Saturday. My watch read 10:15. I bent down and looked through the slit where the shade didn't reach the bottom of the window. Lights were on in the back of the shop.

I pounded on the door, waited thirty seconds, and pounded again. The sash flipped up, the deadbolt snicked, and Kelso opened the door.

"We're closed. Inventory week."

"I'm not here to buy." I barged past him. "I came to talk."

He shut the door, turned, and gazed at me, his stare lingering and intimate. I swallowed my irritation and walked over and chose one of the overstuffed chairs to sit down. Casey sat in the chair opposite mine, crossing his ankle over his knee. His foot beat a rat-a-tat rhythm as he picked at imaginary lint on his perfectly creased, charcoal trousers.

"Okay, Ms. Harrigan, talk."

I brushed at the dog hair on my jeans. "I thought it was time we had a frank discussion."

"Ellie said you'd probably stop in, after last night." He steepled his fingers and regarded me through gold wire-framed glasses. "Someone is harassing you. Why assume it's me?"

"A hunch and the fact that you're threatening a lawsuit. Either take me to court or drop the suit, just stop with the juvenile notes, and phone calls."

He leaned forward, his hair swinging freely about his shoulders, and rested his elbows on his knees. His face held a smug smile equal to the one Ellie had worn, but he had dark circles under his eyes, the kind that a person gets from sleepless nights and problems with elusive solutions. "Sorry, can't help you. Don't know what you're talking about."

"Right." I stood and walked over to the basket display, picked one up and turned it over. The price tag read two hundred. *For a little ol' basket?* "Sell many of these?"

He was out of the chair and plucking the basket from my hands before I could take a breath. "A few," he said, placing the basket reverently back on the shelf.

I had a sudden urge to sweep the entire collection to the floor, maybe shred one before his eyes. I resisted. "I hear Thelma wasn't excited about selling them."

"She got over her aversion once she realized the profit margin." He folded his arms and stood like a sentry before the basket filled shelves.

I sauntered over to the new title section and plucked out David Rosenfelt's latest mystery. Casey was instantly at my side, hovering. I didn't step back, though that was my first instinct. Instead, I looked him straight in the eye.

"Did you know Claude Phoenix was attacked last night?"

A flicker of something crossed his features. Surprise? Fear? Possibly panic? "No, I didn't know."

I maintained eye contact. "He's dead."

This time fear and panic twitched through his brown eyes, but only for a moment before he slipped behind a neutral mask.

"I'm sorry to hear that."

Was he? I remembered the way he'd said goodbye to Claude at the Realtor Gig. Two words, the first one starting with "F" wasn't meant to be endearing.

He placed a sweater-clad arm against the wall, effectively blocking my exit, and leaned in, his face a couple of inches from mine. His breath smelled of stale coffee. "Ms. Harrigan, why exactly did you come here?"

"To discuss . . . things." I placed the novel back in the row, folded my arms, and tried to appear taller. Too bad I'd left the plumber's helper in my car.

"Things? What type of things?"

Did you kill your aunt? Did you bash poor Claude over the head? And if not, do you know who did?

"Mainly the lawsuit." I answered, the picture of poise except for a line of sweat trickling down my spine.

His whole body relaxed, like a slow-leaking balloon. "Mother and I have decided not to pursue it."

He gave me a slight grin. "We both agree that by the time the dust settles, the lawyers would be the real winners."

Relief wobbled my knees. *Okay. Good news. No lawsuit.* Why was the man back to hovering? According to Loralee and Ellie, Kelso was nothing more than a timid, creative genius who ran from confrontation.

"Happy to hear it." I made a show of checking my watch. "Better let you get back to doing inventory."

He lowered his arm but didn't move out of my way. "Then we have everything straightened out?"

My head started nodding like a bobble-head toy. "You bet. Everything is just fine. All dandy and a-okay."

He followed me to the door, unlocked the deadbolt, and opened it wide. "Nice to meet you."

I slipped out and forced myself to walk until I rounded the corner. Then I ran.

Next stop, new cell phone. I pulled into the parking lot of U-break-it-We-fix-it and was happy to see, according to the sign in the window, I was five minutes early. Good, first in line; I slipped out of my car and stood in front of the door. The shop was in a mini-strip mall next to a Mongolian restaurant. The heavy garlic aroma mixed with other herbs seeping through the restaurant's roof vents had my stomach rolling, weighted down by donuts. I couldn't give up my number one slot, other cars and trucks were now coming into the parking lot, so I folded my arms, leaned against the locked doors, and concentrated on my meeting with Casey. Did he know something about poor Claude Phoenix before I gave him the news? Maybe.

He'd suggested selling baskets to Thelma, what else was he doing to make the bookstore's bottom-line more solvent? The open mike idea that Loralee had told me about had appeal to some but didn't seem to be a real moneymaker. And why drop the lawsuit? Not that that didn't make me happy but why the sudden turn around? Why was I even following up on this as though I was a bona fide trained detective?

Gut feeling: something was off but I didn't know what, and couldn't even explain it.

I heard a key inserted in the lock and turned. A guy with an amazing smile unlocked the door.

"Looks like you're first."

I smiled my best smile. "Yes. Reb sent me." He sold me a new phone.

Johnny B Goode's parking lot was filled. I had no choice but to park in the vacant lot next door. I nosed in between a rusty V.W and a lonely clump of Russian Sage.

Reb stood and waved when I pushed through the double doors. She'd secured a table for two beneath the Elvis clock with gyrating hips, which played the first bars of "Jailhouse Rock" every thirty minutes.

"Sorry I'm late." I said, plopping down on the red ice-cream-parlor chair and hauling my new cell out of my purse and wiggling it in front of her.

"Finally, a new phone ... about time, girlfriend. Now please put it on a leash like your pups and drag it with you. Also, listen for

number forty-seven, that's us. I got you a Cherry Pepsi, lots of ice."
She handed me a large drink and took a sip from hers. "Claude's
death has me worried. I don't want to end up behind a dumpster
like he did. That's so . . . yuck!"

"Asking questions hasn't netted much info, but we are getting
weird reactions." I put my cell back in my purse and leaned closer
across the table. "I paid Casey Kelso a visit this morning at the
Bookmark. He assures me the lawsuit is no longer a go, but he
acted strange when I told him about Claude."

"How did you expect him to act? Happy?"

"Okay, strange is the wrong word—try agitated." I twirled my
straw through the ice. "I was thinking about running a credit check
on all of our suspects.'

"Uh-huh." Reb looked at me expectantly. "Because . . ."

I shrugged. "To see if anyone's having money problems."

Reb leaned back against the booth and gave me a look. "That's
it? That's your plan? Harrigan, Thelma wasn't loaded. Unless there
was a fortune in her mattress, killing her wouldn't solve anything."

"At least it's a place to start. Something might pop up. Do you
have a better idea?"

"Well, I do have *one* avenue worth traveling!" She grinned,
paused for effect and took another sip of cola.

The speaker squawked out our number. I told her to hold that
thought and jumped up to get our food.

"What avenue?" I placed the large order of fries and double fry
sauce between us not much nutrition but tons of comfort.

"I'm meeting Ellie Stromberg at her granny's house at four. I'll
butter-up both the appraisal and Ms. Hair, see what happens."

I dipped a golden potato wedge into the light-coral fry sauce
and took a bite. "Think you can wrangle Casey's Social Security
number out of her?"

"Kinda hard to work into a conversation. Why do you want it?"

"Helps if I run into any kind of snag with a credit report," I said.

"Why don't you try asking Loralee Lish?"

"Ms. Vocal Vesuvius might blab to Casey. Hey, what about that loan officer you dated at Idaho National Bank? He could pull up a couple of numbers for you."

Reb shook her head. "No good. He's engaged. Besides, bank people are trained never to give out a customer's personal info, even under torture."

We both ate in silence while trying to come up with a plan. The French fries made my taste buds applaud, but they didn't seem to help my thinking process. Guess I should've ordered the fish sticks.

"How about we go to his apartment when he's working, toss the place, quick like and find something with his Social number on it?" Reb said.

I stopped mid-chew. "Toss the place? Please tell me you're not binging *Miami Vice* reruns?"

"Ha ha. So you in?"

"You're talking breaking and entering? That gets your butt thrown in jail with no get-out-free card."

Reb shrugged. "Only if we get . . . holy crap! There goes your car!"

I looked out the side window. Sure enough, a big red and white tow truck was inching my car's front wheels off the ground.

"Ah, crap!" I jumped up, spilling both my chair and drink, and raced out the door.

Skidding to a halt before the skinny, pimply faced driver, I shouted, "What do you think you're doing?"

"My job." He kept his hand on the button operating the truck's winch and grinned. I stared at his yellow jumble of teeth. Was that a small diamond pierced through his left nostril?

"Well, stop. Put my car down!"

Skinny guy continued to smile; the diamond continued to sparkle.

My poor car continued to rise.

My ears were ringing again, and I wanted to punt something. Maybe I could use my foot to pop the festering zit on his chin.

I took a deep breath, counted off a few numbers, and exhaled. "Please, put my car down. This is all a mistake."

"No can do. Read the sign." He pointed to a dented white rectangle attached mid-way down on a light pole. I could just make out the faded black lettering: Private Property. The lone Russian Sage I'd parked beside obscured the rest of the sign.

"I didn't see the sign when I parked. I'm really sorry." I crossed my heart and held my hand up to show my sincere intent. "I'll move my car, right now. Don't want to damage this *lovely* property," I said, looking at the garbage-littered, weed-choked, barren lot.

"Look, lady, it's like this. Once I've hooked on, I can't release until I get paid." The guy hadn't stopped grinning. He probably pulled the wings off butterflies in his spare time.

"Hey," Reb panted, jerking to a stop beside me. She'd been a couple of steps behind, running in heels is murder. "Let my friend drive away and no one will get hurt. *Comprende Amigo?*"

"Anyone parking on this property is gonna have their car towed, and is gonna pay a fine, with the cost not to exceed one-hunnert dollars per twenty-four hour period." Grinning man tucked the card he'd quoted from back inside the breast pocket of his stained coveralls and sauntered back to the tow truck.

"Okay. Okay! You win," I said, grabbing my credit card from my wallet.

"No card. No Venmo. This is a cash-only deal."

"I don't have one hundred dollars cash!" I explained through clenched teeth.

"I'm not Macy's, Sweet Cheeks. No cash, no car."

Reb marched over and stood close enough to count his nose hairs. "What's your problem? Everyone takes Venmo or cards."

A group of high-school students originally headed into Johnny B Goodes, let the black-and-white checkered door whoosh shut and walked over to watch our drama. Cell phones were hoisted in the air. Great, this whole embarrassing incident would probably become a YouTube sensation.

Grinning Man shrugged and hoisted his skinny rump into the tow truck. "You can pick your car up at Benchmark's auto yard."

I grabbed Reb's arm. "Omigosh. He's leaving. Quick! Where's the closest ATM?"

"Um, couple of blocks south. But you don't have a debit card."

"I know. Give me your card, please! And stall that jerk!"

Reb fished in her purse. "It costs extra if you don't go to my bank." She handed me her card along with her keys, grabbed my palm and jotted her pin number.

"I'll pay whatever. Just don't let that guy leave!"

I sprinted for her Subaru, safely parked at the curb, a lousy five feet away. Squealing onto the street, I prayed that all sane drivers stayed out of my way.

Three broken fingernails and fifteen minutes later, I returned with the money. The tow truck was still parked in the same spot. A crowd surrounded the vehicle.

Grinning Man wasn't grinning anymore. He was barricaded in the cab with the windows rolled up and doors locked. Reb stood on the truck's running board, holding onto the side mirror for support.

I parked behind the crowd, climbed out and shouted, "I have the money!"

A few people turned and looked at me, then turned back to the action. Shouts of "Let the car down," and "Get a life, halfwit," sounded from the mob. *Not good.* The guy was a jerk, but I didn't want his lynching on my conscience.

Reb saw me, whistled, and put her hands up signaling for silence. "The money is here. Thank you for your help. We truly appreciate all of you."

The crowd both cheered and grumbled then slowly began to disperse. No bloodletting today; clearly some were disappointed.

A burly woman in checked shorts and an overtaxed halter top came up to me and glared through slitted eyes. She fisted her hands on ample hips. "She don't look like she's dying. She doesn't even look sick."

I wondered if holding up my fingers with the half-ripped nails would suffice. From the look on her face, I decided no.

"She's in the first stage. The end will be too gruesome for the average person to witness," Reb explained in a stage whisper.

I tried a wan smile. The woman puckered large lips and marched away with three chubby kids in tow.

"I have a fatal disease?"

"Your doctor suspects a rare strain of Ebola," Reb stepped down from the running board. "I thought it added the right touch. Besides, we got a coupon for a free lunch."

Grinning Man barely cracked the driver side window and yelled. "Got the damn money?"

I fanned the cash before his eyes. "That better be the whole hunnert."

"Count it if you want," I answered.

The guy lowered the window and snatched the bills. "Now get back. I don't want no disease, understand?"

I doubled over and coughed, long, low, and gasping. It was almost worth the money to watch the man's eyes bug out while he cranked up the window and thumbed through the bills. Satisfied, he motioned for me to move away before he opened the door. Reb grabbed my arm and hauled me a short distance to the side.

"Thanks," I whispered. "I owe you, big time."

"All in the line of duty."

When my car's front wheels thunked to the ground, I had to fight the urge not to melt against Reb. With the adrenalin rush subsiding, my insides went all gooey. Or maybe hunger made me weak-limbed. Our lunch had been ruined . . . and for what? So some skinny jerk could throw his authority around and charge me for parking on a hard-packed, weed-infested lot?

My stomach shifted from gooey to sour and hot. "Think I could get away with acting rabid, maybe go for his jugular?" I asked Reb as he scurried to unhook my car.

Reb glanced at me and frowned. "Calm down, girl. It's over."

"If he so much as leaves a tiny scratch or dent, he's mine!"

Reb grabbed my arm. "Whoa, girlfriend. You bust him, I'm behind you. But he looks like the type to press charges."

I shook off her arm. Hot tears stung my eyes. "First my tires. Then that stupid note. Now this. I hate feeling so—powerless."

Reb's eyes flew open wide. A slow smile spread across her face. "Oh my gosh, that's it!"

"What's it?"

"Power. That's how we get Casey's Social Security number."

"Tow his car?"

"No. Call Melinda Whosit at Idaho Power and have her pull his application. His Social will be on it."

I gave Reb a high five. "Girl, I love how your mind works."

FIFTEEN

I APPRECIATED EVERY CURVE my Karman Ghia hugged like a friendly embrace as I drove the winding road to my house. My car might be dated but it was the perfect machine for me. After the tow truck brutality, I'd performed a quick scan, making sure there was no damage to her vintage body, told Reb I'd call her later and drove south towards home-sweet-home.

My head throbbed along with my bruised fingers and I wanted nothing more than to cuddle my dogs on the couch and make the rest of this day fade away. Instead, my cell rang as I pulled into my driveway. My new phone showed Candlemass as the caller. Damn.

"Yes," I said, cutting the engine and leaning back against the front seat. A glance at the grease-stained bag of donuts on the passenger seat made me grimace; too stale now, even for a donut loving cop.

"Good to know family honor is back," Yancy said.

I climbed out of the Ghia, opened the backyard gate, greeted my happy duo dancing on their hind legs, and thought about simply ending the call. "Yancy, I've had a long day. No riddles, please. What are you talking about?"

"Claude Phoenix. Harrigan Funeral Home will be handling his funeral in the classic style someone of his stature deserves."

"Good." I opened the backdoor, went to the fridge to get a bottle of water for me and a handful of mini carrots for Bogart and Bacall.

"Good? Mercedes, you are a walking thesaurus and that's the best you can come up with?"

"That's it. Bye."

"No weeping? No gnashing of teeth? Beating of breast? Where's the angst you're famous for displaying? You knew Claude Phoenix, right?"

"Candlemass, what do you want?"

His voice dropped and I had to strain to hear. "The funeral I handled this morning was an unmitigated disaster and since I can't share it with Cassandra I need to tell someone."

Why me? Didn't he have any close friends? Okay, I knew spreading gossip about the Harrigan Funeral Home was a bad, bad idea and I did admire his forethought. I drew in a breath and let it out slowly. Gram would be home from her cruise in a couple of days but Yancy was, no doubt, well aware of her ETA. I plopped on my couch and took pity. "Share away, Candlemass."

"First of all, I'm not a snob!" *That depended on whom one asked about Yancy but I let it go.* "This family claimed they were close to destitute and to save money they decided to make their father's casket. I think the eldest son wanted to show off his woodworking skills but . . . the casket turned out to be a gaudy abomination, ornate carving of deer and pheasants covered the outside. Handles shaped like antlers. The wife and daughter made the interior lining . . . in hunter red and black plaid. Simply dreadful but I worked with it and did my best to make the whole thing presentable at the viewing."

"The son whipped out a casket just like that?" I snapped my fingers for Bogart's benefit. He wagged his tail.

"No. The father was terminal but, according to his children, he was a stubborn old guy, determined to beat the cancer and prove the doctors wrong. Family had about six months to prepare. They worked on the casket in a shed on some neighbor's property. They considered it a final tribute."

"Okay."

"The casket was awful but the eulogy, given by the eldest daughter, turned into a blame game. Dearly beloved Dad never paid attention to her. Mom wasn't much better. Her siblings were like Hell Hounds always nipping at her heels. An hour-long blah-blah gripe-fest of finger pointing and fire and brimstone Bible thumping. At one point, the Pastor tried to intervene, soften her wrath, at least get her to go back to her seat, but she brushed him aside and forged on to the bitter end."

"What did you do?" I asked.

"Vowed to carry earplugs in my pocket from now on."

"Ok, the service wasn't standard, the casket wasn't what you expected, but you've handled odd funerals before. Talk to you later." I decided Yancy had reached my max level of commiseration and I didn't want this conversation to become repetitive like a hamster's run on a wheel.

"You haven't heard the piece de resistance."

"A fight broke out among the relatives?" *Been there watched that.*

"If only I'd had to deal with a fight. The funeral procession finally arrives at the cemetery. The Pallbearers unload the revolting casket, walk it to the gravesite only to discover the homemade nightmare is too big for the grave!"

I'd just gulped some water which spurted out my nose. Good thing it was only water.

"Candlemass you're lying."

"Hand to God, Harrigan." I almost felt his shudder travel the airwaves.

"What did you do?" I was trying to imagine how a mistake like that could happen let alone how to remedy it.

"Sonny-boy came prepared."

"Please tell me the alterations did not include a chainsaw."

"Thank God, no. He brought his toolbox from his truck, took the handles off both sides, chiseled part of the ornamentation off the ends, and it fit . . . just barely. For a brief moment I seriously toyed with asking everyone to drain some oil from their vehicles so we could grease the abomination but after about an hour of chiseling it fit."

"Candlemass this is perfect. You have fodder for an article. Write this up and submit it to The Funeraire Magazine. They published your article about some families preferring Johnny Walker bottles to cremation urns. You could get another byline and get paid."

"The pay was a mere pittance," he huffed. "Besides, I don't know if I have it in me to revisit such a dreadful experience. Right now, I want to soak in Cassandra's lovely claw foot tub with some of her special oils and scrub away my frustration with mankind." His voice became softer as he spoke.

I pictured him sliding down whatever he was sitting on like a limp noodle. "Indulge yourself, you've earned a long soak."

"Speaking of earning, is the scuttlebutt true about Thelma foisting phony exotic baskets on John Q. Public?" All of his distress vanished as he spoke. Obviously, repeating gossip had rejuvenating properties better than fame or fortune.

"Where did you hear that?"

"I have my sources. One source is seriously considering bringing a lawsuit against the bookstore after discovering she'd paid a fortune for a painted thrift store basket."

"Who?"

"Not sure I should divulge that privileged info."

"Candlemass you're not an attorney or a Priest. Give!"

"Gwen from *Butter Your Buns* is raging mad."

"Gwen, tiny mild-mannered woman who looks like Hollywood's version of Mrs. Clause? The one who owns the bakery on 3rd? That Gwen?"

"One and the same, claims she will not be made to play the fool.

Thelma might be gone but her estate better watch out. Woman's out for blood."

Interesting.

"She's painted a bulls eye on the bookstore clerk who sold her the basket."

"Casey? Thelma's nephew?"

"No, some blonde clerk. Gwen said the clerk was very knowledgeable and claimed the basket had good karma woven into it. Just having the basket at *Butter Your Buns* was supposed to double if not triple business."

"Loralee?"

"I think that's the name she said."

Loralee was in on the scam. *Hmm.* Because she was devoted to Casey or because she got a nice commission? Or both? I'd have to check this out. My best guess would be Gwen bought the basket just to get Loralee to stop talking before Gwen agreed to sacrifice her firstborn. But maybe Gwen was into good Karma and believed Loralee's line of B.S.

Was Gwen capable of murder because she was scammed? I pictured her bustling about her small bakery in a starched white apron, serving, baking, chatting with everyone that came in. When would she find the time? I knew she always arrived at the bakery way before dawn to begin mixing and preparing goodies for the day. Maybe, around midnight, before starting her work day she went to Thelma's in a blind rage and . . . no. Committing murder in a blind rage did not include a premeditated thought to find an old toaster, take it to Thelma's, and use the bare wire to extinguish her life.

That was the whole problem. Thelma's murder had been carefully planned. There was nothing spur-of-the-moment about it.

The headache I'd been coaxing to the back of my head sallied forth in all its glory. I told Yancy we both deserved a long soak in a tub and hung up.

As I went upstairs, the conversation that continued playing in my mind turned into the repetitive hamster wheel I'd tried to avoid with Yancy. Two names continued to squeak on the wheel: Casey and Mama Kelso.

Maybe when I got the credit reports I'd find something else to obsess about. In the meantime, I wished Mary Poppins would appear in my bathroom with her magic umbrella, carpetbag full of tricks, and turn the bubble bath I was running into a magical play land where nothing mattered except joy—pure joy. I ran the credit report for the student who wanted to rent the apartment. It was fine.

SIXTEEN

L ATE FRIDAY AFTERNOON, a neat and tidy pile of credit reports
sat on my kitchen table. I printed them so I could make copious
notes on some and doodle on others. Melinda had been reluctant
to give me that many Social Security numbers—until I promised
I'd catch a serious case of amnesia should anyone question where
I got my information. The free lunch I threw in, her choice, didn't
hurt. I had a feeling I'd better start saving in case the lunch happened to be at some little café along the Champs Elysees

Loralee Lish's report topped the pile. A quick scan of the two
pages revealed nothing. She'd purchased a computer, a digital camera, and a deluxe, queen size, pillow-top mattress six months ago
and was current on all payments. *Ms. Dependable all the way.*

A deluxe queen mattress? Did she plan to invite Casey to a
sleepover? That wouldn't be a bad thing. According to Casey's credit
report, the man might need shelter soon. He was overextended on
two major credit cards, and his Suzuki GSXR 1000 would be but a
fond memory if he didn't make the Suzuki shop happy soon.

Whoa! Casey had a crotch-rocket?

Hard to picture him in biker gear, careening down the road
on a motorcyclist's wet dream. The man didn't seem the type. His
girlfriend, Ellie, seemed more inclined to go for the black leather

look: metal-studded jacket, tight leather pants, and spiked-heel boots, maybe a little whip—yeah, definitely, a whip.

Could Casey's gaunt features and surly attitude be the result of collection agents hounding him? Were repo guys invading his dreams? If his landlord decided to boot him, at least Casey wouldn't be homeless. Ellie, Loralee, or Mama Kelso looked like three friendly ports in his financial storm.

Ellie's report showed she'd been in financial trouble a couple of times, but she'd always managed to stay ahead of serious grief. Clever girl; Casey should take lessons.

Right now, she was pretty leveraged. Could be the reason she was in a rush to sell her grandmother's house. I mentally crossed my fingers and hoped Reb could finesse the right info from Ms. Hair when she listed granny's homestead.

I picked up the report on Claude Phoenix; pretty standard except for a sizeable second mortgage. He'd refinanced his home just two months prior to Thelma's death. Interesting—too bad the report didn't state what the money was used for.

Judy Kelso's report was the most confusing. Before her husband passed, they'd owned several buildings in 'Old Town.' Some were small, quaint, others towered three and four stories. About six months after Mr. Kelso's death, Judy began selling commercial properties and buying commercial properties and selling and buying. There didn't seem to be any pattern to her financial planning; instead, there was almost a randomness that could best be explained as impulse buying.

Intriguing data, but what did it prove? Zero, zip, zilch. Sitting on my fanny while my mind wandered was not productive, but, where to go, what to do next?

I could return to the scene of the crime; it worked for fictional detectives. The police had conducted a thorough search of the alley where Claude was attacked and Floydean said they hadn't found anything significant. I wanted to have a look-see myself. I'd read that a place visited by violent death retains the memory, sort of like a cosmic negative. I didn't buy it, but, like a kid on Christmas Eve, I wasn't going to scoff, either.

Shrugging into my Levi jacket, I stuffed my new cell phone into the breast pocket and headed out the back door. The sun hugged the edge of the mountains, casting amber shadows across the sagebrush-dotted hillside. Smoke from a neighbor's chimney teased the cool air. Fall always stirred my appetite, and the crunch of leaves underfoot started my mouth watering for a big, juicy apple—dipped in melted caramel.

With dinner planned, I opened my car door and called Bogart and Bacall. The duo bounded into the passenger seat, and I drove with the windows open; the wind whipped their ears back against their furry heads, while tantalizing aromas teased our senses. The night felt electric, poised on the brink of new discoveries with possible adventure, romance.

Romance? Cruising down the mountain with my two dogs on a Friday night, headed for any alley to scope out some garbage bin, hardly qualified as romantic.

It was more like pathetic.

When we got back home, I'd slip a horror movie into the DVD player and treat myself to two caramel apples, and popcorn, with lots of butter, and—whoa, girl! I wouldn't be able to fit into my car, let alone my pants if I kept up this obsession with comfort food. It was obvious I needed a date and not with the snack genie.

I flipped on the radio. The Eagles crooned "Hotel California," adding exactly the right touch to the night's mystique.

Reb would claim my biorhythms were coordinating with whatever biorhythms coordinate with. I wasn't on board with all her mumbo-jumbo, but something was making my stomach shiver with anticipation—and it wasn't just the pig-out I had planned for later.

Maybe if I stood where Claude had been attacked I'd receive vibes or have another psychic moment with Thelma. Tonight, anything seemed possible.

My cell phone jingled, making me jump. I fished it out of my pocket. "Hello, this is Mercedes."

"Where you at, girlfriend?" Reb asked.

"On my way to check out where Claude got mugged."

"Why?"

"I wanted to look around."

"What do you expect to find?"

"Not sure. Just seemed like a good idea." I didn't want to explain my wanderlust over the phone. "Want to join me?"

"In a sleazy alley?"

"Sure, that's where all super-sleuths meet."

"Right. I just listed Granny's house for Ellie. The place is a real bow-wow, but I gave Ms. Hair one very smooth assessment. She's a happy camper, and I do have stuff to report." Static garbled the rest of Reb's answer.

"What?" I shouted.

"I said, talking like this reminds me of the time I got those walkie-talkies for my birthday."

I smiled. "See you. This is Sadie, over and out."

THE GRAY DUMPSTER HUNKERED ON PITTED ASPHALT next to the sooty red brick wall of the Beijing Restaurant. I panned the flashlight in an arc; the alley looked greasy-wet under the litter. Shattered glass, scattered at the base of a lone streetlight, sparkled with every blink from a neon beer sign hanging in the window. Where the neon sign didn't reach, the alley became shadows stacked upon shadows in the moon's pale glow. I kept reminding myself that shadows have no substance or cryptic agendas.

Nothing leaped out at me. Well, what had I expected? A monogrammed flask dropped on the ground and overlooked by the cops? A library book that could be traced back to the borrower?

"It's a good thing I'm not wearing my new heels!"

I shrieked and whirled. "Damn, Reb, you scared ten years out of me. Quit sneaking up like that."

"I wasn't sneaking. You must be in La-La land. Isn't the city supposed to maintain the alleys?" She wrinkled her nose and kicked a tall beer can against the curb. "Remind me again what we're doing here."

"Looking for clues. Absorbing the aura." I walked slowly around the garbage bin. The battery in my flashlight was dying, along with my enthusiasm. I lifted the heavy lid and peered inside. *Whew, gross.* I let the lid clank shut and stooped to peer underneath.

"You slip and fall on this glass; you'll absorb more than aura. I'm talking emergency room—tetanus shot. Let's get out of here."

"In a minute." I looked across the alley at the eight-foot chain-link fence. On the other side, the Union Pacific rail yard divided the city in half with serpentine ribbons of tracks. "Why would Claude come here?"

"Maybe he got a craving for Chinese. He eats, heads for his car," she said, pointing to the parking lot across the street. "And wham!" She clapped her hands. "Some punks jump him."

"Possibly." I walked partway down the alley, reading the different establishment names above the back doors. The Beijing Restaurant, a hardware store, a dry cleaner, and the Rum Runner Lounge, all had back entrances that opened onto the alley. Floydean said Claude had been attacked sometime between nine and ten. The hardware store and dry cleaner closed at six. All of their customers would've been long gone when the crime occurred. That left only the restaurant or lounge.

The bar's back door was propped open, leaching out waves of cigarette smoke and alcohol-bright voices competing with the blare of country music. I peered inside the narrow, dimly lit interior. It didn't look like the type of place Claude would visit.

"Tell me we're *not* going in there," Reb said, wrinkling her nose.

"What if Claude got a phone call telling him to come to the Rum Runner? The bartender might know something. Some of the regulars might remember something."

"Uh-huh. And the police didn't think to ask questions? They're waiting for Sadie Sleuth to tell them their job?"

I rolled my eyes and walked back to the dumpster. We'd been snooping around for at least thirty minutes and so far, no clues, no vibes, or psychic stirring. If Claude or Thelma was trying to send a message, it probably couldn't get through all the debris and grime.

"Let's get a fruit smoothie from that new java-something place. I'm bursting with info, but this place doesn't inspire sharing details," Reb said.

"Okay. Guess I better get back before Bogart and Bacall hot-wire the car." I hadn't found anything and now wished I hadn't come. Thinking of Claude crumpled in this filth was beyond depressing.

"Terrible place to die," Reb said, echoing my thoughts.

I could only nod in agreement.

We reached the sidewalk, and I stepped off the curb.

Reb whispered, "holy moley," grabbed my arm and hauled me back into the alley.

"What the . . .?"

"Shh," Reb hissed. Back pressed against the building, she inched her way to the corner and peered around the edge. I followed her lead and took a quick peek. Waiting on the corner, half a block away, stood Ellie Stromberg, Casey Kelso, Mama Kelso, and Thelma's neighbor, Esther Clemmens. Esther wore a pearl-gray pantsuit, making her appear almost ethereal in the glow of the street light. She glanced our direction, and we ducked back into the alley.

"This is silly. Why are we hiding?" My whisper sounded louder than I intended.

"I'm not sure, but . . ." Reb frowned and looked up at the moon as though searching for the answer on its anemic face.

"It feels all wrong," I said.

"Exactly. Those people—together—pretty strange."

I peered around the corner again and watched our four suspects cross the street. "Before we let our imaginations run amok, time out for a little logic. Esther decides to eat out and runs into the Kelsos and Ellie."

"They chat while waiting for the light to change," Reb added. "Normal. Nothing strange about it."

"Sure."

"Logic prevails, right?"

"Nope." I shook my head. "I'm not buying it."

"Me neither."

"Gut feeling?" I asked.

Reb nodded. "Gut feeling."

That settled it. Whatever was happening, it wasn't mere coincidence.

"Want to follow Kelso?" Reb asked. "See where he's headed?"

"He knows my car," I said, hurrying to catch her as she jogged across the middle of the street.

"We'll use mine. If sleuthing is your new vocation, you should get another set of wheels." Breaking into a run, Reb pushed the unlock button on her key chain. Ten feet away, parked next to my Ghia, her car beeped and flashed both front and taillights.

"Get real. The Ghia's a classic," I said, inching my hand through the slightly opened window to calm my barking hounds.

"Whatever. Get in, we're taking mine." Reb climbed behind the steering wheel and started the engine.

"Wait. We need to think this through. The Kelsos won't talk to us just because we show up. Esther is the one to visit."

"On what pretext?" Reb said.

"No idea, I'm making this up as I go. Quit arguing and either follow me or climb in. I can't leave the dogs."

Reb gave me a look, shut off her car and slammed the door. "You win. Get this hunk of junk rolling, and I'll tell you about Ellie and Casey while we drive."

Opening the driver-side door, I herded the dogs into the back.

A pair of headlights blinked on directly behind us. Reb screamed and dove into the Ghia. I couldn't move, couldn't blink, my brain was trying to catch up to this new development as I stood still like a transfixed deer.

"It's Kelso. We're dead," Reb moaned.

"Lock your door!" I dove into the front seat, slammed the door and heard a familiar voice.

"What's the problem?"

I stopped trying to ram the key into the ignition and leaned back to get a better view of Officer Jack Killian grinning through my windshield.

SEVENTEEN

"**Y**OU'RE SERIOUS?" Seated in a booth across from us, Killian looked down at his hands folded on the wooden table and shook his head. A devilish grin indented his dimples. Damn, the man even made smirking sexy.

Reb rotated her smoothie cup, creating overlapping rings on the table, and remained quiet. It had been her idea to invite Jack to join us at Mocha Madness and explain everything. She'd left nothing out. Now, I had the pleasure of watching her squirm. Of course, I also looked the fool. But, hey, most pleasure comes with a price.

Reb quit playing with her cup. "The police department doesn't consider slashed tires and threatening notes serious?" she asked, voice whisper soft.

Oh-oh. If Killian was smart he'd stand up and leave. Calm before the storm is never good where Reb's concerned. By her immobility, I figured she was a couple of milliseconds away from an epic hissy fit.

"I did not say that." Jack stood and held his hands up. "I have to see a man about a horse. We'll continue this when I get back."

"Count on it," Reb called as he made a quick exit. She turned to me. "Man about a horse?"

"Code for needing to use the restroom."

She nodded then scowled at Killian's retreating form. "What if he's going to the little boy's room to laugh. Let me out, I want to listen at the door."

I gave her a slow shake of my head and kept my bottom planted in the booth, blocking her exit. "Let the man have some peace, will you. Even cops have to answer nature's call. He's coming off a double shift."

"But he doesn't believe me—er—us. Doesn't that make you angry?"

"A little. Just give him some time to digest the info. Process it through those law enforcement channels in his brain."

Reb exhaled. "All right. But one quirk of those divine lips and we're gone."

"Right with you." I took a sip of my Chocka Mocha. Not bad, except the caffeine would keep me wired most of the night. Being awake in the wee hours wasn't all bad. I'd work on a story. A visit from the witching-hour muse could be worth the sacrifice. Thinking of witches, I asked Reb what she'd learned from Ellie Stromberg.

My question stopped the staccato beat of Reb's fingernails against the laminated tabletop. She glanced over her shoulder at the restrooms and snorted.

"Granny's house is in a low rent area, and mega-dated. I'm talking avocado shag carpet with a permanent traffic pattern, gold, and black velvet wallpaper." Reb grimaced and sipped her smoothie. "Bad roof, weed-choked lot, a tiny garage that's one nanosecond from imploding. But Stromberg thinks a slap of paint, here and there, and the house will bring around a hundred grand . . . after realtor fees."

I whistled. "Where is this beauty?"

"On Second Street, close to Ross Park."

"That long row of houses that backs up to the railroad hump?"

Reb nodded. "Probably the reason granny's deaf. All those boxcars screeching down the incline."

I shuddered. At times the rail yard can broadcast sounds like demented souls crying for release. "Are you going to list it?"

"Of course. It's the perfect excuse to gather info. Eventually, I'll inform Ms. Hair it's time to either renovate, which means shelling out more money, or do a sacrifice sell."

Killian returned; face appropriately neutral. He slid onto the bench opposite from ours. "I don't like the idea of you two playing detective, but a couple of your theories have merit. I can run them past my captain, see what he thinks. But this whole toaster thing . . . not a standard weapon, you know."

"It is innovative," Reb said.

"And unreliable unless you use it to bash someone. Then, it's awkward. A cast-iron frying pan is a better choice."

"But it could be a murder weapon, right?" I said.

"Almost anything can become a weapon," Killian agreed.

"Exactly! Using an appliance no one suspects is near perfect. Our murderer is quite the devious thinker," I said.

"*Our* murderer?" Killian raised his eyebrows.

Reb crossed her arms and tilted her head. "There are certain people who'd benefit from Thelma's death."

"Like?" Killian said.

"Casey Kelso, for one," I said. "Thelma's nephew is up to his eyeballs in debt."

Killian looked at me and shrugged. "Lots of people in that situation. Doesn't make 'em murderers."

"Unless their employer suspected them of taking home more than their paycheck, and said employer threatened to go to the authorities!" Reb gave me a knowing look.

Both Killian and I stared. She wiggled her eyebrows and sipped her drink.

"Omigosh! That's your news?" I said. "It took you long enough, spill it."

"This type of info needs a proper buildup. It can't be done while snooping around a filthy alley." Reb crossed her eyes and shuddered.

"Wait a minute," Killian said.

"Ms. Hair told you Casey was embezzling from the bookstore and Thelma was going to report him?" I asked.

How had Reb managed to cozy up to Stromberg-the-ice-maiden in one afternoon?

"Who's Ms. Hair?" Killian asked.

"Not in so many words," Reb hedged. "Ellie hinted her boyfriend was in financial trouble. That's the reason she needs to turn a big profit on granny's house. I simply commiserated."

"You commiserated and poof." I clicked my fingers. "She spilled everything?"

"I had to do a little reading between the lines, but that's essentially what she said."

Killian cleared his throat, leaned across the table, and took Reb's hand. "Who is Ms. Hair?"

While Reb explained about Ellie Stromberg, I wondered how much between-the-lines reading my amigo had been doing. Ellie didn't strike me as the confiding sort. Reb has a way of wriggling secrets out of people.

"Earth to Harrigan." Reb waved her hand in front of my face.

"What?"

"You want to come?"

"Where?"

"My house. We can discuss Thelma's death—Jack's itching to play devil's advocate." She gave Killian a wink. "I'll make popcorn, and we can watch *Invasion of the Body Snatchers*." She turned to Jack. "Play a vintage scary movie and Sadie's brain kick-starts into hyper-drive. She's amazing when she thinks outside the box . . . sort'a like putting her in a think tank."

Movie? Popcorn? When had our serious discussion turned into a date with me cast as a ghoulish Einstein third wheel? How attractive.

"Thanks, but I better get the dogs home. It's way past their bedtime. And a story in the works needs two or more finishing touches."

"Let the dogs snooze at my house, fix the story later. Come on, it'll be fun." Her words might say yes, but her eyes begged for a private twosome.

"Call me tomorrow." I drained the last of my mocha and scooted out of the booth.

"Be careful, Sadie," Jack said, his voice gruff . . . with concern? My insides tingled and the room grew warmer. "If anything happens, I mean anything out of the ordinary, call the station."

Lucky for me, Killian doesn't have x-ray vision. My stomach thudded back down and started whining about too much coffee. I nodded and left, hoping my face hadn't betrayed any of that little emotional drama. The Ghia's yellow paint radiated warmth under the streetlight I'd parked next to. I slid into my car happy I had an easy exit and Killian and Reb could do whatever.

Bogart and Bacall, snuggled tight in the passenger seat, raised their heads and fixed me with sleepy eyes as I started the car.

"Next stop, home."

Satisfied, they resumed sleeping. I turned left onto the near-deserted street, changed my mind and flipped a U-turn As long as I was in the vicinity, might as well check out granny's dilapidated house.

Taking a right onto Dunn Street, I drove two blocks and turned left onto Second. Some of the homes are cramped side-by-side while others enjoyed extended lawns large enough to graze a small herd of sheep. The architectural scheme resembled early hodgepodge, but most of the houses had aged gracefully, the yards well kept. Granny's turned out to be a real weed among petunias. Ms. Hair expected to get a hundred grand? In her dreams, maybe.

I drove past, noticed lights on in the front window, and flipped another U-turn. I stopped a couple of houses back and cut the engine.

"Why are the lights on?"

Bogart yawned and stood on his hind legs to look out the

window. Bacall joined him, but neither answered my question. As we watched, another light came on . . . then another.

"Ah-ha!" Bacall looked at me. I shrugged, not sure what I was ah-ha-ing about, but I intended to find out.

"Stay here. If I'm not back in twenty minutes call for help," I eased out of my car, pushed the lock button, and gently shut the door. Bogart began to bark, Bacall whimpered and whined. A couple of neighborhood dogs joined the chorus. So much for stealth.

Hugging the shadows, I made my way to granny's driveway. A car similar to Ellie's stood silent on the broken cement—hum? I crouched by the car, watching the house lights wink on and off, progressing from room to room. Either Ellie was searching for something or else a thief—with Ellie's taste in automobiles—was prowling the house. As a concerned citizen, it was my duty to find out.

I crept to the nearest lighted window, glad for the giant bush that covered the side of the brick house. Ignoring the prickly brown spears, I pushed my way into the dying shrub and stopped. I figured the bedroom light had just snapped on. I needed to take a quick peek, but what if I saw more than I wanted to? What if it was Ellie? And Casey? And my leather and whips scenario wasn't that far off?

The blind snapped up. My heart lurched, I ducked closer to the hard-packed dirt, praying I hadn't wet myself in the process. I held my breath, listening for banging doors, angry shouts, thudding feet . . . nothing.

Slowly, I inched back up the rough brick and took a quick peek into the room. A bedroom, all right, with plenty of leather; although Ellie wasn't wearing it.

Neither was Casey . . . in fact, Casey wasn't even in the room.

A large, bald man with a red handlebar mustache, squat neck, and arms tattooed with writhing green and black snakes stood next to the bed. Dressed in tight leather pants, leather vest, studded neck collar, and black army boots, he paced the length of the room and back. He then marched into the closet and did a quick chin-up on the wooden closet rod.

Ellie sat on the bed, legs crossed, silk skirt hiked up. She kicked off her heels and began messaging her right foot with her left, skirt hiking higher as she rubbed.

The man turned to her and grinned. She smiled and nodded. Part of me wanted to turn away. A bigger part wouldn't let me. It was like viewing a car wreck in slow motion. The man started toward Ellie, stopped, and turned to look at the mirror over the dresser. He scowled.

Oh damn!

Too late, I realized the mirror faced the window I was peeking into. I ducked and did a quick crab crawl out of the bush. Had he seen me? Was I dead and didn't know it?

I'm not the best runner and scurrying out from the bush crouched like the Hunchback of Notre Dame didn't help. I skirted a tall pine tree, chanced a quick glance back, and saw the front porch light come on.

Adrenaline gave me wings. I reached my car, tennis shoes slipping in the gravel along the curb and grabbed the Ghia's door handle. Bogart and Bacall yipped a greeting as I fumbled to open the lock. I flung open the door, cursing the overhead light, and threw myself into the seat. A car idled slowly past in the opposite direction as I slammed the door and punched the lock buttons down.

Jamming the key in the ignition, forcing myself not to stomp on the accelerator and kill the engine, I pulled away from the curb.

The rearview mirror revealed an empty street; no leather-clad madman chasing me on foot or otherwise, no red-light flashing cop cars dashing to arrest me for peeking in windows.

I blew out a long sigh of relief, picked a couple of dead twigs from my hair, and glanced at the scratches on my arms. "Color me stupid."

My dogs wagged their tails in agreement.

As my heart slowed and my breathing returned to semi-normal, I went over my mistakes. One: in the event of a fast getaway, never lock the car. And Two: never park in such a visible area. I looked at my happy twosome curling together for a quick nap on the ride home.

"You guys are more hindrance than help. We need to work on the appropriate times to bark." They didn't reply. Guess there wasn't much to say. I just prayed tattoo man hadn't jotted down my license number.

As I turned onto the dark, winding road that led to the top of Mink Creek, I couldn't shake the feeling that something wasn't quite right. As far as I knew, I'd gotten away with my silly escapade. If the cops *did* show up on my doorstep, I planned to claim insanity. I didn't feel safe. I felt—exposed.

As I pulled next to my house, the thought that had been lurking in the dark basement of my mind jumped into the spotlight . . . the car! The damn car that had cruised past as I scrambled to make my getaway. I'd only caught a glimpse, but the driver looked familiar, and whoever it was had enough time to scope out my actions.

I let the dogs out and urged them to hurry with their nightly business. The wind moaned high in the trees. The night seemed alive with moving shadows. *Think, Harrigan, think:* A big white car, headlights glaring . . . cruising slowly past—me opening the door—dome light coming on, turning to look.

Oh crap.

I hoped I was mistaken.

Maybe even delusional. I shivered, but not from the cold wind. Unless I was wrong, the witness to my hasty retreat was Mama Kelso.

Eighteen

My cell shrilled and vibrated in my back pocket as I herded the dogs into the house, jangling my nerves and mind. I grabbed it and whispered, "Hello."

Willie's throaty voice crooned, "Darling, I've met her. With my help, she will become superlative."

"Met who?" I locked the front door and collapsed onto the couch, happy, for once, it was Willie babbling on the other end and not the long arm of the law—or worse.

"Teeny, of course."

Of course, how silly of me. "Willie, I'm not in the mood for games. Who the hell is Teeny?"

"Big part of your problem, dear, you never are in the mood." Willie sighed and spoke slowly, enunciating each word. "Teeny is Cary's latest squeeze. Your brother is simply ga-ga over her."

I thought about making static noise so I could claim a bad connection and hang up. "We're talking about a grown woman who goes by Teeny?"

"A nickname which fits her perfectly, she's simply adorable." *Translation: Teeny had sucked up to Willie, big time.* "But FYI, her real name is Tina Louise Bickmore. Tomorrow, we're doing lunch and shopping. Under my tutelage she will emerge from her chrysalis, spread her colorful wings and fly!"

Having been under Willie's tutelage most of my life, I pitied Teeny. At least she rated chrysalis status. In Willie's mind, I would forever languish in hairy, green caterpillar mode.

"Sounds great," I murmured. Talking about butterflies made me think of Casey Kelso. Seemed different women wanted a hand in making sure his wings were the right color.

"I invited your brother to share in Teeny's transformation. A recreation of that marvelous shopping scene in *Pretty Woman*. She could put on a private fashion show, twirling, shimming, doing the whole vogue thing."

"Uh-huh."

Wait, butterfly was the wrong analogy. Casey seemed more— Chameleon—always changing colors to meet different people's needs. If Leather Man was any indication, Casey wasn't satisfying all of Ellie's needs. Then throw Mama Kelso, Thelma, and more-than-ready-to-gossip Loralee Lish into the melee—whew, what a mess.

"Of course, your brother claims he's too busy, teaching all those snotty-nosed brats to surf. He simply does not catch the vision."

"Too bad."

I bet Kelso found it exhausting trying to please everyone. Pretty soon all the different chameleon colors would run together, turning dark and mottled. Say Reb was right, that Thelma discovered money problems at the store. She confronts Kelso, maybe even accuses him and threatens to go to the police, then—whammo! The man snaps!

"Mercedes McCambridge Harrigan, what is wrong?"

"Huh?"

"You are way too agreeable. What's going on?"

"Willie, I haven't the foggiest what you're implying. I thought we were just having a marvelous conversation." As a diversion I lapsed into Willie-speak. She eats up antique clichés like *foggiest*.

"You haven't heard a word I've said."

So much for diversion. Willie lived for intrigue. Any hint I was involved with a murder, and she'd be on my doorstep, ready to borrow my car, clothes, and money—especially money. I shuddered at the thought. "Just got a lot on my mind," I answered.

"Man trouble, darling? Tell me what—or hopefully who's been keeping you up nights?"

Okay, time to pull out the big guns and end this. "It's the apartment business. See, property taxes are due in a couple of months, and the city council has voted to raise . . ."

"Darling, you know I don't have a head for business. Lord knows, there are more fulfilling ways to occupy one's mind. Why don't you run yourself a tub full of bubbles and forget those nasty financial problems for now."

I sniffed my armpits. The woman did have a point.

"Great idea. Kiss, kiss and chat later." I hung up before she launched into fifty ways to take a sensuous bath.

Stuffing my cell into my back pocket and grabbing a couple of candlesticks from the mantel, I headed upstairs to my lovely claw-footed tub. Bubbles and candlelight seemed the exact combo to get my creative juices flowing.

Twisting on the taps, I added Pina Colada bubble bath and sat on the edge of the tub shucking off my sneakers while my mind wandered. What if a young woman, preparing for a leisurely soak, found a vampire in her bathroom? A night stalker that reeked lust at first sight—they'd met earlier that evening at a poetry reading at the library.

He'd seduce the unwary woman with slow lingering kisses, gentle caresses, exotic brown eyes hypnotizing away any reticence. During an intimate embrace, flesh to flesh, hearts beating in synch, he'd morph into his true self: pointed fangs, eyes glowing red with gnawing hunger . . .

My phone shrilled Reb's tone, I dropped my sneaker into the bubbles, and all thoughts of handsome hickey-makers dissolved. Damn! Wasn't she with Killian?

I twisted off the water and answered, "Yellow."

"Do you still have that Ouija board we used to goof around with?"

Ouija board? Talk about a blast from the past. "Why? You and Jack looking for a cheap spectral thrill?"

"We'll need it to contact Thelma."

"You and Jack want to contact Thelma?"

"No, silly. Jack fell asleep watching *Invasion of the Body Snatchers*. He's on my couch making cute little snoring sounds. I'll cover him and pin a note to the blanket explaining we're holding a séance. When he wakes, he can call me."

"A séance?" I looked longingly at the bubble-filled tub. "Tonight?"

"Night is usually best, Harrigan."

A memory of lavender with a hint of formaldehyde filled my senses, and I was transported back to the summer between our seventh and eighth grade. Reb got a Ouija board for her birthday. We'd spent hours in Gram's mortuary asking the Ouija spirit outrageous questions about cute guys we liked and popular girls we loathed.

"The idea hit me during the movie. We want answers to Thelma's death. Best place to go is the source, right?"

"Giant alien pods taking over a town made you think of contacting Thelma?" I tested the water. Ah, just right. There was no way I'd let Reb talk me into *this* harebrained scheme.

"Don't tell me you've forgotten," she said. "Our summer of the Ouija? The marathon spooky movie fest?"

"That was kid stuff."

"What about the one time—middle of July, ninety-five degrees in the shade, except in Cassandra's viewing room, so damn cold we could see our breath. The stylus moved on its own. You threw the board under a casket and we high-tailed it out of there."

Oh, yeah, I remembered. I felt the hair on my arms spring to attention and suddenly candlelight wasn't enough in my little bathroom. I fumbled for the light switch, keeping my eyes averted from the mirror in case some ghoul or ghost peered out and scared twenty years off my life span.

"So?"

"So tonight feels—I don't know, sort of mystic. Like there's a portal open and maybe we really could reach into the beyond."

With a sigh, I yanked the tub chain and watched the lovely bubbles gradually shrink from view. Reb's words might be hokey, but who was I to argue? Earlier, the night's undercurrent had spoken to me. Now the preternatural siren was calling to her.

"Phone the couple who rented Thelma's apartment and ask if we can borrow . . ."

"No way!"

"But, Sadie . . ."

"Forget it! Your idea, we'll use your house."

"We can't use mine. I'm not cosmically connected to Thelma." Reb paused. "You were her landlord, she contacted you in the cemetery. Your kitchen will probably work."

"I only smelled toast that one time. I could've been just hungry, might've hallucinated the whole thing."

"Oh ye of little faith. Don't make me call Yancy for backup. He's into Ouija."

Not surprising, Yancy liked playing Ouija. How Reb knew this bit of info was the bait I wasn't about to take. Plus, my spectral encounter in the cemetery was not public information. I intended to keep it that way.

"You bring Yancy and I'll burn the board."

Reb huffed a sigh. "Chill some soda, I'm coming over. Alone."

I hung up and retrieved my soggy shoe from the tub. Thelma had never been in my kitchen. The whole thing was ludicrous—about as ludicrous as searching around a greasy alley waiting for some kind of mystical contact.

AN HOUR LATER, LEGS NUMB from sitting lotus-style on the hard linoleum, I longed for a large bottle of water, something covered in chocolate, and the bubble bath I'd drained.

"Thelma, we beseech thee to come to our aid. Can you give us a sign?" Reb had started out very no-nonsense, but she'd slowly lapsed into verbal singsong.

I pried open my gritty eyes. Reb sat opposite me, eyes squinched shut, upper body swaying slightly from side to side. She began to hum.

"Beseech?" I took my hands from the stylus. "What's with the old-English? Thelma died. She wasn't transported back in time."

Reb opened one eye. "Hush, you've got to help, you know."

"I am. I'll probably never walk right again."

Reb opened the other eye. She lifted her hands from the stubborn triangle and used her right hand to massage the back of her neck. "Have you smelled anything? Felt anything?"

"Rigor mortis." I groaned and uncrossed my right leg. "Face it, Reb. You've asked Thelma for a sign, for help, for the next winning lotto numbers." I manually straightened my left leg and blew out the candle on the floor beside me. "She's not answering. Time to give it a rest."

"Harrigan, you of all people should know spirits can't be rushed." Reb said, slowly rotating her neck.

"Are you saying Thelma's mind is willing, but her spirit is weak?"

Reb rolled her eyes.

"We could always wait 'til she gets a membership to Ghoul's Gym."

Reb gave me a look that said, *eat dirt and die.* I was searching for another mortician pun when Reb's eyes grew wide and her mouth dropped.

"Uh-uh-uh," she managed to squeak while pointing at the window behind me.

Yeah—right—not falling for that old gag.

I simply smiled at her lame enactment.

The whites of her eyes grew larger, and the squeaking turned into a mewling deep in her throat.

I swiveled, saw two white faces with hooded eyes pressed against the window above the sink, screamed, leapt to my feet and tripped over Reb's shoe. We ended up on the floor, in a tangle of arms and legs.

A sharp rapping on the glass had us on our feet, ready to do the fight-or-flight thing. Bogart and Bacall plunged down the stairs barking and dancing under foot.

"Mercedes. It's me, Loralee Lish."

Racing for the living room, I stopped mid-stride and squinted at the window. In the pale moon light the figure looked like Loralee, but stories of shape-shifters slithered through my mind.

Warily, I inched forward, the dogs guarding my shoelaces. Good thing the pet door was latched. Loralee smiled and waved her fingers. I focused on her teeth . . . no pointy ends.

"Loralee, it's past midnight. Why are you peeking in my window?" My voice sounded calm compared to my thundering heart.

"Checking to see if you're home. This is Alex Phoenix, Claude's grandson. Can we come in?" A semi-familiar male with blonde hair and dazzling bedroom eyes peered over her shoulder and gave me a crooked grin.

Of course. I'd seen him at Thelma's funeral. I looked back at Reb for a yea or nay vote. Crouched against the far wall in some sort of kung-fu stance, my brave friend lowered the spoons she'd turned into a makeshift cross and shrugged.

Pretty sure I'd regret my decision, I opened the door and flipped on the kitchen's overhead light. Loralee and Alex walked in, Bogart and Bacall bolted out. *Deserters!*

"Oh a Ouija board. How quaint." Loralee picked up the last lit candle and blew it out. "Is this how you get ideas for your stories?"

I looked at Reb. "Sometimes."

Reb stepped toward Alex and offered her hand. "I'm Rebbie Russell. So sorry about your grandfather."

He took her hand in both of his. "Thank you."

"Alex flew in for the funeral tomorrow. Guess you know the Harrigan Funeral Home is handling the affair. Glad they decided against the Waygo pink palace." Loralee gave me a knowing wink.

.I managed to nod.

Loralee roamed the room, examining my salt and pepper shakers, rearranging my canisters. "Alex dropped by the bookstore to say hello. We got to talking, and I told him about my novel and how you're helping me." She ran a fingertip along the yellow tiles on my counter.

"He wanted to meet you, so we took a chance, drove up here and voila, we find you deep in the creative process." She looked at me, face flushed with excitement. I half expected her to clap with glee. "This is so cool. Isn't this cool, Alex?"

"Cool," Alex murmured. He ran a hand through his rumpled hair and looked at his shoes. "Sorry if we disturbed you. I wanted to talk to you about Granddad."

"Please, come in." I led the way into the living room, wondering why Alex wanted to discuss Claude with me. I knew him . . . but not that well. I settled into the chair by the fireplace and watched Reb and Loralee bookend Alex on the couch. Any closer and they'd be in his lap.

Alex seemed unaware of the pheromone cyclone swirling around him. Claude's death had sucker-punched the poor guy hard.

"You know, Granddad was good at wheeling and dealing—and not just cars." He stopped and stared into the fireplace with an expression I'd seen countless times at viewings and funerals. Alex wasn't seeing my sooty fireplace, but instead viewed some distant memory through his mind's eye.

"He could take any venture—some were really crazy—and usually make a profit." Eyes bright with unshed tears, he took a deep breath and let it out slowly.

"I'm really sorry for you and your family," I said. "Claude was good for Thelma. A true gentleman."

"And charming," Loralee chimed in. "I loved whenever he came into the bookstore. We had some deep conversations." Her brow wrinkled, and she fiddled with her black-rimmed glasses. "You know, Claude introduced Alex and me a couple of years ago." Grinning, she patted Alex's knee. "Don't you think there's a strong family resemblance? I bet Alex will have a gorgeous white mane, exactly like Claude, when he gets older."

Alex frowned at Loralee.

Reb patted Alex's other knee and sighed. "Death is never easy, but to know he was brought down in that filthy alley is beyond awful."

Alex winced and began clasping and unclasping his hands. I toyed with the idea of shoving both Reb and Loralee outside with my dogs and locking all the doors.

"About my novel. What do you think?" Loralee asked.

It was my turn to wince. "You know, I've been so busy I haven't had time to give it the attention it deserves." The words tasted bitter spilling out of my mouth. Reb did a quick eye roll.

"Oh. Of course—sure. Like I said, there's no rush." Loralee took her gasses off, gave them a quick spit and polish before replacing them on her little nose. "The apartments keep you busy, and then there's the murder investigation and all."

"Loralee, I'm not involved . . ."

"It's okay, Sadie. I explained everything to Alex. That's why he wanted to come and see you."

Alex nodded. "Loralee says you're trying to prove Thelma's death was not an accident." He stared at his hands, then at me with such intensity I gulped. "Well, I know Granddad's death wasn't a random mugging."

Nineteen

"**Y**OU HAVE PROOF?**" Alex's words made me want to do a tiny dance of joy. "Great. Tomorrow we'll go to the police and . . ."

Alex shook his head. "Proof, no. Nothing concrete. That's why I came to you instead of the police."

Terrific. "Why me?"

"Because you are willing to look beyond the obvious." Alex leaned forward; elbows braced on his knees. "I talked to Granddad the night before he died. He was worried, said he was either losing his mind—or someone had been following him. At first, I thought he was kidding, pulling some kind of joke . . . even told him I wasn't falling for it." He rubbed his temples as though in pain.

"Did he say who he thought might be following him?" I asked.

"No. Said he'd caught only glimpses, wasn't sure if the person was male or female. But he *was* positive someone was tailing his movements."

"How long had this been going on?" Reb asked.

"He said it started a couple of days after Thelma died. At first, he chalked it up to grief, mind playing tricks, that sort of thing. But his feeling of being watched persisted, and then came the weird phone calls."

"The kind where you answer and there's only silence?" I asked, a shiver streaking through me.

Alex nodded. "That's why he called me, wanted to get my take on the whole thing." He hitched in a deep breath and blew it out. "I told him to hang tight, if the calls continued, I'd come down and see if I could help."

Great. Perfect. Alex was positive his grandfather's murder was premeditated. But we still had nothing to make the police department stand up and holler.

"Feelings should never be ignored." Reb touched Alex's shoulder, turning slightly to look into his eyes. " I'm very intuitive, you know, and I have the strongest feeling that Thelma's death was not an accident. That's why Sadie and I are investigating all avenues."

I glared at Reb. She ignored me.

Loralee touched Alex's other shoulder. She met his look with a raise of her chin. "I wish Claude had confided in me about those strange feelings. I would've been happy to help."

She turned to me. "When I lived in Denver, I dated a fellow, Justin Kerry. We were serious, talking marriage, the whole bit. One night Justin decided to take a short-cut, we were late going to see a movie. I got this weird premonition to stop and just go back home. Justin poo-pooed the idea. We ended up in a road-rage thing and Justin was shot point-blank in the chest. He died in my arms." She squinted up at the far corner while a single tear slid down her cheek.

"That's terrible, Loralee," I said.

She swiped away the tear and leveled her gaze at Alex. "See, that's why strong feelings should be acted upon. They're like cosmic warnings!"

Alex patted Loralee's hand and continued. "If Thelma and Granddad's deaths are connected, it had to be someone they both knew."

Reb narrowed her eyes and nodded. "Like Casey Kelso."

I darted Reb a shut-the-hell-up look.

Loralee gasped, hand flying to her heart, and leapt to her feet. "You are delusional! Where did you get that piece of info? Casey would never hurt anyone!"

Reb stood and squared her shoulders. "I can't divulge my sources but let me say you're blind if you can't see what's happening right under your nose."

Loralee stepped closer, hands on hips. "Like I said, delusional. And, if you persist in spreading lies about Casey get ready. I know a lawyer who would love to take on a defamation of character suit."

Terrific. Dress both in tee-shirts, add water, and some serious money could be made on this catfight.

"Sit down!" I barked. The duo looked at me. "Both of you." They glared but took a seat on the couch. "No one is accusing anyone of anything."

Alex cleared his throat and began bumping his knuckles together. "There's more. Granddad told me he and Thelma had a big blowout a week before she died."

He raised his eyes and looked at me.

"They squabbled over some money he'd loaned me. And there was something else, something concerning Casey. But he didn't say what, said he needed to investigate it a little further before he acted."

"Did he give a hint what 'it' was?" I asked.

Alex shook his head.

Arms folded; Loralee slumped back against the couch. "Must be pick-on-Casey-night, guess I missed the memo."

"Loralee, I'm not saying Casey did anything wrong, but you know he's always resented my grandfather. It started when Granddad and Judy were dating."

"It's natural for a kid to be jealous of his mama's dates," Loralee shot back. "If we're going to talk suspects, what about that Zoetwilder lady? She didn't approve of either Thelma or Claude."

Alex's mouth quirked, and he scratched his cheek. "The old, arthritic neighbor?"

"Don't let her fool you. Claude said she's a hateful old bat." Loralee slumped further down and looked at me. "Is Casey your only suspect?"

"Everyone's a suspect," Reb said.

Loralee ignored Reb and glanced at her watch. "Wow, look at the time. We better go."

Alex stood and stretched. "Right. We can talk tomorrow, after the funeral."

"Sure," I said. "I'll meet you at the cemetery after the graveside formalities are over."

"We'll both be there!" Reb gave me a dark look.

I opened the back door, and the dogs rushed in, anxious to see what they'd missed. Loralee grabbed Alex's hand and they left.

Reb folded her arms, brows slanted, eyes flashing. "What's this 'I' business—thought we were a team."

I grabbed a box of doggie treats and tossed a couple to my dancing duo. "*We are.* I didn't want Loralee to get the impression she's invited."

Reb sighed. "Poor guy. He looked so dazed and forlorn. Now he must ride home listening to "misunderstood Casey" stories."

"Are you kidding me?"

"What?" Reb asked.

"You're accusing Loralee of running off at the mouth after you announced Casey is our main suspect?"

Reb stuck out her lower lip and looked at the floor.

"Uh-huh. No pouting," I warned.

"Not pouting; thinking." She sniffed and glanced at me. "Guess I'm a real washout as a sleuth."

"Don't start with the tears, either. Hell, we're both out of our element."

"Fine." Reb folded her arms. "What's your take on Loralee's story about her fiancée dying in her arms?"

"Sad. And weird. She loves to broadcast drama, yet this is the first time we've heard about her fiancé. And she sheds one lone tear?"

Index finger tapping her pursed lips, Reb looked first at the ceiling then her boots. "I'm pretty sure I've run across her problem in my psychology book, she fits many of the basic Romeo and Juliet complex symptoms."

"Really? Might explain why she's such a space cadet," I agreed before Reb put on her pop-psychology hat.

From the living room, Reb's cell twanged a little ditty. She gave me a sly grin. "Sounds like Killian woke up."

She hurried to answer, and I looked down at the candle wax puddles splattered across my linoleum. The floor resembled a giant connect the dots puzzle. Killian or not, Reb wasn't leaving until she helped me clean up. I knelt beside the Ouija board and started scraping at a small red puddle with a knife from the silverware drawer."

"Gotta run, Jack's awake." Reb stood in the doorway, pulling on her coat.

As she passed, I grabbed her ankle and pointed to the wax splotches. "Not so fast. Start scraping."

She held up her recently lacquered deep maroon nails. "I'll get some gloves and help tomorrow."

"I've got gloves."

She groaned and knelt down. "Whoa, Harrigan, look at the Ouija."

"What?"

"The stylus. It moved!"

"You saw it?"

"No. But I remember when Alex and Loralee left, the triangle pointed at the word Goodbye, which seemed very appropriate. Now it's setting smack on the letter V."

"So? Someone bumped the board, or the dogs moved it." I blew a strand of hair from my eyes.

"Oh ye of little faith. Thelma is trying to communicate, and you refuse to open your mind." She thumped me lightly on top of my head with a manicured nail.

"Okay. We'll try again." I grabbed the board and plunked it on the table. "But this time I get to ask the questions."

"Nope." Reb sniffed the air as though seeking a phantom smell. "The mood is gone. Too many negative vibes. We need a new plan. Claude's funeral starts at ten-thirty. Be at my house by nine-thirty." She stood and hustled out, letting the screen door bang shut.

I thought about doing a running tackle and dragging her back. No, too much effort. I sat at the table and placed the stylus on the letter V, fingertips lightly skimming the triangle. "Okay, Thelma. Here's a head start. Do your stuff."

The clock on the mantle ticked away the seconds while I stared at the stylus until my eyes felt fried: nothing.

"Please, Thelma. One tiny sign. Anything to let me know I'm not chasing a bogus idea."

I waited. And waited some more.

Again, there was nothing.

Maybe my attitude did need adjusting. My floor definitely needed cleaning, while my body longed to crawl into bed. My body won.

As I punched my pillow into the right shape, I thought about the letter V. Violet was the obvious choice. But what if Thelma had manipulated the stylus before Reb noticed? V might not be the beginning letter of the word or words. Maybe the message was in code.

"Maybe I need my head examined for listening to Reb," I told my bedmates. Bogart yawned, turned around three times and arranged his body in a nose-to-tail circle by my feet. Bacall nestled her body closer to mine. Okay, I could take a hint. Things would look clearer in the morning.

FOUR-THIRTY FOUND ME WILLING MY COFFEEMAKER to dribble faster while my mind percolated over the different conversations from the night before. At four a.m., my eyes had snapped open, mind reaching for some elusive bit of information. I was

ninety-nine percent certain someone had said something perti-
nent last night, and that something was working in my head like a
grain of sand in an oyster.

My dark side whispered, *call Reb*. A deliciously naughty thought
but useless. She'd just share a couple of expletives and hang up.
However, if I showed up on her porch with a nice cappuccino and
some sticky buns from Mocha Madness . . .

I threw a coat over my flannel pjs, raced out to the barn and
forked hay into Eclipse's feed bin. He greeted me with a sleepy
nicker. I stroked his neck then ran back to the house and up the
stairs. Bogart and Bacall raised their heads, gave me a bewildered look and snuggled deeper into the blankets. They're not
much for mornings.

I pulled on the jeans I'd shucked off mere hours ago and stopped.
What if Killian had stayed the night? No use rushing over there
looking like an unmade bed. And I couldn't go to Claude's funeral
looking homeless. Yancy would bar the door and Gram, when she
heard about it, would be embarrassed beyond words.

There was enough time to take a shower before I annoyed Reb.
Arranging the shower curtain around the tub, I noticed headlights
jerking down the road outside my bathroom window. Who in the
world? I let out the breath I didn't realize I'd been holding as the
lights continued past my driveway. Must be the neighbor going to
feed his horses.

Stepping under the warm water, I lathered apple-scented
shampoo through my hair and felt the exhilaration of being part of
an elite group: up before the crack of dawn, slogging through the
trenches. Okay, I wasn't doing much slogging, but I was going forth
to stand for truth, justice, and sticky buns.

The day promised to be a long one, so I took extra time to dry
and curl my hair and applied my mother's motto when I picked up
the can of hairspray: everything in excess.

I dressed in my new retro suit with its short black jacket and
black and white checked skirt. Slipping into thigh-high patterned

stockings, I shoved my feet into forties-era suede pumps I'd found at Shabby Chic and looked in the mirror: M.M Harrigan, lookin-hot and ready for action.

Slipping my cell phone, a mini-can of hair spray, and black flats into my shoulder bag, I hurried down the stairs.

I opened the panel to the doggie door, poured a quick cup of coffee and savored the dawn coloring the clouds, hovering over the gap from which our town got its name. Bacall came into the kitchen and pushed her food dish across the floor.

"Right." I scooped dry food into both bowls. "Here you go, Babe."

Bogart raced in from the living room with a hunk of paper in his mouth. I gave him the evil eye and snatched it from him. "You are so dead if this is from my office!"

I opened the tattered wad and spread it on my counter, trying to make sense of the half-chewed, fill-in-the-blanks puzzle. The paper was plain white with a simple sentence printed in red block letter: "B—f or yo—n-xt."

Red ink . . . Ba—f or yo—n-xt?

Hmm.

It was like a Wheel-of-Fortune puzzle without Vana White's dazzling aid to reveal the correct letters.

I tried squinting as I looked at the code. My breath caught in my throat. "Back off or you're next!"

TWENTY

"You're taking a shower at the butt-crack of dawn, and someone just happens to slip this under your front door?" Reb stood bleary-eyed and alone at her kitchen door. She yawned, rubbed her eyes, and studied the wrinkled note. "How quaint."

"Easy for you to say. The damn thing wasn't there when I locked up last night." I pushed past her and sat two Styrofoam cups and a bag of caramel pecan buns on the kitchen table.

"Good thing you have your hounds. The shower scene in *Psycho* would've played a lot different if Janet Leigh had had a dog." Reb opened the lid on her Chocka-mocha and took a sip, sighed, and handed the other cup to me. "Have you tried this? You gotta' try this. Sheer Heaven."

I sipped and set the cup down. Goodies were not the answer. What I needed was reassurance that my life wasn't turning into a crappy made-for-TV thriller. "I can't see simple pranksters creeping around so early."

Reb munched on a bun and nodded. "Average punks don't lose precious sleep to terrorize. Psycho punks, on the other hand . . ."

"Let's not think about that hand." I peered into the living room and down the hall; no sign of Killian. "Don't supposed Jack is handy to run this past?"

"When I got home last night, he was gone. But I found the sweetest note and a rose on the table."

"A rose?"

Reb shrugged. "A yellow one from that silk arrangement in my bathroom, but it's the thought." She gave me a wink. "Want to read the note?"

"No. I've read enough notes for today." I sat down across from her. "Think back to last night's conversation. Did any of it strike you as odd?"

Reb tapped the wrinkled paper with her fingernail. "You think Loralee or Alex is behind this threat?"

"I hadn't considered those two." I gave myself a mental shake. "No, something important was said last night. So important, it woke me up."

"What?"

"That's just it, I don't know. I feel it's vital but, my mind is blank."

"You woke up obsessing about the conversation with Alex last night?"

"Yes." My fingers drummed the table. "Think I'm losing it?"

Reb nodded and took another bite of her bun.

"Well, given time, something will jog my brain."

Reb tapped the paper again. "Time is something we may not have. Buttons are being pushed, and those buttons might belong to someone who doesn't have all his cornflakes in the box. This isn't funny anymore."

"Do I look like I'm laughing?"

"No, you look the way I feel. Scared!"

"Well haul your scared self to your closet and get dressed. We have suspects to view at Claude's funeral."

"Have you called Floydean Mollicker about this latest note?" Reb asked as she walked down the hall.

"No. But I will." I grabbed a gooey bun from the bag, licked caramel from my fingers, and took a giant bite. Worrying about a couple of pounds on my hips took a backseat to death threats. I rummaged in my purse, found my cell phone, called Floydean and asked her to meet me at Claude's graveside.

I spotted the Harrigan Funeral Home's dark burgundy awning stretched over the gravesite as we pulled behind a glistening white Cadillac. Yancy Candlemass had all the chairs in regimental rows. He looked self-assured and in charge as he ushered people to their respective seats. I didn't know if Gram would find Yancy's expertise in her absence reassuring or not, but he was basking in the limelight while playing head mortician. He caught my eye and gave me a nod. I returned the gesture and took a couple of steps back from the milling crowd. Yancy was resplendent in a dark suit, navy tie, and a white shirt with cuff links. His patrician face was appropriately solemn and caring. He'd pulled off the perfect Funeral Director look.

Except for the group of car dealers and city government muckety-mucks, the crowd at the cemetery was identical to the one gathered to pay their last respects to Thelma.

"Yancy seems to have everything under control," Reb whispered. "Glad the family decided on Harrigan's over the Pepto-Palace."

"Amen to that."

"I didn't know Agatha Heckathron knew Claude very well."

I looked where Reb was pointing and spotted Agatha talking to a group of people. Palm open, my resident hypochondriac passed her hand back and forth for everyone to examine. "She's sort of like old man Burlington."

Reb shuddered. "The guy with that giant gaudy headstone, always wore the same old suit and showed up at every funeral even if he didn't know the deceased?"

"That's the one. Some people look at funerals as a chance to broaden their social life."

Reb looked appalled.

I shrugged. "Whatever floats your boat."

I continued scanning the crowd. Unless Dexter had come and gone, it looked like Agatha was the only representative from the apartment complex. Too bad, I was hoping Dexter would've had a chance to pay his last respects. I noticed Floydean Mollicker making her way around the tented seating and waved her over.

"Hey Sadie, Rebbie. Let me see this latest note." Looking very official in crisp white shirt and navy skirt, Floydean took the paper and studied it. She motioned for us to follow her a short distance from the crowd. "Did the last note have block letters?"

I nodded. "And red ink."

"You threw the first note away?"

"I was hoping it was a hoax," I said. "Guess I should've hung onto it."

"There's a chance I could've pulled some strings and had a comparison run. But . . ." she tapped the paper against her palm. "I'm still thinking prank." She handed me back the note. "Keep this one, just in case."

"What about fingerprints?" Reb asked.

"Unless the author has a record, we get diddly."

"So basically, you're saying until one of us turns up dead, we're not top priority?" Reb asked.

"'Fraid so." Floydean laughed at Reb's expression and wrapped her arms around our shoulders. "Not to worry, I'm on alert, along with officer Killian." She dropped her arms and gave us a wink.

"What if I told you someone was stalking Claude Phoenix before his death?" I asked.

Floydean raised an eyebrow. "Who?"

"I'm . . ." I looked at Reb. "*We're* not sure."

"Did Claude tell you this?"

"No. He told his nephew, Alex." I pointed at the group of mourners. "He's the one standing just outside the tent."

Floydean rolled her eyes heavenward.

"Before you pray for holy intervention, just hear him out, okay?" I said.

She muttered something that sounded a lot like "pain in the butt" as the color guard lined up to give a twenty-one-gun salute.

After the last strains of taps, I wiped my eyes and sent Floydean a pleading look.

"I have forty-five left before my shift," she said.

"Then we better haul." I looked at the crowd. The graveside rites were over, but I knew it would take some time to separate Alex from all the well-wishers.

Floydean read my mind. "Leave this to me."

"OFFICIAL POLICE BUSINESS." Seated at Jimmy John's sandwich shop a half-mile from the cemetery, I looked across the table at Floydean. "Girl, that was slick, but did you get a look at the mourners faces when you hauled Alex off?"

Floydean shrugged. "Not my problem. You have thirty minutes, better start convincing me." Guess the smell of rising bread dough wasn't making her feel all warm and mellow.

"Right." I cleared my throat and looked across at Alex. He stared down at his triple Hoagie with extra mustard, as though it was something foreign.

Sitting beside him, Reb patted his shoulder. "Tell Floydean what you told us."

He raised his head, brown eyes moist, and took a moment to compose his thoughts. "Ms. Mollicker, I know my granddad died at the hands of a murderer, probably someone he knew. I know it, feel it, but can't prove it."

Floydean stared hard at all three of us, index finger tapping her lips. "Okay, tell me precisely what you have."

Alex repeated the conversation from last night.

"Besides the phone calls, did he receive any threatening notes?" Floydean asked when he finished.

Alex frowned. "If he did, he didn't mention it. I know it's not much to go on but ... "

Floydean held up her hand. "There seems to be a couple of strange coincidences. Too much coincidence bothers me, bothers a certain detective I know, too. The guy's pretty perceptive. I'll run this whole thing past him and see if it raises his hackles."

Alex released the breath he'd been holding. "I can't thank . . ."

"Hold that thank-you. Until I get back with you three, no investigating on your own. Got it?"

"What about . . ." Reb said.

Floydean shot her a squinty-eyed look. Reb clamped her mouth shut.

"Do we all understand?" Floydean dabbed her lips with her napkin, stood and gathered her purse. "Nod if you do. Good. I'll be in touch. Might take me a day or two, but I will get back to you."

"You sure she works dispatch?" Alex watched Floydean walk out the door. "She'd make a great undercover officer. Or Pit-bull."

"Uh-huh." I waved and waited until Floydean had pulled out of the parking lot. "Alex, this is what Reb and I have so far."

I filled him in on my slashed tires, weird phone calls, and cryptic notes. I ended with Casey's sad financial situation and the black-leather-clad man I'd seen with Ellie.

"You didn't tell me about Leather Man." Reb's eyes grew wide. "Holy Hannah, doin' the naughty tango right in her granny's house! So, like, how much did you see?"

"Nothing. He saw me, and I ran."

Reb rolled her eyes and snorted.

"How did you find out about Casey's money woes?" Alex asked.

"We pulled up his credit report. Pitiful with a capital P." Reb said.

Alex drummed his fingers on the table. "Last night, Loralee talked a lot about Ellie Stromberg, claims she's the reason Casey's in debt. Plus, she still thinks the Zoetweilder lady is worth looking at."

"Don't forget the mattress money and the bad feelings between Thelma and Ms. Humane Society across the river," Reb added.

"But that wouldn't involve Claude," I said.

"It might. What if the murderer thought Granddad knew something incriminating?"

Alex and I munched on our chips and contemplated that point while Reb answered her bleating cell phone. After a brief conversation, Reb stuffed the phone back into her bag, stood and smacked her forehead with her hand.

"What?"

"I forgot to cancel a meeting with a client. They're at the house I'm supposed to show them. It's not far from here, come on."

She marched out, Alex followed while I dumped the sandwich wrappers and chip bags into the garbage. The sun beat down in true Indian summer fashion. I took off my jacket and tossed it behind the driver's seat of my car.

"Okay, we can all fit if we scrunch together. Reb you get in the middle." I pulled my white blouse away from my clammy back and thought about shucking off the fancy thigh highs.

Alex opened the door and looked inside my little car. "Thanks, but I think I'll walk. Granddad's house isn't far from here. I better head over and see how my mom's doing. Call you later."

"Later," Reb said and climbed inside. She shut the door and waved as we pulled from the parking lot. "What a gentleman, saving me from straddling the stick shift. Okay, Harrigan, do your pedal-to-the-metal thing."

The house was in an older section of town where unique architecture made the streets interesting. Built before cookie-cutter subdivisions, the trees and bushes had grown tall and stately. A big weeping willow dominated a corner of the yard. Two little girls chased each other around and around it, laughing and screaming as I cut the engine. The parents stood under it looking less than happy. Reb got out of the car spouting apologies, took the woman's arm, and led her into the house. The man grabbed both girls around their waists and hauled them inside.

I sat on a small wooden bench under the vacated tree and tried to assemble the facts as we knew them: lots of arguments, money trouble, jealousy, but nothing I could see that would warrant murdering two people. There had to be a dark, ugly secret we had yet to discover.

Whoever we were dealing with had tried hard to make Thelma's death appear an accident, and Claude's homicide look like random violence. A lot of thought had gone into both murders.

And what about the threats I'd received? If the person considered me a liability, why threaten? Why not bump me off? *Cheery thought.* And why hadn't Reb received any threats?

I felt the need to get home. I wanted to lock the doors, wrap up in a quilt with my dogs, watch silly movies and eat vast spoonfuls of peanut butter.

The family came out of the house looking happier than when they'd gone in. Reb followed; her lips spread in a cheesy grin. I got in my car and waited while she said her final spiel before she joined me.

"Did you make a sale?" I asked as she climbed in.

She shook her head. "Not sure. The woman loved it, but the guy is hard to read." She brightened. "My schedule is clear for the rest of the day. Want to come to my house and pig out on guacamole?"

"No. I'm feeling . . . beat."

"So feel something else. I have plenty of junk food. Come on, kick off your shoes and join me. We can eat and rethink the case."

Part of me wanted to, but a bigger part needed to hibernate for a while. "My brain is mush. Let me go home and regroup. I'll call you later."

I dropped Reb off at her house and turned onto Fourth Street. My phone jingled its vapid generic tone. I would have to download something fun on my new cell—something I could relate to.

"Hello, this is Kim Kasai. Sorry to bother you. We are having trouble with our back door."

"What kind of trouble?" I crossed my fingers and hoped for something minor. The workings of toilets I knew a little bit about, doors remained a mystery.

"The deadbolt will not open."

Uh-oh. A locksmith, I wasn't. "Is the key stuck?"

"No, key work okay. But from inside, latch will not open deadbolt."

This was not good. I had images of the Kasais trying frantically to get out of their burning apartment, trapped in the kitchen, huddled together by the backdoor where the firemen would find their charred bodies. Where did that macabre vision come from? It was proof I needed some down time, maybe even a nap.

Before calling a locksmith, I'd swing by and see if I could whack the lock into submission.

Inside Thelma's kitchen, correction—the Kasais kitchen, I fiddled with the obstinate deadbolt. It would turn only about midway; my guess was a shot of WD-40 would do the trick. I didn't have a can of the magic stuff with me, but I was pretty sure Dexter might.

I told Kim I'd be right back, went out the front and rapped on the Zoetweilder's screen door. Dexter answered, shoulders slumped, face drawn. I started to ask why he hadn't been at Claude's service but stopped in case Violet was nearby.

"Sadie, how's it going?"

"Good. Toilet working okay?"

He nodded. "Sorry she bothered you the other day. I could 'a fixed it in a jiffy." He lowered his voice and glanced over his shoulder. "It's those damn cotton balls Violet uses. I tell her to throw them in the garbage after she takes off her makeup, but it doesn't do much good."

I nodded, really not in the mood to hear about Violet's personal hygiene routine. "Do you have a can of WD-40?"

"You bet. What's the problem?"

I explained about the sticky deadbolt. Violet appeared, blanket wrapped around her solid frame. One side of her hair was flattened against her head and her eyes were red-rimmed. "What's all the noise, Dexter?"

"Nothing. Go on back and rest. This will only take a moment." He disappeared into the kitchen, reappeared a second later, stepped out onto the porch and firmly shut the door. "Violet has one of her sick headaches. Doesn't like the young couple who moved in next door."

"Why?"

"Claims the way they look—brings back memories of the war." His mouth pinched into a sour grimace. "What war? She was still wearing diapers in WWII."

A couple of squirts of lubricating oil, and Dexter had the bolt sliding as smooth as bald tires on ice. Standing on Kasai's back porch steps, I felt a chill as gray clouds dimmed the sun and a gust of wind whirled leaves around our feet. A storm was moving in fast from the south. Time to get home, batten down the hatches, dig out the peanut butter. A quick round of handshakes, and I was out of there.

"Yoo-hoo, Sadie."

I turned and saw Esther waving to me through the fence from across the river.

"Hi, Esther."

"When you get done there, come on over."

I tried not to grimace. "I'm kind of in a hurry," I called back.

"This won't take long. I have excellent news."

How could I say no to excellent news?

When I reached her house, Esther stood on the sidewalk nearly bouncing in her tasseled loafers. "Spanky and the woman I placed him with are inseparable. By the way, that's a lovely suit. Very vintage."

"Thank you. I just came from Claude Phoenix's funeral."

Esther tsk-tsked. "Such a tragedy. And weird, following on the heels of Thelma's death."

"Weird is right." I looked at my watch and smiled. "But great news about Spanky."

"You know Thelma's death has produced some amazing results." Esther's exotic cheekbones reddened, and she shook her head. "Sorry, let me rephrase that. After the funeral, I had a nice chat with Thelma's sister, Judith Kelso. It's amazing the connections that women has. With her help, the Humane Society has been able to purchase an older home where we can house our foster cats."

"Judy's selling her house?"

Esther laughed. "No, she introduced me to her son's fiancé, Ms. Stromberg. Ms. Stromberg is going to sell her grandmother's house to one of our members. He's been looking for a larger home to accommodate the strays we can't house at the shelter. Ms. Stromberg hasn't signed with any realtor yet, and without any fees, she can let us have the house for a great price."

Unless Ms. Hair had two houses to dump, this news was not going to make Reb's day. I congratulated Esther, turned to leave, and stopped. "This cat lover, is he a big man with multiple tattoos?"

"Oh, you know Tiny Tim?"

Leather Man's real name was Tiny Tim; perfect. I mumbled something about seeing Tiny Tim with Ellie and made my escape, my head whirling with this information.

As I turned into my driveway, I eyed my mailbox: an ordinary gun-metal gray mailbox, attached to a white post, nothing to be afraid of. It wouldn't hurt to change clothes and walk the dogs down to check the mail. If there was another threatening note, I'd feed it to my mini shredders.

Killian's truck was parked next to the barn. The sight of it made me feel a little more secure. I opened the back door to silence . . . dead silence. There was no happy barking, no scrambling down the stairs. I rushed into the living room calling for Bogart and Bacall. More silence. Upstairs, I took a quick look then raced back down to the kitchen.

Nothing.

Kicking off my heels, I turned and bolted out the back door. In the far corner of the yard, I spotted Bacall pawing at something. I called her name. She ignored me. I ran, heart beating faster with each breath, my fear focusing on Bogart lying in a small heap, shaking, drooling, eyes streaming.

"Oh, please God, no!" I knelt beside him, tears blurring the sight of my pitiful little buddy. He raised his head and whimpered. I scooped him up, turned, and ran smack into Killian.

"What the . . .!" He took one look at Bogart, grabbed my elbow and hustled me to his truck. Eclipse, sweaty and still saddled, stood tied to the arena fence. He whinnied as Killian opened the passenger door.

I pointed to Eclipse.

"He'll be okay. Come on." He helped me onto the seat, boosted Bacall up, then ran around to the driver's side and maneuvered the truck onto the road.

"Where's the nearest vet?" he asked above the engine roar.

"Two miles down Bannock Highway. In the Greenway complex." I swiped at my tears and pleaded with my dog. "Hang on, Bogie. Hang on, little guy."

Twenty-One

A YOUNG ASSISTANT USHERED KILLIAN AND ME into an empty examining room while Dr. Gerstner took Bogart and rushed to the back of the clinic. The examination room was standard with the exception of an industrial-size bathtub. Inside the tub, a turtle with a ragged hole in its plate-size shell stood in a murky pool of water. Looking at the poor reptile started my tears anew. Bacall threw back her head and proceeded to howl. Killian groaned, snatched her up and mumbled something about taking her with him while he tended to Eclipse.

"No! Don't leave. Please." I reached for Bacall, burying my face in her soft, long fur.

He put his arm around me. "Sadie, I must go back and take care of Eclipse, can't leave him tied to the corral. Bacall is upset, let me take her with me. I promise I will not let her out of my sight."

He gently pried Bacall away, holding her in his strong arms. "I'll hurry. I promise."

Left alone, I paced, worried, and prayed.

As the second hand on the wall clock plodded along, I stopped beside the tub and explained my situation to the turtle; in case he was wondering about the hysterical woman sharing his room. His calm demeanor and ageless eyes helped soothe my frantic thoughts.

A very empathetic listener, my new pal. We'd concluded that Nazi torture was too good for animal abusers, when Dr. Gerstner burst into the room.

Her round face was all smiles. "Good news. Bogart's going to be okay. The atropine is working."

I erupted into a fresh round of tears.

"Come on, Sadie. Buck up. The worst is over." She handed me a tissue from a box on the counter. "Come see for yourself."

I wiped my eyes, blew my nose, wished the turtle luck with his recovery, and followed my miracle-working vet out of the exam room.

The narrow hall led to a big room full of cages. Bogart lay on a plaid blanket in the bottom kennel of a long row. When he saw me, he raised his head and thumped his tail.

I knelt down and pushed my fingers between the bars to stroke his head. "Hey, Bogie. How's my big guy?" He rewarded me with a slow finger bath.

"See, he's doing great." Dr. Gerstner patted my shoulder. I sniffed and wiped my eyes.

"What a beautiful sight." Killian stood in the doorway, arms full of a struggling Bacall. "Okay, go check out your buddy." He bent down and Bacall leaped from his embrace to race across the cement floor on stubby, churning legs.

Killian stood and pulled a plastic sack from his back pocket. "Found these on the ground near the back fence. Could be the culprit."

Dr. Gerstner took the sack and held it up. Clumped in a corner was something that resembled dandelion-colored salt crystals.

"Uh-huh. Looks like fly bait, irresistible to most dogs. Also pretty deadly." She turned to me. "Been havin' a problem with flies?"

I shook my head. "There's a couple of fly strips hanging in the barn. I've never even heard of fly bait."

"Some people use it to poison coyotes," Dr. Gerstner said. "Maybe someone in your area got overzealous."

"Maybe," I muttered. I didn't want to go into what I really thought. Not until I had proof. "Can I take Bogart home?"

She shook her head. "I want to monitor him tonight. You can pick him up tomorrow morning, any time after nine."

I was to leave Bogart alone? In a cold, metal cage? Dr. Gerstner must have sensed my panic. Putting a firm arm around me, she guided me to the door. "I'll keep a close watch. If I think there's a problem, I'll call you."

I looked back at Bogart. He lay with his eyes closed, breathing softly. Suddenly this back room with all the wire cages and blankets seemed like a nice safe place to spend the night. Part of me wanted to bolt the doors and hunker in with my dogs, secure from the approaching twilight and the crazy world. But a bigger part wanted to find the person responsible for this and make them pay—over and over again.

"Found these on the back porch." Killian held out the orange-rubber clogs I wear to muck out the stables. "Thought you might want something on your feet."

I looked down at my big toes poking through my new, over-priced shredded thigh-highs. My new suit was wrinkled and covered with dirt and dog hair. Add the orange clogs and, voila, it was the perfect Halloween Nineties grunge outfit.

The waiting room, filled with people and animals, all quieted when we walked out. Dr. Gerstner promised to call me if Bogart's condition changed. She picked up a folder and called out the next patient's name. I could feel every eye in the room examining my attire. *Time to exit, stage right.*

"You okay?" Killian asked, as he followed me out.

I climbed into his truck and cuddled Bacall in my lap. "Yeah. Thanks for your help. If you hadn't acted so quickly, Bogart might have . . ." I stopped. I couldn't say the word. If I did, it still might happen.

"Listen, we'll go to your house, make sure it's safe and poison-free, and order a pizza."

I nodded, and we rode in silence for a couple of miles. The wind had picked up and dark clouds rode the horizon.

"Jack, do you see a connection between Thelma, Claude, and my rash of accidents?"

He looked at me, and his expressive features turned presto-chango into no-comment-neutral.

"There could be a connection." He held up his hand to stop my reply. "But I'm not saying there is."

"It takes a real sicko to poison innocent animals," I said, stroking Bacall. "Anyone like that wouldn't have a problem murdering a person."

"I agree. But, Sadie, it comes down to motive. Thelma's death had to benefit the culprit in some way."

"Thelma might have oodles of money hidden somewhere?" *Had her mattress contained thousands? Even a million?*

He shook his head. "Doesn't have to be about money. Could be someone considered her a threat."

Was Thelma a threat?

A week ago, the idea had been laughable. Now, I'd learned how Violet Zoetwilder, Esther Clemmens, Ellie Stromberg, even nephew Casey had all felt Thelma's wrath. But could one of them commit murder?

"By your silence, I guess you have a suspect or two?"

"Sort of."

"Sort of?" Killian pulled into my driveway and cut the engine. "Want to fill me in?"

"Thelma had a real Jekyll-Hyde thing going. Around me she was sweetness and light, but she could also be hard-headed and vindictive. Very vindictive. Yet nothing I've learned was serious enough to warrant murder."

"We're back to coincidence."

"Too much coincidence bothers some people on the force," I replied.

He raised an eyebrow. "You mean the Portneuf Gap force?"

I matched his cynical eyebrow and added an angry squint. "No. *Star Wars*."

Grabbing Bacall, I climbed from the truck and stomped into the house. The red light on my answering machine caught my eye. I ran and pushed play, praying it wasn't Dr. Gerstner. Two calls were from telemarketers wondering about my car's warranty and my credit score. I jabbed the delete button and looked around for something to pummel or drop kick. The screen door slammed. Killian walked past me, opened the fridge, and rummaged around.

He stood, Pepsi in hand. "Want to talk?"

"No—yes. I don't know. I just feel . . ." I gripped two handfuls of hair and mimed yanking it out.

"Like punching someone out?"

"Yes."

"Typical reaction. Go change and meet me in the backyard."

"You offering a boxing match?"

He smiled. "Better hurry while there's still enough light."

"I'm coming up with squat," I hollered above the howling wind.

For the past half-hour I'd been crawling around my backyard, looking for clues and poison. The sandwich baggie stuffed in the back pocket of my jeans remained flat and empty.

Killian popped up from behind a porcine sagebrush on the other side of the backyard fence. He twirled his finger in the air. "Spiral search, Sadie, ever-increasing circles."

He grinned and disappeared behind the brush. Damn the man, he was getting a real kick out of teaching me Evidence Gathering 101. I sat on my heels. The wind pushed the slate gray sky from north to south. The storm had yet to break through leaden clouds that smothered the dying sun's descent below the horizon. Probably a half hour of light left before I could attend to my grumbling stomach and Bacall's howling from behind the locked pet door.

"Bingo!" Killian waved a wrinkled Burger King sack in the air.

I met him at the fence and peeked inside the sack. Plastic gloves, the kind used for applying hair color, lay in the bottom. Killian withdrew a glove and held it at eye level. "There's yellow crystals on the thumb."

"The killer left that behind?" What were we dealing with, one of the world's dumbest criminals?

"Found it in the weeds by the road. The perp may not know he dropped it. I didn't see any more fly bait, but I'll use the barn hose and spray the area." He folded the sack and put it in his back pocket.

I raised my eyebrows. "What about fingerprints?"

Killian smiled. "Too much TV, Sadie. Chances of getting anything are slim."

"But forensics might find something, right?"

"Forensics?"

"You hand the evidence over, and they work their magic." I clenched my hands to stop my explanatory pantomime. Didn't the man know his job?

"I will report this . . ."

"Damn straight!"

"But I'm not sure what steps Animal Control will take," he said.

"Animal Control? Jack, someone tried to kill my dog . . ."

"The investigation . . ."

". . . not to mention two people have prematurely joined the cemetery crowd." I folded my arms and stared at him.

Killian shook his head, hooked his thumbs through the chain link and looked at the restless sky. He snorted. "I'll run this past a few people. Okay?"

No, it was *not* okay. I wanted action, justice, a public hanging. I brushed my hands off and nodded. If that was the best Jack could do, so be it.

Good thing I wasn't shackled by policy. Vengeance is the Lord's, but the undertaker eventually deals with everyone. It was time for this undertaker's granddaughter to do a little dealing!

Killian mistook my silence for total acquiescence. "All right. Let's eat. You up for pizza?"

I shrugged. "Sure. What flavor?"

"Big and with lots of cheese. What pizza joint delivers up here?"

"There's no delivery in the boonies. I meet any delivery guy down the road at the Tee Box convenience store across from the golf course."

"Okay. Order a large pepperoni with extra cheese. I'll meet the guy and pick up some beer. Corona okay?"

"Fine." I opened the door and Bacall bounded out, barking at invisible intruders. Before ordering the pizza, I checked my phone: one voice mail. I let out the breath I was holding while I listened as Reb's voice complained about my ability to lose track of my new cell then she invited me to come over and binge a couple of Brad Pitt movies. I glanced out the window at Killian. *Sorry, Reb, a hunk in the hand was better than one on the screen.*

The message light on my vintage answering machine blinked a soft red against my white kitchen wall. I pushed play, heard Floydean Mollicker's modulated tone and stopped looking through my cell numbers for a pizza place.

Her message ended, and I pushed replay. "Sadie, tried your cell, where are you? Alex Phoenix was involved in a hit and run. He's been taken to Portneuf Gap Regional. Watch your butt."

My cell rang as the screen door banged shut behind Killian. He started to say something, but I held up a finger and said, "Hello."

"About time," Reb said.

"Been a little busy with a crisis . . ."

"You up for a movie or what?" She pushed on.

"Can't. All hell is breaking loose." I explained about Bogart, the Burger King bag, and Alex Phoenix.

"Damn, girlfriend. Meet you at the hospital. I know Alex will be more than happy to see us. We can put our heads together and figure out who tried to turn him into road kill."

"You poor, poor man." Reb grasped Alex's hand tightly against her sweater-clad chest. From the hospital bed, Alex gave her a goofy grin. Too much pain medication? Or was it because his arm lay cradled between the cashmere mounds of Mount St. Rebbie? Bad news: he had some serious road-rash going down the right side of his body, his eye was swollen shut. Good news: he was propped up and talking.

"How did this happen?" I asked, scooting my rear onto the tiled window ledge. Portneuf Gap Regional is situated on a hill with the entire city spread below. Lights winked on as night claimed the valley. The storm had finally broken and rain slashed against the windowpane with a cold fury.

"One minute I was crossing Fifth Street, the next I was flying. Flying's not bad, but the landing sure sucked. Got some bruises and this." He pointed to the thigh-high blue cast on his right leg cradled in a sling. "Guess I'm pretty lucky."

"The person driving didn't stop to see how you were?" A shiver tickled my spine. Portneuf Gap is known for its friendly people. No one would simply drive off . . . unless it was intentional.

"Nope. Didn't even slow down. A couple of other cars stopped and some guy on a bike. Next thing I know, the paramedics are loading me into the ambulance."

"Someone contact your family?" Killian asked.

"Yeah. You just missed them. Dad took Mom back to Granddad's condo to get her migraine medicine. They were supposed to fly back to Seattle tomorrow." He shifted his body and groaned. "Stupid accident changes everything."

Killian perched like a stalking panther on the edge of the only chair in the small room. "Do you recall anything about the vehicle that hit you?"

"Big. White. The grille looked like a grinning shark. Don't remember much about the driver, couldn't tell if it was a male or female."

"Get any license numbers?"

Alex frowned. "A witness at the accident told the first officer that showed up, Dixon I think, the car was local. One-B, followed by a two, eight, maybe four. Something like that."

Big? White? Hmm.

Dexter and Violet drove a silver VW Rabbit. I wasn't sure about Esther Clemmens, but I did know who drove a big ol' white Buick.

I turned to Killian. "Check out Judy Kelso's license plate."

Rebbie dropped Alex's hand. "You think Mama Kelso ran this poor man down?"

Alex stared at me. "Casey's mother?"

I shrugged. "I know she drives a white Buick. Wouldn't hurt to look into it."

"Sit tight. I'll make a couple of phone calls," Killian said and left.

"You think Judy Kelso killed her sister?" Alex shook his head and winced, pressing both temples as though to steady his brain. "Why?"

Thunder rumbled in the distance. I scooted off the windowsill and leaned against the wall. "I don't know. Sibling rivalry gone berserk?"

"Of course." Reb tilted her chin and gazed at the far corner. "I should've thought of this. Matricide is more common, but sistercide does happen."

Sistercide? I suppressed a groan. Heaven help us, Wonder Psychologist was making an appearance. I prayed for strength and Killian's quick return.

"Okay, maybe she'd hurt Thelma," Alex said. "But I can't see her smashing Granddad over the head. You know they dated."

"Uh-huh, he dumped her—classic example of a woman scorned. Hell hath no fury, you know," Reb said.

"I'm not sure who was the dumper or dumpee. Besides, that's ancient history," Alex said.

Lightning shattered the darkness, thunder crashed a second later. Reb walked to the window and twisted the vertical blinds shut. "Sometimes revenge is best served cold." She turned and favored us with a knowing smile. "See, on the outside Judy appears to take the breakup all calm and cool. But inside, her anger is simmering. Eating away at her. Until one day—wham—she loses it and goes on a killing spree."

"What?" Alex frowned and stared at Reb.

Red blotches colored her cheeks. She slumped into the chair and folded her arms. "That's one possible scenario."

"But why turn me into road-kill?" Alex asked.

"You're a threat," I said, warming to Reb's idea. Talk about perfect . . . who would suspect an aging Barbie doll?

"I've never threatened . . ."

"No. No, Alex, think." I walked over to his bed and took his hand. "You must know something, or Judy thinks you know something, that could point to her."

"Yeah, right. Sadie, I don't . . ."

"Have you talked to Judy lately?"

"No. I saw her at Thelma's funeral, but we didn't speak."

"What about Casey?" I asked. "Have you talked to him?"

"Sure. Last night when I dropped by the bookstore. He and Ellie were both there. We talked about how bizarre life is—Thelma and Granddad dying so sudden."

"That was before you came to Sadie's house, right?" Reb said.

"Yeah."

"Did you tell Casey about your suspicions'?" I asked.

"Alex rubbed his temples. "No. I only told you and Loralee."

Reb and I looked at each other and mouthed "Loralee" in unison.

Killian sauntered into the room, a sheet of lined yellow paper in his hand. "Judy Kelso's plate is a possible match. Along with twenty other people in Bannock County."

"Cool! Let's go grill the woman." Reb popped up from the chair. "I get to play bad cop."

Killian grabbed her arm. "Wait a minute. No one is grilling anyone."

"But . . ."

"But nothing. I'm not getting my ass chewed or sued for harassment. Time to have a *friendly* chat with Judy Kelso. See if she won't let me take a look at her car."

"Let's get moving." I patted Alex's hand. "Take care. We'll see you tomorrow."

Out in the hall, Killian stopped. "Okay troops, fun and games are over. This is now official police business. I'll be talking to the woman all by my lonesome."

Fun and Games? I'd just served the man murdering Mama Kelso on a platter. No way was he giving me the brush off. I took two steps, making sure our toes touched, and stared him dead in the face. "You wouldn't know diddly without our hard work. We're coming."

Killian took a deep breath and let it our slowly. "Three against one will only alarm the woman."

Reb smirked. "You haven't met Mama Kelso."

"A situation I intend to rectify right now." Killian's eyes darkened from green to the color of angry seas; pure intimidation. Anger stiffened my spine—I didn't budge. After a moment, he neatly sidestepped and started down the hall.

"You can't stop us," I said, striding to catch up with him.

He stopped, looked at the floor and sighed. I'm pretty adept at reading sighs; Killian's was long, heartfelt, and translated into: "God, why me?"

"You're right. I can't stop you." He raised his head. "But I'm asking, as a friend, please let me do my job."

The quiet sincerity in his voice punctured my righteous indignation. I glanced at Reb. All the steely determination had left her face, leaving her eyes gooey soft with understanding.

Killian took each of our hands. "Thank you. I promise, I'll let you know what I find."

Then he was gone, leaving the two of us standing in the hall, hospital staff bustling around us.

I looked at Reb. "I think we've just been played."

"Big time. Probably learned that trick in some police psych course."

"Still a free country," I snapped.

Reb nodded. "Until someone slaps the cuffs on you."

I held out my wrists. "No cuffs here."

"Your car or mine?" She asked, striding for the elevator.

Hey, a sincere please only goes so far.

THE STORM HAD STOPPED by the time we reached Judy's neighborhood. We spotted Killian's truck in the center of Judy's circular driveway. Floodlights mounted on the garage lit the wet asphalt and most of the manicured front yard. There was no sign of Killian. Reb parked her Subaru next to his truck, looked at the house, and whistled.

"Would you look at this?" She pointed at the yellow ranch sprawled across what looked to be half the block. A tall, white wrought-iron fence lined three sides of the professionally landscaped yard. "Thelma should've taken Judy up on her offer to move in."

"And live with Mama Kelso?"

Reb climbed out of the car. "With a house this big they'd never see each other."

Our breath pluming in the air, we walked up the flagstone path and climbed the three steps to the porch. A motion light near the front door blinked on. I rang the bell. It sounded like a gong echoing inside a cave. No answer, so I tried the door; it was locked.

Reb pushed the bell again. "Doesn't seem to be anyone home."

"Time for a look-see." I pressed my face against the front picture window. Reb joined me. Lucky for us, the drapes were open. Guess Judy felt the pink sheers gave her enough privacy.

"Lots of French Provincial," Reb said. "No dead bodies lying around. That's a positive. I'd give my eye-teeth to list this. If she's guilty can she still list property from prison?"

"Not funny!" I craned my neck, trying to see down the dark hallway to the right. "No lights. Let's check the garage."

It was hard to see anything through the tiny windows of the double-wide garage door, even standing tippy-toe. "Looks empty." I said.

Reb nudged me with her shoulder. "It's dark, how can you be sure?"

"The yard lights shine in a little, and I don't see any car-like shapes."

"She's not home." The voice deep and slightly pissed sounding came from directly behind us.

Reb and I yelped and jumped away from the garage.

"Talk about heart attack," Reb hissed, clutching her chest.

Killian raised an eyebrow. "Window peeking is frowned on around here."

Reb folded her arms and shot him a look. "Not if one intends to make a citizen's arrest."

"Citizen's arrest?" He thunked his hand against his forehead. "Damn, why didn't I think of that. Judith Kelso will surely confess to hitting Alex with her car because you made a citizen's arrest." Killian grinned and shook his head.

"Ha ha." I looked at my watch: eight-thirty. Most people Judy's age were plunked in front of their TV sets by now. "Kinda weird she's not here."

Killian shrugged. "Maybe she's helping people in Hell strap on ice skates. Or teaching flying pigs to sing opera." Again he gave us a lopsided grin.

"Come on, Jack, this is serious. You've put out a BOLO or APB on her, right?" Reb asked.

To Killian's credit he didn't smirk or grin. Instead, he took her hand. "Not quite to that stage, yet. First, we need to eyeball her car . . ."

"And if she's running in said vehicle? You're just going to let her vanish into the night?" Reb waved her free hand toward the road.

"Trust me." Killian started a slow thumb massage on Reb's knuckles. "If she's responsible for the hit and run, we'll get her." The thumb thing was working; Reb snapped her mouth shut and nodded.

"It might look like the department's not rolling on this, but wheels are turning."

"What wheels?" I asked.

"Wheels." Killian emphasized the word. "The investigation's rolling through proper channels so some fancy-ass lawyer can't waltz in and ruin the case." Killian checked his watch. "I'm thinking of going to the new indoor archery range. Gotta sight-in my new bow. Wanna come? Shouldn't take long. Afterward, we can all go for pizza."

My stomach rumbled at the thought, but I didn't want to witness Reb's total loss of self-control. She's always had a thing for Robin Hood. Guys holding bows on the cover of hunting magazines made her hot. Now, heaven have mercy, Killian had just invited her to the archery range.

Before she started to rip at his clothes with her teeth, I thought it prudent to make a quick exit. "Thanks for the invite. I should get home, check on Bacall. Batten down the hatches, keep a sharp look-out, beat a cliché to death."

"Sure, Sadie," Reb said, her voice low and husky. Her eyes never left Killian's face as she fished into her coat pocket and tossed me the keys to her car. "We'll touch base tomorrow."

Killian, having picked up on the thrumming sexual vibes, didn't say goodbye or adios, just waved and helped Reb into his truck. They roared off and left me guessing if they'd even make it to the archery range.

I didn't feel left out—or lonely.

Not me—uh-uh—I had an agenda of my own. With Reb's generic car I could roam the town looking for Judy Kelso's big, white Buick. I'd start with Casey's apartment and work outward in an ever-widening circle, just like Killian had taught me. The storm had passed, and a bright harvest moon rode the sky. With any luck, Reb wouldn't be the only one to score tonight.

TWENTY-TWO

REB'S SUBARU JERKED TO A STOP in my driveway, and I slammed the steering wheel with my fist. Sleuthing was turning into one giant pain in the arse. I'd cruised nearly every street in town, even bouncing down a couple of pockmarked alleys, and what did I have to show for my diligence? I had Reb's car running on fumes and a hunger headache that craved massive amounts of anything with a large Pepsi, and no sign of Kelso or her car. She'd probably freaked and was halfway to Reno.

Only the tiny kitchen nightlight shined through the side window. The rest of my house was dark. A week ago that was business as usual. Now my heart started flip-flopping with my stomach. Battling my cowardice, I climbed from the safety of Reb's car, shut the door and heard Bacall's welcoming bark.

I scanned the area lit by my sensor light and peered hard into the surrounding shadows. Everything appeared normal. Opening the gate, I stepped into the back yard and repeated my surveillance. All was calm, and thanks to the full moon, all was bright. Eclipse nickered from the corral. *Damn.* In all the excitement, I'd forgotten to feed the big guy. Killian might have, but I wasn't sure. I couldn't stuff my face before checking.

"Hang on, Eclipse, help's coming."

I left my purse hanging on the gate for safety from the nibbling horse, and hiked up the hill to the barn. Eclipse met me at the paddock's rail fence and nuzzled my pocket for sugar cubes.

I turned my pockets inside out. "Sorry."

He whinnied and tossed his head.

"How about some nice hay?" I patted his rump and he trotted to the far side of the arena. Hum, maybe he wasn't hungry.

As I pushed the side barn door open, a pungent odor assaulted my nose. My hand stopped in mid-grope for the light switch.

Gas!

The whole place reeked like a gas pump gone berserk.

Okay, Harrigan, don't panic.

A match or spark might turn my barn into a pyro's dream. Was the guilty person still in the barn? I took another whiff. Whew, not likely. No wonder Eclipse was staying away.

Backing out, I left the door open to help air the barn out and inched my way to the far corner of the barn for a quick peek around the side. The grass swished and fallen leaves seemed to snicker a warning.

A big white Buick hunkered in the weeds, moonlight gleaming from its grill. Alex was right, it did look like a grinning shark.

While I'd wasted time looking for the woman, Judy Kelso was at my house; poisoning Bogart, spreading gasoline, and giving me ulcers.

Staying in the shadows, I crept closer to the car, hoping she was inside. I'd drag her out and, if she gave me any grief, I'd slap a ton of makeup off her face.

I popped up next to the driver's door and jerked it open—empty. *Damn and double damn.*

I turned and stared down at my house. And stared some more as dread twisted my guts. I should've left Bacall with Bogart at the Vet clinic. Now she was at the mercy of Psycho Mama. If Kelso hurt her in any way . . .

Sprinting down the hill, adrenaline pumping, ready to yank every bottle-blonde hair from her head, I reached the back door and stopped. I had no clue where Kelso might be lurking. Getting bashed over the head, or worse, wasn't tops on my list. But if I could sneak in unnoticed—maybe drop down the old coal chute into the basement—vengeance would be mine.

I crept to the side of the house and gave the ancient rectangular iron door a quick yank; nothing. Planting my feet, I grasped the handle with both hands and pulled. The door budged a little, its rusted hinges screeched like a banshee. I froze, listening for anything louder than my thumping heart. Only the soft thud of Eclipse's hoofs reached me. I let out a pent-up breath, slowly pushed the door open, then peered into the inky basement.

There was only black silence, except the air didn't feel empty.

Swallowing a lump of fear, I turned and wiggled feet first through the butt-size opening and dropped into a crouch on the packed-earth floor. Ancient coal dust tickled my nose. I sneezed into my hands to muffle the sound.

Ears straining, hands out in front of me, I fumbled my way to the corner post of the dank room. Considering the maniac keeping her company, the soft click-click of Bacall's nails on the kitchen floor above was comfort of a sort. The snuffling, pawing and whining at the basement door was not. Damn, why hadn't I left her with Bogart?

A loud, "Move it" followed by a thump and squeal put an end to Bacall's efforts to reach me.

Kelso was so dead when I got my hands on her scrawny neck.

The basement door creaked open and the single bulb in the stairwell snapped on, creating a weak puddle of light on the cracked cement floor. Shadows from a jumble of stored furniture lining the perimeter of the basement projected strange shapes onto the floor.

"I know you're down there, Sadie." That voice wasn't Kelso's! Too little-girl tinny. "Don't make this difficult."

Loralee?

What was Loralee doing here?

Where was Mama Kelso?

I scurried from the coal room, frantic for a place to hide, under the stairs? No, that would be the first place I'd look.

"No place to run to ba-by, no place to hide." Loralee's rendition of the old R & B tune was way off-key, but her footsteps rat-a-tatted sharp and clear. Sounded like she was tap dancing down the stairs.

The overhead fluorescent bulbs flickered to life as I squeezed behind an old console TV. Crouching down, I thought about my gun and gave myself a mental head-slap. Along with my cell phone, the gun was safely tucked inside my purse . . . the same purse I'd left hanging on my back gate.

Smooth move!

"Ollie-ollie, Oxen-free." Loralee sang out, her voice echoing from under the stairs.

I peeked around the side of the TV. She backed out from beneath the stairwell, and I saw the cannon clutched in her right hand. Where did she get such a big gun, and a better question would be, could she actually shoot it?

Pulling my head back, I did a frantic search for a weapon; there was nothing at ground level but dust and cobwebs. The sagging shelf high above me held bottled beets covered in protective layers of mold—botulism against bullets? It was a no-brainer there.

"Come on out, Sadie. I'll make it painless, just like Claude."

I thought of Claude's bashed-in head and shivered. That was painless?

"Make me hunt, and you'll be sorry. Judy Kelso made me hunt for her."

Loralee had killed Mama Kelso? My prime suspect? So much for my powers of deduction.

She began humming, "Who's Sorry Now," while my heart threatened to beat its way through my rib-cage. There didn't seem to be enough oxygen in the basement. The room decided to swim. Maybe I'd be lucky and pass out before Loralee turned me into Swiss cheese.

"Okay, I'll give you to the count of three. One." Her voice sounded closer. "You and your dogs are such a pain in my ass."

My dogs? The dizziness faded. If I died, Bogart and Bacall would be orphans.

"Two."

I gritted my teeth and peered over the TV. Loralee faced away from me, inching toward the coal bin. I stood, snatched a bottle of beets off the shelf and chucked it at the far corner.

She whirled and fired the gun into the shattered mess.

Ears ringing from the explosion, I did a flying tackle, my head connecting somewhere around her middle. The gun discharged again, breaking one of the overhead fluorescent lights. I landed on top of her, fists swinging. She groaned and lay still. Mindless fear propelled me toward the stairs.

The gun thundered. A stab of heat shot down my right leg. I yelped in surprise, whirled off balance and grabbed at air as my leg collapsed under me. My right hand connected with something slick, smooth—a vase?—then I was sitting on the ground, looking at the remaining light flickering like a demented strobe.

I tried to stand. Pain, hot and sharp, roared through my leg making me scream.

"Now you're gonna pay!"

Loralee stood over me, blood streaming from her crooked nose, turning her white blouse into a giant Rorschach blot. With one eye closed, she sighted down the gun barrel. "Thelma tried to get away. Almost did, except her crummy back door stuck. Too bad she had such an inept landlord."

I blinked away tears. With anger-fueled strength, I hurled Aunt Vie's Chinese vase at her head.

I missed. The vase struck her collarbone. She screamed and grabbed for her left shoulder, knocking her glasses askew. The gun remained clutched tight in her fist.

Move! My brain screamed. I tried to stand; but no go.

"I had it made—the old toaster, old wiring. Police chalked it up as an accident. Just like my fiancé in Denver, his murder remains unsolved. Maybe someday one of producers of Cold Case Files will decide to focus on his death. Make a big production, interview everyone. But nothing will come of it. I know how to cover my tracks. And, everything was going as planned with the bookstore and Thelma's untimely death until you started snooping. Then Claude gets a burr up his butt about the authenticity of the baskets. I tried to warn you both away." She took a step closer, adjusted her glasses and attempted to aim the wavering gun one handed.

"You're both too stupid to take a hint. Too stupid to live!" I watched the emotions she was struggling with turn rancid and run down her over-bright cheeks.

"Well, your novel stinks!"

I slammed my heel into her ankle. She collapsed on top of me. I grabbed for the gun. It roared again. Keep this up, I'd either be deaf or dead. Pain exploded through my right shoulder. The scum-sucking witch had shot me . . . again!

I latched onto her right hand and sank my teeth into soft flesh. She squealed. I bit deeper, jaws clamped like a Pit-bull. She head-butted me. I yelped as my head bounced off the floor. Stars flickered in my vision. Loralee gasped, her weight shifted off me. I closed my eyes, willing death to be quick. Instead, I heard the most beautiful male voice ask, "You okay?"

I opened my eyes and saw Killian restraining a struggling, red-faced Loralee. Out of her mouth spewed a torrent of four-letter words that would've netted her a good tongue-scrubbing with Ivory soap from Aunt Vie.

"Holy moley, Harrigan! We came to feed Eclipse and . . ." The color drained from Reb's face as she knelt beside me. "You're bleeding."

"Tell me something I don't know," I croaked. I grabbed her shaking hand and held on tight. A furry missile suddenly launched from partway down the stairs landing near Reb's feet. Bacall whined and licked my cheek. In the distance I heard sirens.

Reb picked Bacall up and stroked her soft head. "Okay, okay. Don't panic. Everything's under control."

The first time Reb uttered those words, we'd been caught raiding ol' Hal's cherry orchard. Back then, I'd nearly ended up with a backside full of rock salt. Too bad Loralee chose real bullets. However, this time Reb was right. Everything was under control.

TWENTY-THREE

"**R**EALLY THINK YOU OUGHT TO STAY the night," Killian said.
Right words, wrong place.

The puke green walls of the closet-sized examination room reeked of antiseptic. I was propped up on a standard ER bed and shook my head feeling floaty and free. Wonderful stuff, painkillers; no more hurt, no more hassle. "I want to recoup at home with my dogs."

"Plus a jar of peanut butter and a couple of Hershey bars," Reb added. "And plenty of Pepsi to wash down the pain pills."

Does my friend know me or what?

Killian snorted, scratched his chin, and leaned against the bed's safety rail. "Quit the hard-nosed act and stay like the doctor advised. You'll be admitted to a regular room for observation, not spend the night in the ER. One night of peace and quiet."

"Peace and quiet lying in a bed with rails? Ha! A full night's sleep in a hospital is impossible. Weird machine noises echoing down hallways, and nurses coming to take patients temperature or blood pressure or something every hour."

"Not to worry." Reb switched her smile to high-beam and patted his folded arms. "I'll take her home and make sure she limits her activities to low-impact knitting and dusting her navel."

"Right." I agreed. I'd agree to eating raw liver if it got me released from the hospital. "Has anyone found Judy Kelso?"

Killian nodded. "In the barn."

Gory images flashed through my head. Had Judy's body begun to decompose like her sister's? "How bad?"

"Scrapes, rope burns, and a couple of hefty knots on her head, but she'll survive. She's been screaming for Loralee's blood since an officer discovered her, trussed-up and gagged in Eclipse's stall. Loralee planned to make Judy's death look like suicide. We found a note in Judy's car, claiming responsibility for all the murders." Killian fixed me with a summer lightning glare. "Including yours."

"Good thing I interfered with Loralee's plan." I grinned and watched Killian's scowl deepen. The giddy euphoria I felt wasn't all pain-pill induced. My dogs still had their mama, and I'd saved Judy from a fiery death.

"Good thing you're not lying on a slab in the morgue." Each word came out as unyielding as a granite gravestone.

I folded my arms, a stab of pain made me wince. The two-sizes-too-big hospital gown shifted against my bandaged shoulder. "I bet Mama Kelso's grateful she's not a crispy critter. Bet she's happy I interfered."

"She hasn't said. Since being admitted, her new hobby is pressing the call button. Nurses are ready to throw her out, but at least she's doing the sensible thing and staying the night for observation." Killian gave me a raised eyebrow.

"She gave me a message for you," Reb interjected.

I returned Killian's pointed stare. "And?"

Reb splayed her hand across her heart and gave a tormented sigh. "The poor woman is wounded to the core. How could you possibly consider her the culprit of such heinous crimes?" Reb removed her hand. "The woman is a born martyr."

"What about Loralee?"

"She gave some garbled explanation claiming she did everything for Casey," Killian said.

"Casey?" I squinted at Killian, not sure I'd heard right.

He nodded. "Casey had been embezzling from the bookstore to pay off some debts."

"Like we pointed out," Reb said.

Killian ignored her. "Judy intervened and promised to pay Thelma back, so Thelma let him off with a warning. But, when Thelma discovered the baskets, she'd been selling as antiques were really doctored fake baskets, she went ballistic. Threatened to turn both Loralee and Casey in for fraud. She wanted both of them behind bars."

"Loralee went to Thelma's and killed her with an old toaster." I favored Killian with my best told-you-so grin.

Killian's cheeks took on the faintest hint of color. "She tried pleading with Thelma for another chance. Thelma refused and Loralee used the old toaster she brought along in case Thelma didn't capitulate. She got the idea from the show Forensic Crimes."

"And she killed Claude when he became suspicious," I said, feeling the first twinges of guilt. Would Claude still be selling luxury cars if I hadn't started digging into Thelma's death?

"Loralee has turned mute since she was read her rights." Killian put his arm around me and gave me a gentle squeeze. "She won't stay mute for long; we have experts who can weasel a confession out of a rock."

I relaxed against his warm chest, feeling safe and secure for the moment. Then a traitorous tear slipped down my cheek; all my giddy euphoria erased by guilt. "Guess Claude, Mama Kelso, even Alex are my fault."

"How do you figure?" Reb handed me a tissue from the box on the counter.

"Asking questions, poking around." I swiped at another tear.

"Playing detective where you had no business," Killian added.

"Solving Thelma's murder," Reb said. "A murder that was officially ruled an accident." She turned the last word into three syllables.

"Right." I twisted out of Killian's embrace. "An accident. Like the murder in Denver."

Reb's eyes widened. "You mean . . ."

I nodded. "Told me everything was going as planned, just like in Denver."

"Denver? What about Denver?" Killian said.

"Before the experts interrogate her, they might want to look into a cold case, the death of her fiancé in a road-rage incident."

"She's done this before?" Killian folded his arms and glared at me. "Son-of-a-bitch. You've no idea how close you came . . ."

"Wait." I placed my fingers against his lips. He stopped his tirade, exasperation curved one corner of his mouth, but concern colored his eyes. I removed my fingers. "You can chastise me, yell at me. Whatever. Just please wait 'til I'm home."

A slow grin indented his dimples. "Fair enough. Let me go see if I can't round up some release papers."

He disappeared through the beige curtain, cowboy boots echoing down the hall.

Reb grabbed my hand. "We did it, girlfriend. We got the crazy witch. Damn if this hasn't been exciting."

"Exciting? I have six stitches in my shoulder, more in my thigh."

"Both bullets just grazed the skin, doctor said there's no permanent damage. Hell's bells, we took a certified psychotic out." Reb gave my hand a squeeze. "Who knows what other warped plans Loralee had in mind. With her fatal attraction for Casey, Ms. Hair might've been the next victim."

Reb had a point. Loralee's idea of love was obsessive, twisted, dark and terrible.

"Besides, if you get the chance to compare scars with a couple of macho types, you'll have real braggin' rights."

"What?"

Reb huffed a sigh. "Hello, remember the first time we watched *Jaws*? We always felt sorry for the sheriff cause all he had was a wimpy appendix scar?"

She was right. While the rest of our friends had freaked out about all the blood and the shark's huge teeth, Reb and I had felt sorry for the sheriff who's only scar was from an appendix surgery compared to hand-to-hand combat with denizens from the deep.

"Casey is involved in the basket fraud?" I asked.

"Who knows. Like Jack said, Loralee's mum and Casey's insisting he's innocent."

Killian pulled aside the curtain and pushed a wheelchair up to the bed. "All set?"

I looked down at the faded hospital gown. "Am I wearing this lovely thing home?"

He held up a plastic bag with Portneuf Gap Medical Center printed in big, bold letters. "Your clothes if you want 'em."

Oh goody. My crusty, blood-smeared shirt and jeans. Gathering the excess cloth of the gown, I scooched off the bed, climbed into the wheelchair, and took the bag. "I think I'll eighty-six these."

Killian bent down and tucked a dangling curl of hair behind my ear. A tingle shot through my nethermost region. "Does this mean you're hanging up your Nancy Drew hat?" he asked.

"Probably," I said.

Probably. Definitely. Maybe.

J. W. HODGE LOVES COMMITTING MURDER on paper. She believes it's very therapeutic. She did grow up playing in her grandmother's mortuary so her view of death might be a little skewed. She and her husband are kept busy cleaning and repairing their many apartment complexes. When she's not cleaning or writing she's busy rescuing dogs, feral cats, and battling with a flock of wild turkeys for the rights to her back hillside. She's a member of Sisters in Crime and belongs to two local writer's critique groups.